The Match Game

D.W. Brooks

Cover design by 100covers.com

Editing by Danyelle Briggs, *In The Write Dyrection LLC*

Formatting by *In The Write Dyrection LLC*

Publisher's Cataloging-in-Publication Data

Names: Brooks, D. W., author.

Title: The match game / by D. W. Brooks.

Description: Houston, TX: Life: The Reboot LLC, 2026.

Identifiers: LCCN: 2026901637 | ISBN: 979-8-9890807-9-3 (paperback) | 979-8-9890807-8-6 (ebook)

Subjects: LCSH Physicians—Fiction. | African-American—Fiction. | Man-woman relationships—Fiction. |

Dating—Fiction. | Romance fiction. | Love stories. | BISAC FICTION / Romance / African American &; Black

| FICTION / African American &; Black / Women | FICTION / Romance / Contemporary | FICTION /

Romance / Medical | FICTION / Romance / Later in Life | FICTION / Women

Classification: : LCC PS3602 .R66 M38 2026 | DDC 813.6-dc23

Printed in Houston, TX

Contents

dedication

To the women out there who are getting better with age
Smarter, more creative, more understanding, more beautiful, more standing in
your truth
Just MORE
Don't let anyone dull your shine, mess with your plans, interfere with your goals,
or destroy your self-esteem...
Dance in the sand, sail on the ocean, break that glass ceiling, fall madly in love
Do one or all if you choose.
But ENJOY your MORE because you deserve MORE of whatever you want in
this life.

content warnings

Welcome to my world.

First things first— thank you so much for picking up *The Match Game*. This story means everything to me, and I don't take it lightly that you're choosing to spend time with these characters. I'm so excited (and a little nervous) for you to meet them, root for them, and maybe even yell at them a little along the way.

That said, I want you to go into this book feeling informed and safe. *The Match Game* explores themes that may be heavy or triggering for some readers—and while those moments serve the story, they don't need to catch you off guard.

This book contains:

Explicit sexual content (multiple detailed scenes)

Strong language throughout

Depiction of past sexual assault (non-graphic, disclosed in narrative)

Past sexual trauma and its long-term emotional impact

Divorce and past relationship trauma

Themes of trust, betrayal, and emotional vulnerability

Family conflict and dysfunction

Brief references to parental infidelity

Discussions of absent and difficult parents

You deserve to read stories in ways that honor your emotional well-being. If you choose to read *The Match Game*, I hope it's a story you enjoy—deeply, fully, and without surprises you weren't ready for.

prologue

grace

This was not how the night was supposed to end. After the ceremony, I was supposed to be in my hotel with a bottle of Louis Roederer Cristal and the kind of silence you only earn after surviving a month of last-minute wedding chaos.

I was supposed to be eating another slice of piña colada coconut cake—because I picked that cake, and I deserved it. I was supposed to be in my hotel bed... *alone.*

Not pinned against a counter by the ex-husband of the bride.

Not letting David Witten—Mr. Bad Idea in a tailored suit—put his mouth on my neck.

David Witten. Former European professional basketball player. Professional flirt. The man I teamed up with nine weeks ago to shove MacKenzie and Evan back into each other's arms.

Not doing this with somebody I promised myself I would stay away from months ago. So, why was my ass on a marble bar top in a guest suite at my ex-mother-in-law's house?

I'll give you the answer.

It's because there was a gorgeous, totally inappropriate man dismantling my boundaries like they were suggestions and not walls that I'd put up on purpose. My floor-length green silk dress was bunched around my waist while I kissed rum-raisin ice cream off David's mouth and he returned the favor—almost greedily, as if he'd been waiting on this all night.

It was complicated, sure.

It was also stupid as hell.

I was just drunk enough to wrap my legs around his waist, pressing my core against him. I could feel his erection through only my lacy thong, and I knew this was going to be a moment of problematic ecstasy. Emphasis on *problematic*...

That thought didn't stop me.

David slid the spaghetti strap of my slinky wedding attire down for access to my bra-less left breast... swirling his tongue around my nipple and teasing it to a pebble. I threw my head back to further expose my neck. He blazed another trail of kisses up the column of my throat to my ear. Our hands were moving frantically all over each other, tugging at clothes, hair, limbs—anything that was in the way. Rational thoughts buried deep in my champagne-soaked brain tried to surface, but I ignored them. David probably hadn't considered the consequences of where this was headed at all.

I apparently didn't care either.

Except I was lying to myself. I knew this would just be sex. Nothing more than a quick fuck. David didn't do "more" with me. Not like that.

And I would regret it. Probably before he even finished.

But I was drowning in my feelings and needed something, *anything*, to distract me.

What could it hurt?

I turned my head to capture his mouth as our tongues danced against each other. His hands slid down my back and under my ass to pick me up off the counter. I wrapped both arms around his neck as we swung around in the suite searching for the bedroom.

David growled in my ear, "Which of these doors leads to the bed?" The suite was dark, but he moved like he knew exactly where he wanted me.

Either room would work. I wasn't pretending to be picky.

Either room would work for me...

"I think it's the second one over there. I don't know if we need a bed—" It didn't matter. I was so wet it was embarrassing. It had been a while since I had had sex with a person and not a toy. I kept repeating to myself: *I need this. It's only once.*

It was a lie I didn't even believe while I was saying it.

This could mess up my relationship with MacKenzie. With Evan. With everyone. And still—I stayed wrapped around David as if he were the only solid thing left in the room.

With all this flying around in my head, David gracefully opened the correct door with me still draped around him.

After he gently placed me on the mattress, he paused.

"Are we doing this?" David asked, searching my face in the dim light.

I stared into his eyes briefly and heard myself say, "Yeah." I couldn't believe what was coming out of my mouth. During our brief relationship, David and I had worked so hard to maintain our boundaries, and here I was, tossing them out like they didn't matter after one tough day.

And so?

"Stop talking and fuck me." I reached up and pulled him down on top of me.

A few hours earlier, I'd smiled for pictures and blown bubbles like I wasn't the groom's ex-wife.

I watched as Evan and MacKenzie finally rectified the biggest mistake they ever made. I even caught the bouquet. I laughed. I played my part. But once Evan and Mac made their way to the limo, something happened that shifted my feelings. Evan had reached out to steady Mac as she stumbled on a crack in the pavement. Nothing major—just instinct. . The move didn't even affect their momentum towards the limo. It was just that small...

But that small action sent me spiraling....

Because he used to do it for me.

For a split second, my body remembered before my pride could intervene. We weren't meant to be together. We both knew that, but he had always supported me. Now he was going to be there for our son. Not for me. I wasn't really part of his family anymore.

Within a matter of minutes, our entire dynamic had changed. This wasn't new information for me. Evan and I had discussed it after he and Mac decided to get married.

But now I *knew* it. I *felt* it. I didn't even get a goodbye wave.

And it hurt. I didn't expect it to hurt like that—to cave my chest in where it was a little difficult to breathe.

Gabe nudged me after taking a glance at my face. "Are you okay, Mom?"

I smiled brightly back at him—at least I hoped I did. "I'm fine, son. I'm thrilled that this worked out for them."

Which was true. Didn't mean I was prepared for how it made me feel. I wiped away a tear that had trickled down my face, hoping Gabe didn't notice.

So, I continued to blow bubbles with a pasted-on smile as Evan and MacKenzie disappeared into the SUV limo to ride off into their shiny new future in Miami.

And my future? All I could see was a bottle of expensive champagne—maybe two—and maybe waking up alone under a table.

After the reception, I moved fast. I had to get Gabe settled with Evan's family, make sure he was good, and then I could disappear before anyone could look at me too closely. Gabe and MacKenzie's son, Alex, were going to stay with Evan's people for a few nights meaning I would be able to have my pity party in peace.

Dropping Gabe off with Miss Lorraine, I walked away before my face did anything embarrassing. This whole weekend came with a new label for me, whether I liked it or not.

Ex-wife.

Not "family," not "daughter-in-law," not even "complicated." Just... moved aside to make space for MacKenzie. Space that should have been hers to begin with.

I knew Miss Lorraine, though. If I'd said more than goodnight, she would've said something kind and I would've fallen apart in front of everyone, messing up my plans for a drunken party of one.

Weaving through the crowd and furniture, I first grabbed a bottle of champagne off one bar as I walked by. Then I made my way to a corner of the backyard behind the temporary pavilion. The pavilion where the wedding quartet entertained the crowd with beautiful romantic songs a couple of hours ago. Ironically, after all the bliss and love associated with it, the building was now deserted like a ghost town.

A perfect place to hide.

Once I was sure that no one could see me in the fading light, I let the tears flow.

I was crying for the naïve 26-year-old who first laid eyes on Evan during an inpatient consultation and was a goner from the beginning. For the 31-year-old who was crushed to learn that her husband was capable of all-encompassing love—just not for *her*. For the 33-year-old who pulled on her big-girl pants and asked for a divorce, knowing he never would have. For the almost 42-year-old who desperately wanted that endless love that my parents and Evan and Mac had. Where I wasn't the one who was always pushing the relationship forward. Where the man simply breathed and wanted only *me*.

I had never been in that type of relationship before, and that left me melancholy and ripe for drunken shenanigans... which is why I needed to remain alone tonight. Under my table. *By myself.*

Taking a long gulp of champagne, I tucked my legs under my bottom and leaned back against the support beam, telling myself that nobody was looking.

Unfortunately, someone was. David. The ex-husband of the bride.

Shortly after meeting, we conspired together for a week to facilitate this reunion—despite what it might have cost us personally. Over the course of the week, David and I became friends. Friends who had been in the unenviable position of being married to someone who was in love with a shadowy, absent figure from the past. That shadow, that ghost of a long-lost love, was always lurking around the edges of our relationships and occasionally took its place right in the center.

We didn't have to explain much to each other. We already knew what it felt like to come in second to a memory. Then the wedding happened.

"Grace!" he looked slyly at me with a devilish grin as he doubled the number of syllables in my name. He had a bottle of whiskey—that Black-owned brand out of Nashville—tucked under his arm as he sipped the brown liquid from a small snifter glass. "This is your hiding place? You really weren't trying, were you?"

I glared at him. "Why are *you* still here? Isn't Alex gone with his step-grand-mother?" I asked as I took another long swig from the champagne bottle.

"I could ask you the same thing. Gabe's gone too. And you're now the ex-wife once removed or something like that. *¿Por qué sigues aquí?*"

I looked away. He had a point. I could have called an Uber to my hotel room and continued my pity fest alone and in peace. Maybe I didn't want to be alone.

David could sense my discomfort and tried to redirect the conversation "So, what are your plans for the rest of this weekend?"

"Nothing really. I expect to be nursing a wicked hangover *alone*. And you? Do you have a number or two to call while you're in town?" The jealousy underneath it irritated me more than the question itself.

"Nah. None of my roster lives out here. Besides, I need to decompress a little. This wedding run- up was stressful!"

I peeked at his profile as he looked out over the backyard with the white altar and rows of cloth-covered chairs lined just so. Given how close he and MacKenzie are, I could believe that he had been handling a bunch of last-minute details and taking care of Alex. I did something similar for Evan.

We were both suckers in that regard.

"Did you get any of the Azucar ice cream?" I asked, trying to shift the mood. The melancholy atmosphere was getting a little oppressive. The ice cream came from a shop in Miami and played a role in the newlyweds' journey to marital bliss.

"You know I did. I even have some hidden in the freezer in the—what is it—the in-law suite?"

"Really? Which flavor?" I put the champagne down and placed my hands on his arm.

He sipped a little more whisky. "The one with the rum and raisins. Forgot the name. But I stashed some away. If you're nice, you might get a spoonful."

I laughed at his facial expression. It was the lightest I had felt since the couple left in the limo. Maybe talking to David was what I needed to get my emotions back in check. I hooked my arm through his.

"I think you will be the one getting only a spoonful. I claim dibs on the container itself." He offered the whiskey. I took a sip. It burned...and it helped.

David's grin widened like he'd just watched me make my first bad decision of the night.

A slow song drifted out from inside the house. David held out his hand.

"Come on," he said. "We're not doing this tonight. No moping."

I took his hand. He pulled me into his arms and for the first time, I realized that I fit right under his chin. We had hugged each other before, but this felt a little different. I finally felt comfortable despite the stresses of the day.

The song ended, but we didn't move from our embrace immediately. Instead, we stood there for a second letting the silence fill the space. Finally, I stepped back to disentangle our limbs—a small warning bell going off in my head. That bell was extinguished when David looked at me and held out his hand again.

Second bad decision: I took it and followed him.

"Let's go get some of that ice cream. I'll show you where I stashed it."

And that's how we ended up *here.*

His hand slid back under my skirt and up my thigh, and I let him because I was already past the point of pretending that I was making smart choices tonight.

I need this, I need this…

"Oh! I'm sorry! We didn't know anyone was in here," an unknown voice blurted from the doorway.

David and I froze in place. *Perfect, just perfect.*

We stared toward the doorway, caught mid-mistake.

Helpfully, the voice turned on the overhead light which was more humiliating. After the initial acclimation to the sudden light, I saw a young man in a waitstaff uniform with a pretty young woman whom I remembered worked with the florist. The young man absolutely tried to sneak a peek. The young woman tried to avoid eye contact.

Oh, my GOD! Fuck, fuck, fuck.

Blushing, I quickly scrambled into a sitting position and had to nudge David so he would move his hand from my thigh and roll off me. I tugged the dress strap back into place and tried to smooth my dress back down.

"Sorry, we didn't mean to interrupt—" the young woman stammered, clutching the young man's arm. He giggled as they backed out.

When she joined in the laughter as they left the suite, I wanted the mattress to swallow me whole. I exhaled and covered my face with my hands. The hottest thing that I had done in years quickly turned into the most disconcerting within moments.

David got out of bed and walked into the kitchenette. I gingerly followed him while trying to get my haywire emotions and body back under control. Opening the freezer, he pulled out another container of Azucar rum raisin ice cream. I watched him grab a spoon and eat some with a shrug. He offered me a second spoonful while I declined, staring at him as if he were insane.

Typical David, nonchalant as always.

Another reason that this had been such a bad idea.

I turned to walk out of the suite, pride in the gutter.

What the fuck was I doing?

1

grace

Two months later, on a brisk, October morning, getting through my weekly ritual reminded me of how much I missed my kid.

On Saturday mornings after his swim practices, Gabriel and I used to visit the Ferry Plaza Farmer's Market together to pick out fruits, vegetables, and other foods for the upcoming week. He still tried to hustle extra sweets into the basket—one more piece of fruit for an extra cookie, like I didn't know his games. We'd argue, laugh, and leave the market with too much bread and not enough produce. It was our thing.

On the rare mornings Evan came with us, the two of them would team up and turn the whole trip into a baked goods heist. Gabe loved those days. I did too, even when I pretended I didn't.

Now that Gabe was attending an elite swimming academy in Miami for the next 10 months, I was alone this Saturday morning. Training for the Olympics was his whole life right now, and my role in that dream was to step back and let him chase it. So here I was, shopping solo for one. Missing my son. Considering my life choices.

I scheduled weekly phone calls with Gabe and flew to Miami at least once a month to see him. Still, I missed his teenage chatter and all the wayward clothes left all over the house. When he was home, I swore his shoes reproduced overnight. Now I'd give anything to trip over them. Strange what you miss when it's gone.

I walked my usual route on autopilot, past bins of apples and pears stacked like they were posing for a fall photo shoot. Someone had put out pomegranates, and I almost bought one out of habit—until the reminder hit: Gabe wasn't here to demolish it.

"Hey! Those are nice melons!" A loud, masculine voice boomed out over the general din near me.

My head snapped up as I searched for whoever had made the offensive statement. The comment couldn't have been aimed at me. I was in a University of California, San Francisco sweatshirt, old men's Levi 501s, and a crossbody bag. Nothing about me was giving "catcall bait," and my sweatshirt wasn't exactly a billboard. If I had 'nice melons', my sweatshirt would have offered sufficient cover.

Finally, I spotted the culprit: a man probably in his 40s with his wife and two children making a morning of shopping. He held up a honeydew melon, and she gave him a gentle nudge and ducked her head blushing—it looked like an inside joke between the two of them. While their parents were distracted, the kids quietly added more sweets to the shopping basket. Typical Ferry Market shenanigans.

I felt a brief pang of jealousy and loneliness. It wasn't even about the melon joke. It was the ease of them—family as a unit, bodies moving together like they belonged to each other. I had close friends—even though they were all married—and family in the area, so I was not completely in my lone wolf era. But this morning still felt quiet in a way I didn't like.

The family with the melons had completed their selections and moved as a group through the crowd towards another booth. I watched them briefly and then searched for my own melon. I started thumping a couple. My mother did it when she bought melons, so I did too. I found one that sounded about right and handed it to the booth worker.

"I saw you. Do you know what you were listening for?" the woman asked with a smile as she rang my purchase.

I ducked my head. "No. But it makes me feel like an informed adult when I do it!" I slid the melon into my basket and adjusted the handles on my wrist. The Olympic rings tattoo on the inside of my wrist—new enough to still be tender—peeked out when my sleeve rode up. I got it for Gabe. For his dream. For the way our lives revolved around a stopwatch and pool laps.

I could hear her laughter as I turned around to make my way to the exit. Out of the corner of my eye, I spotted a booth with fresh sourdough bread. I turned toward it and bumped directly into a tall, attractive Black man who appeared to be around my age. Of course, every piece of fruit that I had carefully selected flew out of my basket and went bouncing across the walkway.

"Oof! I'm sorry! Excuse me," I yelled to the man as I tried to prevent the falling fruit from getting away from me. People stepped around my runaway produce like it was an obstacle course, and I dropped into a crouch to scoop everything up before a honeydew took someone out.

The gentleman winked at me, and then he went after my melon, which had rolled under another booth. Crawling under the shelving, he came directly into contact with a pair of legs.

"Excuse me," the woman who owned the legs said, kicking at him and backing away. Once she realized what was happening, she bent over to pick up the melon.

The helpful but now embarrassed man backed out from under the shelves and stood up blushing. "Thank you. I was just trying to help her," he stated, pointing at me. "I'm sorry—no harm intended," he added as she handed him the somewhat battered fruit.

Backing further away from her kiosk, the man continued to apologize the entire time. By then, the woman in the booth was laughing at his embarrassment.

I felt my own face heat up. All of this because I can't walk straight when food is involved.

With a lot of apologies to the shoppers that I was blocking, I had placed everything else back into my basket by the time he reached me to return my honeydew. He gave me a goofy grin as he handed it over.

"I can't say that this was not a worthwhile endeavor," he said as I accepted his offering.

"Thank you for risking life and limb to rescue my breakfast!" I replied, blushing.

The man was quite handsome in a boyish way, with medium brown skin and a neatly cared for beard and low- cut afro. Dressed for a casual day at the market, he wore a Tennessee State University (in Nashville) sweatshirt and loose-fitting jeans.

"Anything for such a lovely young woman."

I barked out a laugh. Hearing myself referred to as a 'young woman' made me laugh as a 42-year-old lady. I wasn't old, but I was dancing towards middle age. "That's very nice of you to say." I could feel him staring at me, scanning my body intently. To shift his focus, I said, "I see you've stocked up on veggies. May I ask, are you a vegetarian?"

"Almost," he smiled.

His smile was lovely and drew me in. A couple holding hands had to separate to walk around us and gave us dirty looks for obstructing the center of the path. "Hey, I would love to chat for a few more minutes and not draw the ire of our fellow shoppers. Would you like to get a cup of coffee at that market coffee stand?" he added, pointing to the nearest one.

He motioned about 100 yards down the path to one of the bustling coffee stands in the market. The vendors there sold locally baked goods along with a variety of coffee drinks. I knew the stand. The woman behind the counter knew my order. That alone should've made this feel safe.

I eyed him cautiously but relented. *What could it hurt?*

2

grace

I should have known better than to say yes to coffee with a stranger.

But there we were, weaving through the crowd to the stand with four or five people ahead of us in line. At least it gave us a chance to talk.

"We haven't even properly introduced ourselves. My name is Curtis. Curtis Young. Coming over here once or twice a month is one of my guilty pleasures." He looked me up and down again, which made me uncomfortable again. "I picked the right Saturday to visit. What's your name?"

"Hi. I'm Grace. I come here most Saturdays to get ready for the week. I'm surprised we haven't run into each other before."

"This is a little early in the morning for me. I usually come later. Are you from around here?"

"Not too far away. I live in the Laurel Heights neighborhood right now."

"Laurel Heights, huh? That's a very nice area. Must be nice. There aren't many brothers and sisters living over there." Before I could respond, he quickly changed the subject, tilting his head towards the menu board. "What would you like to drink?"

"I'll get it. I almost caused you bodily harm with my clumsiness and flying fruits and vegetables. Consider it a reward for putting yourself out there and risking injury on my behalf." I tried to shake off the comment with a smile. Maybe he meant nothing by it, but I wasn't convinced. I recognized I lived in a nice, relatively expensive area—relative compared to other neighborhoods in expensive-ass San Francisco. I didn't know him though, so immediately assuming ill intent on his part was only going to feed into the bougie behavior most people in my neighborhood had.

He squinted at me and gave in. "Okay, you win. So, Grace, what do you do besides making kind men to risk their lives on the weekends?"

I hesitated at first before finally responding. "I'm a GI doctor over at UCSF. What do you do?"

"Oh, we both work in health care. I work at a natural health product company in Oakland. I used to work at a similar company near here, but I took a promotion at a better company on the other side of the bridge."

"Wow, congratulations." Something in my gut tightened. Natural health could mean a lot of things, and not all of them were benign. "Did you move to Oakland, or do you fight the traffic every day back and forth?"

We moved closer to the front of the line.

"Oh, I always lived in Oakland, but I grew up in Tennessee. My family still lives there. San Francisco is too expensive to live in for most, but since you're a doctor, I can see why you can. How did you end up in San Francisco as opposed to other places? Did you ever consider moving down south?"

There it was again—money, assumptions, the little test questions dressed up as conversation. This was going to be an issue. I could tell. "I grew up in Berkeley. My father and mother worked at the college. I went to college and medical school there." I kept it vague on purpose. I didn't feel like defending my life to a stranger in a coffee line.

Red flag. This would not end well.

"So, you're one of those..." He started. "I went to Tennessee State University. May I ask: are you mixed or adopted? Just asking. Parents working at Berkeley? Odds are that one or both are white. And while you are rather light-complexioned, you obviously aren't white."

I recoiled visibly, then shook my head slowly—surprised I was having this invasive and rude conversation with this man I didn't know. "Both of my parents are Black. I'm Black. Let's change the subject because I just met you, and I will not defend my family and our choices for where we live or how we live. If you don't mind."

I could already feel myself mentally backing away. Get the coffee. Pay. Leave. Don't get dragged into this. This was the fastest that a potential suitor outed himself as not the right guy for me...

"Fair enough. How did you end up in gastroenterology? That is what GI means, right?"

I shrugged. "I found the GI system fascinating. I also love the ability to improve and possibly save lives by diagnosing colon cancer, especially in our people. The earlier, the better."

We moved closer to the kiosk counter. "Well, at least you aren't one of those doctors who push unsafe treatments. There are so many natural options to treat so many conditions that the establishment is trying to hide. The company I work for has a vaccine substitute that you should look at. Do you know any pediatricians? I'm sure they would enjoy having options."

And there it was. The reason behind the bad vibe that I got from him. All his questions led to this moment.

Before I could reply, we hit the counter. Emma, the woman working the counter, greeted me happily.

"Grace! I haven't seen you in a couple of weeks. Have you been avoiding my little coffee stand?" She asked with a smile as she typed in my standard order: a cup of Kenyan coffee with one brown sugar and vanilla creamer and three chocolate croissants. "Still correct, right?"

I nodded, returning her grin. "Still correct," I confirmed, because Emma was a safe island in the middle of this. Then, because I have manners even when I'm annoyed, I added, "He's got an order too."

Curtis tipped his head at me and said, "I would like a medium caffe macchiato, if that's okay." The look he gave me made me even more annoyed, and I looked away and exhaled loudly.

We quickly got our drinks, and I paid for them. Emma hid a smile as she handed me the receipt. I took my croissants and placed them in my basket with everything else. As Curtis and I walked away from the booth, I looked at my phone to check the time. "Oh wow! I really must get going. I'm having brunch with my girlfriends today."

"Are they all doctors too? That sounds like a fun time." The sarcasm dripped from his words.

It didn't sound like a fun time the way he said it. I ignored his statement because I was almost free from this 'date'.

"You know, it was really nice to meet you today. I'm sure I'll see you again at the market sometime." I held out my hand for a polite shake and nothing else. Curtis was feeling brave today; he had both arms out—cup of coffee in one hand—to hug me.

I cringed and continued to hold my hand out.

He looked at it suspiciously and then reluctantly shook it. "I would love to take you out sometime. Show you around Oakland, take you to places that you haven't been before."

Like I had never been to Oakland?

Like he was about to introduce me to things I'd seen as a teenager. His audacity was starting to piss me off.

He thought I was a bougie princess he could educate about that life. Probably true if that's what I was looking for. Whatever story he'd built about me in his head, I didn't want any part of it.

I flashed an apologetic smile. "I don't think so. But thank you for saving my breakfast, and I hope you have a wonderful day."

"Oh, that's it? It's like that?" Curtis pulled a pout and then backed up. "I can walk you to your car."

"That's okay. It's not far. I don't want to put you out or anything."

He squinted at me again but decided to let it go. "It was nice meeting you. I'm sure we will see each other again around here one day."

I nodded and quickly turned on my heel to get to my car, heart thudding anxiously. I kept my free hand in my crossbody bag, where my pepper spray was. I peeked over my shoulder several times—I didn't see Curtis following me. At least he didn't know what car I was driving. Besides, I wasn't alone out here. It was a busy Saturday morning with people scattered everywhere.

I stood in front of my black Mercedes G wagon that Evan had bought me right before I asked for a divorce. The black G-wagon sat there like a flashing sign that said: get rid of me now if you ever want to move on from your ex-husband. As I unlocked the key fob, I heard a step behind me. I whirled around, pulling my pepper spray canister out at the same time. Face to face with Curtis, who instantly held his hands up.

"Hey, hey! I just wanted to make sure you got to your car safely, and I wanted to give you my card just in case you wanted to contact me." He looked scared by my defensive stance. Good. Let him be scared.

My pulse slammed hard enough to make my hands shake. I exhaled loudly again and climbed into my driver's seat. I said nothing to him, nor did I accept the card from his outstretched fingers. Closing the car door, I stared at him until he tucked the business card under my windshield wiper, mumbling about how I didn't appreciate a good man trying to be nice.

At least he retreated quickly. Once he was out of my line of sight, I sat there for a second with my hand still wrapped around the pepper spray, breathing like I'd just run a sprint. Bullet dodged.

My phone buzzed through the car's speakers before I could even pull off.

"Glad I caught you. Are you still at the market?" Autumn De Luca started talking without greeting, per her habit. "Theo just asked for some of the chocolate croissants that you always buy at Ferry Street. No biggie if you aren't—we can have some delivered. Maybe bring a dozen or so, because he'll eat them all week. At least if I let him, he needs to make sure that he eats right--"

Sometimes, I have to crash into Autumn's train of thought just to get a word in edgewise. Autumn didn't greet—she launched right into whatever it was she wanted to talk about. "I'm just pulling away. And I'm not going back in there right now because I met an unpleasant guy who I made the mistake of having coffee with. I really don't want to see him again!"

"Gi-r-rl-l! Just come on over here, just in case he's following you." Autumn loved true crime. Investigating the supposed stalker guy would be right in her wheelhouse. "But I'm impressed: you saw a red flag and removed yourself from the situation," she added.

To change the vibe, I said, "I have to change. I know you keep saying we don't have to dress up for these functions--"

"You don't. My home is your home. We're friends. Claudia and Zoe have agreed not to come dressed to kill today. Can you manage that?"

The easy answer was to go home and lock my doors.

The smarter answer was to be around people who loved me.

"Yes," I said before I could back out.

"Good," Autumn replied. "Now drive."

3

grace

The second Curtis disappeared from my rearview mirror, my body decided it was safe to feel everything at once. My hands were still shaking on the steering wheel as I pulled away from the curb. I kept my eyes flicking from mirror to mirror like I was searching for a ghost. I'd been a doctor long enough to know adrenaline when I felt it but experiencing it in my own body always pissed me off.

Like, great. Now I have to be scared *and* inconvenienced.

I told him Laurel Heights.

Rookie. Mistake.

I hadn't really dated in so long I'd forgotten the rules: the ones you only remember after you break them. Don't hand strangers details. Don't explain yourself. Don't smooth things over when your instincts are already in fight-or-flight. And yet I did all of it because a man asked me to get coffee.

At the next stoplight, my eyes dropped to the passenger seat—croissants, fruit, the stupid honeydew, all sitting there like evidence of my poor judgment. My mind wouldn't let the scene go. It kept replaying the worst parts like it was trying to make sure I learned the lesson the hard way like it was grading me. One mistake at a time.

Are you mixed or adopted?

I'd met men like Curtis before—men who thought they had a right to decide what kind of Black you were and then punish you for the answer.

"One of those," he'd said.

As if I were a problem that he'd already decided upon.

I exhaled through my nose, forcing my shoulders down.

I told myself to calm down, because that's what I always do. Talk myself out of it. Act like my body is being dramatic.

Except my nervous system didn't believe any of it. The city moved around me as normal, but my brain kept zooming in on threats that weren't there, all because a man decided to turn coffee into an interrogation.

By the time I hit Geary, my heart rate had finally started to come down. That's when I remembered the business card. I could still see him tucking it under the windshield wiper as if he were so sure that I was going to give him a call back.

"You don't appreciate a good man," he'd muttered.

As if a good man had to announce that they were good after following you to your car.

Finally, I reached my neighborhood where my two-bedroom, one-bath Laurel Heights home welcomed me. I loved everything about my little house: the size, the floor plan, the décor. Evan and I used to live a few blocks over in a bigger place—back when we were still pretending we could outwork the cracks in our marriage. After the divorce, I downsized on purpose. I wanted a house that didn't feel like it was still waiting on the life we'd planned. It was just enough space for me and Gabe whenever he came to visit. If I moved next year, I would rent it out instead of selling it. I loved this home and thought it was a brilliant investment.

Dropping my purchases on the kitchen counter, I went to my bedroom to pull out the outfit I had planned to wear. A long, flowy blue sundress—dressy but not that dressy. I didn't trust Autumn when it came to clothes. She had an entire wing of their house dedicated to clothes, shoes, and makeup, and I rarely saw her without a full face. She really didn't care what we wore, but my mother raised me to match the occasion and my surroundings. At my house, a sweatshirt could pass. At Autumn's? Not a chance. Eating brunch off real china with actual silver did something to a person. It made you sit up straighter, even if you tried to pretend it didn't.

I frowned. I needed to steam my blue dress because it seemed to have wrinkled itself up again. And I wanted to wear it. Autumn could swear up and down she was in Juicy Couture all she wanted—my mother's voice would still be in my head.

I hung the dress in the bathroom, turned on my portable steamer to knock out the main wrinkles, and returned to the kitchen. Checking my watch, I saw it was 10AM. Brunch would start around 11. Plenty of time. At least in theory.

I put my fruits and vegetables into the refrigerator. I told myself I'd meal prep later. That was a lie I'd been telling myself more often lately. After a quick shower. I checked my hair. In its natural state, it was curly with a tendency to frizz at the slightest sign of humidity. The shorter I wore it, the more manageable the curls were, but I had been letting it grow since June. It was going into a bun today.

While I was getting dressed, my mother, Lena Billings, called me. I put her on speaker.

"Hi, Mom! What's up? I can't talk long. I'm running late for Autumn's brunch." I quickly steamed my dress as we talked.

"I just called to make sure you were still coming tomorrow, and that you hadn't invented a reason to skip dinner."

"Yes, I'm still coming," I said. "Are Victor and Stacia coming too?"

The silence on the other end told me everything I needed to know. My brother and I still lived in the San Fransico area, but our sister Celeste had moved to Korea after getting married. With Gabe in Miami, my mother had been on a mission to keep everybody she could within arm's reach. Monthly dinners were her new hobby.

"As far as I know, he is bringing that woman. It's going to be a long afternoon with her there. Please, Lord, help me maintain my manners. I would love to tell her what I think of her."

"Mom, try to relax. We don't know what goes on behind closed doors."

"Nothing good, as you can see. Get to your brunch. See you tomorrow."

I disconnected, feeling tense about tomorrow's festivities. Knowing my family, things could get ugly. Slipping into my dress, I twirled in front of the three-way mirror in my closet. I loved the way the dress cascaded almost to the floor so I could wear my Chucks without drama. It was sometimes challenging to find a dress that long as I was 5'9" but Autumn always directed me to reasonably priced tall clothing options. As a former model, she knew where to go.

Hopefully, my dress would be the most dramatic conversation piece on Nob Hill today.

It wouldn't be. I knew that the second I thought it.

2

Somehow time got away from me.

As I headed over to Autumn's, I glanced at the dashboard and swore under my breath. Late. Not "Autumn-late," but late enough. Right on cue, my phone rang as I turned onto her block. This time it was Claudia Booker, MD—calling from Autumn's phone.

"Where are you, G.? I'm actually here on time and child-free for three hours and you aren't here. We want to eat, and Autumn's making us wait until you arrive. I'm starving! I can finally eat without a starving preteen or sticky-fingered children swiping food off my plate. Hurry up!"

Claudia and I came up together at UCSF. Residency does that—turns coworkers into family whether you like it or not. She married Xavier, her residency boyfriend, and somehow, they were still disgustingly solid... even with three kids and the twin four-year-olds running their home like tiny CEOs. When my divorce finalized, she threw me a party I didn't ask for and absolutely needed. "No Evan talk," she'd announced. "Not one tear. We're celebrating you." It helped me get through.

"I don't know what happened to the time. I thought I had this scheduled this out better."

Autumn chimed in from the background, "Probably stressing over the weird coffee date."

"Coffee date?" Claudia echoed. "I thought you went to the farmer's market?"

I heard Claudia lower her voice. "She found a man?"

Autumn hissed something I couldn't make out, but it sounded a lot like, "Stop talking."

I raised an eyebrow. "What are you two whispering about?"

"Nothing," Claudia said too fast. "Just hurry up."

I narrowed my eyes at the road like it had answers. "Is Zoe there yet?" What were these two up to? And honestly, it would serve me right with all the meddling I did with Evan and MacKenzie. At that point, I was on Autumn's street, so I held my fire for now.

"Yes," Claudia said, and I could hear the grin in her voice. "But she's in the bathroom. We might not be seeing her much today."

Zoe was pregnant. Violently so.

Autumn made a sound like she was personally offended by the concept. "I don't know how you all did it." She shuddered. "When my momma had my little sister, I was twelve and I knew then that it would never happen to me!'"

"Twelve, girl?" I teased. "I thought it was ten,"

"Either way," Autumn replied, dead serious. "Traumatic."

By then I was on Autumn's street, and the gate to their home was coming up. There was a guard, Isaac—Theo's guy, though at this point he felt less like security and more like a friend. Isaac saw my car, lifted a hand in greeting, and opened the gate electronically without me even slowing down.

I drove down the curved driveway to a small courtyard where the brunch participants parked their vehicles. I didn't see Theo's Rolls, which meant he'd likely told his driver to take him out for a while so Autumn could visit with her girls in peace.

I scrambled out of my car, peeked at myself in my car window and gave my hair a pat. Claudia was waiting for me at the door.

"I have been pacing around waiting for you to get here!" Claudia yanked the door open like she'd been counting down the seconds. She looked too excited for a woman with three kids and a medical degree. She was a tall woman—actually, all my friends were tall, 5'9" like me or taller—and she was an inch taller than me.

After kids and aging, she had become a fuller-figured, shapely woman with round hips and ass. Xavier loved her when she was thinner, but now? He acted like he'd won the lottery and wanted everybody to know it. The way he touched her, the way he stared at her like he was still surprised she was his... plus what Claudia had shared over wine when she was feeling bold. Yeah. They were doing just fine.

Claudia spun me around after giving me a hug. "I do love this dress!"

Autumn appeared from around the corner, eating a sushi roll. She still looked like the model she had been twenty years ago with a clean face, mascara, and a touch of lip gloss. To my surprise, she really was wearing a Juicy Couture tracksuit. In true Autumn fashion though, she had on some designer sneakers and a designer tank top. I didn't recognize either brand. I didn't need to. Autumn's outfits always looked expensive even when she swore they weren't.

Claudia frowned at Autumn, then at the sushi in her hand. "Hey! You said we had to wait!"

Autumn hugged me like she hadn't just been caught red-handed. "Technicalities," she said. "She's here now. Let's eat. We have other things to do."

Brunch at the De Lucas was always a veritable feast, and Autumn treated the menu like a suggestion, not a theme. Pancakes, French toast, Eggs Benedict, quiche, shrimp and grits, pastries, smoked salmon, fruit and yogurt plus Autumn's favorite—sushi. A mimosa bar sat ready. The platters were family heirlooms, so Autumn served us on reusable plates and flatware. Nobody wanted to be the one who broke Theo's great-grandmother's china.

The staff moved around us like they'd been trained to be invisible. Claudia and I sat down, and plates appeared in front of us before I even finished adjusting my dress. Autumn quietly asked Zoe if she was coming out of the powder room where she had camped out. Morning sickness had taken over her life and at this point, even Autumn was concerned.

Zoe was 43 with a thirteen-year-old daughter—I met her at Gabe's school when both children were in kindergarten. She and her husband, Cooper, had waffled for years about whether they wanted another child. Finally, at forty, they decided no more, and Coop got a vasectomy. Then they fell victim to that tiny chance of failure everybody jokes about, and nobody expects. Surprise, Zoe was pregnant and hating every minute of life right now.

Almost immediately, Autumn returned with Zoe trailing behind her, looking a little green around the gills and a lot like she wanted to fight her own body.

"Hi Zoe," I said as she came over and gave Claudia and me both hugs. I thought it was risky for her to sit at the table while we ate, but it looked like she was going to try.

"Hi girls. I hope you two are feeling better than I am," she said as she asked the butler to bring her a dry waffle and a glass of ginger ale. "Fucking vasectomy and fucking anniversary. Let me tell you, Claudia—don't celebrate your anniversary riding Zay cowboy style without protection. You might end up like me," she added with a wry grin as she put her hand gingerly under her nose.

Claudia blushed, and Autumn and I started laughing. Claudia's obvious discomfort with blunt sex talk when sober made it worse. I forgot about my suspicions about my friends' plans.

Like they lulled me into a sense of calm. Little did I know what was coming...

4

luke

Fitzgerald was giving me the look again.

My chocolate lab sat beside the chess table, head tilted, brown eyes full of pity. The "you're getting your ass kicked" look. Even my dog knew I was losing.

"Can we get this over with?" I leaned back in my chair and twirled my Stanford class ring. My father had insisted I get this ring as proof I'd attended and graduated. He'd paid for it. I didn't wear it regularly until he passed when I was thirty-three. My nod to him.

Kyle Washington, my best friend and the bane of my chess existence, was studying the board like he wasn't sure what to do next. Which was bullshit. He knew exactly what he was doing.

"You're dragging this out," I said. "The abuse of your friend and business partner is not pretty."

Some of the spectators around us laughed.

We were at the Chess Club at The Mechanics' Institute—longest-running chess program in the US. Their Chess in the Community event drew a crowd. Other players were waiting impatiently for us to clear the table.

Kyle adjusted his glasses and made a show of his decision. At my loud exhale, he laughed and made the obvious move. "One day, I'm going to stop playing with you like that. Checkmate." He stood up to let the next person take his chair. "And let's go."

I followed his lead and pulled my chair out for the next young woman who'd been waiting. She appeared to be in her twenties and batted her eyes at me. "Thank you! Are you going to stay and watch? Maybe we can play next round."

I frowned. I was old enough to be her father. Though I appreciated the flattery. "Not this time. I have some errands to run. It's a beautiful day. Enjoy your game."

As we walked away, Kyle laughed. "Even the young ones are still chasing you! And you can't find one woman who keeps your attention for more than a moment?"

I shrugged. "I haven't had a lightning-bolt moment like you did with Jada. Don't frown at me. Remember, I was there. All ability to create coherent sentences immediately disappeared—unfortunate since she was asking you questions for an article for the school paper. Lucky for you, she thought you were cute and made sure the article didn't make you look like a clown."

Kyle waved the story off. "Maybe so. But your time is coming." He glanced at his watch. "Anyway, are we stopping somewhere? The kids will kill me—actually, the wife will too—if I come back without something sweet for everyone."

We headed to the bakery two blocks from the chess site. The place served dog-safe items, so Fitzgerald trotted along happily. After Kyle carefully evaluated the pastry options, he selected one for each kid and two for him and Jada to share. He also ordered coffee. I got chai, a muffin, and a dog-safe muffin for Fitzgerald.

We sat outside. The conversation devolved into trash talk about chess, then football—one area where I could definitely beat him.

"So, how's the company doing?" I asked.

Kyle grinned. "Closing in on three billion. Can you believe that?"

I shook my head. Sometimes I still couldn't wrap my mind around it. Sloane-Wash Sciences had started during our senior year at Stanford when Kyle discovered an adapter for a common medical device. I'd been a football player determined to get my biomedical engineering degree because my chances of making the NFL were slim. Kyle was the pre-med student working in a lab who needed funding for a prototype.

I'd just gotten my Pell Grant money. I handed it over to him.

That prototype sparked investor interest. Kyle had set up a C-Corp and made me VP with 50% ownership. I didn't even know about it at first until I was at the NFL combine. An undersized, aggressive linebacker from Stanford who somehow caught scouts' attention.

Kyle called me while I was testing. "Our little company is worth millions now."

Just like that, I was a millionaire.

An NFL team drafted me in the late rounds. I made it onto an active roster for a couple years. Made up for my lack of size—six-three, two-twenty—by throwing my body at anybody coming at me, no matter how fast or how big. Teammates admired me. I got injured a lot.

After three years, I was tired. Done. But I didn't know what to do next.

I lounged for a couple months, chased a few women. But interest in me had changed since I was a *former* football player. I got bored. I was twenty-five with a Stanford engineering degree. I had choices.

Kyle offered me the option to join the company full-time and finally put good use to that biomedical engineering degree.

The life of leisure wasn't cutting it, so I did.

Best decision I ever made.

"Three billion," I repeated. "Your wife know she married a genius?"

"She reminds me daily." Kyle bought flowers for Jada on our way to the parking lot. "If you ever find that woman, buy her flowers all the time. Keeps you out of trouble. Trust me."

We reached the pay lot. Kyle's driver, Trevor, was pulling up in the Phantom. I leaned against my new electric BMW i7—my first real splurge on a car. Kyle joked that I held onto money like it would disappear. Until this car, I'd only driven used BMWs.

"You coming into the office this week?" I asked.

"I will be on the investor calls. And I have a meeting in Seattle. But I am taking Jada and the kids with me. Divisional football game. I haven't been able to convert her to an SF fan—she's still into the Seahawks and slowly turning the kids against the Niners."

"So why are you helping her?" I laughed. "Expect the kids to come back wearing 12th Man shirts."

"I know. I have a plan—box seats, food, meeting players on the field. If that can't sway them, I've got nothing."

"Might be too late." I grinned. "I'll be in the office one or two days this week. Checking on the latest study results. The investors need an update to decide whether to publish the phase III results before year-end."

Kyle smiled. "I knew that biomedical degree would come in handy. And to think you almost became a man of leisure."

We dapped each other up. We talked several times a day—business and personal. He was the brother I never had. His family had been my family, especially after the mess with my father's divorce and remarriage.

I wouldn't have the life I do without his help.

Kyle climbed into the Phantom. I watched him drive off, then looked down at Fitzgerald.

"What do you think, buddy? Should I finally settle down like Kyle keeps saying?"

Fitzgerald tilted his head.

"Yeah. That's what I thought."

I climbed into my car. Saturday stretched ahead of me—wide open, my own plans, nobody waiting.

Exactly how I liked it.

Or at least, that's what I kept telling myself.

5

grace

After we'd eaten ourselves into a stupor, we moved to the sitting room—our usual post-brunch routine to catch up on family, work, and whatever drama was happening in the world.

But today, Autumn went straight for my throat.

"So, tell me more about this unfortunate date." She sipped her Bellini. "Why did you have coffee with some guy you met at the market? Was he a farmer?"

I frowned at the sudden spotlight. Usually, questions about my life were an afterthought—I'd chime in when there was something to share, which was rare. It was far more interesting to hear about everyone else's lives. My contributions were typically dating fails anyway.

"It's simple," I said. "I dropped my fruit. He helped me chase it down. I thought it would be nice to buy him a coffee. I didn't think it would turn into a national incident."

"But it wasn't nice or fun at all?" Autumn set down her glass. "Hmmm. You were aiming too low again."

I rolled my eyes. "Here we go."

"Look, we get it. Your *modus operandi* in relationships is control—especially since Evan."

"Yes. For me, the fairy tale of getting swept off your feet generally leads to tears, heartbreak, and misery. I don't function well in that headspace. We saw how poorly things went before."

"You picked the wrong guy to try to get swept up with," Autumn said. "Now you've swung too far the other way. You pick guys who you know aren't *the guy*. Someone you think you can control your emotions around. Like today. And your new way isn't working either. They still manage to make a mess in your life."

"How about if I promise to take more chances? Can we not do whatever it is you people are about to unleash on me?" I crossed and uncrossed my legs. I had my keys in my hand, ready to run.

Claudia had been staring at me so intently, I subconsciously touched my face to make sure I didn't have food around my mouth. "Grace, admit that you've had a—how should I put it—an *interesting* social life over the past few years. You're a gorgeous, smart woman with a brilliant career, and yet you continually find the most unserious men. We want to liven up your life a bit—"

Dread crept over me as I looked at each of my three friends. Both Claudia and Autumn looked back at me with glee. Zoe had her eyes closed—the nausea must be coming back.

This was my karma for my matchmaking shenanigans in Miami.

I was about to be handled.

An attractive young woman walked into the room from the kitchen and stopped in front of my chair. I didn't know who she was, but I expected she was part of the "surprise" my friends had planned.

She appeared to be about thirty, average height, with her hair in an Afro wrapped with a scarf.

Autumn stood next to her with her arm around the young woman's shoulders.

"Grace, this is Harmony Zee. The girls and I reached out to her." Autumn sat down next to me. "You've had a tough stretch of relationships, as you must admit. Today included!" She looked at the other two women for support.

Claudia jumped in. "It's been over eight years since you and Evan divorced. We don't expect you to get married, but we know you like having companionship. And most of the guys you've dated since your divorce have been...uh...how can I say this?" She looked around for someone to fill in the word.

"Shitty. Like I feel," Zoe chimed in. She was curled up in another chair, truly green at this point. "I'm sorry, girl. I love you, but it's like you pick a boring guy with red flags on purpose. Then struggle with why things are going to shit. That is now my favorite word. Shit or some variation of it. And if you'll excuse me, I'm going to go throw up."

The four remaining women watched her lurch out of her chair and back to the nearest powder room. Autumn grimaced but turned back to me and Harmony.

"We want you to allow someone else to help select your dates for a bit. You can just relax and see what you think of each guy. No pressure. Maybe it'll help you get back to knowing what you want and feeling comfortable taking it."

"I didn't ask for that kind of help. No offense to you." I directed the second comment to Harmony. She seemed uncomfortable with how the conversation had started and made a move to respond, but I kept talking. "I know my dating acumen has sucked for years—maybe my entire life. My therapist and I decided that my perfectionist tendencies could be a factor. I get it may be difficult watching me struggle, but this? I can't believe you three did this—no offense."

Harmony didn't look offended at all. "None taken. I would've been surprised if you'd responded any other way," she stated firmly. "The cases where friends have hired me to help someone who's been having a difficult time in the dating department have all started this way. The friends trying to explain themselves and the client getting a bit in their feelings. Typical."

I sat there with my mouth open, unsure how to respond. I was angry, but a small part of me could see their point. Even if we didn't talk about my dating woes as a group, I did have conversations with individuals in my circle. Even MacKenzie got treated to occasional complaints.

Maybe letting someone else take the reins could be good... although this young woman looked like a girl. What could she know? Had she even successfully matched anyone older than a teenager?

"Putting you in charge of my love life seems like a bridge too far. No offense. Again. What are your qualifications? Where did you all find her? No—"

Autumn rolled her eyes. "Please stop saying 'no offense.' You know that means it's offensive—just don't be mad at *her* about the situation."

I opened my mouth to reply but Autumn continued talking. "We found her online. Google is free. We wanted a Black woman. A matchmaker in San Francisco. Then we contacted the people who had testimonials on her site to make sure they were real. Better Business Bureau. We did our due diligence. But no guarantees, right?"

Harmony held up her hand. "It's okay. We don't have to make this an exclusive deal. Dr. Robertson can just try a few dates with my service—and keep doing what she's doing too, if she chooses. As long as you let know about any extracurriculars. I bet she'll find that she'll meet someone interesting and compatible through me." She turned to me. "I want you to see what it feels like to not have to work so hard for your relationships. This is just from what they've told me."

I was going to reply, but that statement—*not working so hard*—stopped me. I had to sit with that for a minute.

As if she could read my mind, Harmony walked back into the kitchen and returned with a personalized leather messenger bag that said "Harmony Zee." She pulled out a stack of papers and handed them to me.

"Just so you know, I'm certified by the International Coaching Federation. I have a psychology degree from UCLA. My everyday job is school social worker. I've matched several couples, but my best matches were the ones I did in high school."

Claudia walked over to peek at the papers. "Matches in high school? You were doing this back then?"

Harmony got a faraway look in her eyes. She told us about two couples from different high schools that she matched together who were married now—each had dated through high school and college.

That was impressive, I had to admit. Getting someone together for a couple dates was difficult enough. Finding soulmates for high schoolers was diabolical.

"What are these?" I eyed the front page. It looked like an interest form. Flipping through, I noticed a place for my signature. "This is the contract?"

"Oh, this is the form where you tell me about what you want. Your past dating experiences. What was good about them? Tell me about your marriage. I need information to build a profile for you and a profile for the type of guy you want to spend time with. Notice I didn't say the guy you want to marry. Marrying you off is not the goal here. Just having some fun!"

The packet contained fifteen pages. No way in hell was I filling all those out. Remembering any of my less-than-optimal relationships wasn't fun, but all of them one right after the other? Triggering.

"I'll fill out a few pages, but not all of this! You can ask me questions instead."

Harmony looked at her watch. "Do you have some time right now? It's almost two. Could we spend ninety minutes chatting at most—just chatting? I'd like to get a feel for what you really want without your friends around. I know they have expectations. But I want to know about *your* expectations. They may have paid for my services, but you're my client. I won't be sharing anything with them either."

Claudia and Autumn both jumped in. "What do you mean we can't get any updates?" Autumn asked, crossing her arms.

"You can. From her." Harmony pointed at me and stood up. "If you can meet me at my office for our intake chat, I can get started today. I have some ideas. And I can explain how I find your dates."

"That's it?" Claudia crossed her arms too.

They looked ridiculous, and I burst out laughing. Served them right.

Harmony left after our conversation. The butler walked her out. I followed them to the door as Harmony texted me her office address.

I had a very limited understanding of her at that point. But I still agreed to meet her in an hour at her office. I still wasn't totally sold on this experiment, but this had to be better than whatever I was doing.

When I walked back into the room, Zoe had reentered the mix, and my three friends were anxiously awaiting my comments.

"So? Are you excited? A little?" Claudia asked.

"I have nothing to say yet. I need to check her – and this -- out."

"Please keep an open mind. We're only trying to help," Zoe added.

That comment almost brought me to tears. "I know."

I packed up my belongings and went around and hugged each of them, planning to leave before I started crying. "Anyway, this is my karmic payback for my previous matchmaking sins from this summer." I gave them a weak smile as I walked out.

The butler walked me to the door. By the time I made it to my car, tears were streaming down my face. I felt horrible and grateful at the same time. My friends thought I was so bad at dating that I needed outside help.

And I agreed with them.

But they cared enough about me to try to do something about it.

My heart couldn't handle it.

6

luke

I was running through my afternoon schedule—three-mile run, pool laps, maybe get some meal prep done—when my phone rang through the car speakers. Harmony. My half-sister's timing was impeccable as always.

"Hey, did you survive?" Her voice filled the car, warm and amused. "Or did Kyle wipe the floor with you again?"

"Complete annihilation." I merged onto Geary, heading toward the Marina on autopilot. "What's up? You sound like you're in a good mood."

"I just signed a new client! I'm really excited about this one. Just met her at a friend's place in Nob Hill. It seems like such a great fit for what I do."

That caught my attention. "She's got friends in Nob Hill? Is she Black?"

"Yes, she's Black. And no, I'm not telling you anything else about her." Her tone shifted, protective. "You know you can't help yourself from offering opinions, and I don't need your commentary on my clients."

I had to laugh at that. "Fair. I did overstep that one time. But in my defense, most of your clients are actively hunting for a ring and a baby carriage. Not exactly my speed, so you're right—I don't need details."

"Good. Now listen, I need you to swing by my office today. I've got preserves Mom made for your mother, and my mom is on my case about still having them. Since you're driving right past on your way home from chess, can you grab them? Where are you now?"

I checked the intersection. Already past 25th. "I'm already past your office, actually. But I'm seeing Mom for dinner later. Can I come by then?"

It wasn't entirely true—I could turn around—but backtracking would throw off my entire afternoon. I lived in the Marina, and Harmony's office was out in the Outer Richmond. Even if I were heading straight to Mom's, it'd be a detour. I had a system: chess, breakfast, run, pool. I'd already missed too many workouts this week to start improvising now.

"What time?" She didn't sound convinced. "I'll wait here after my client leaves. Just tell me when."

I glanced at my watch. "I told Mom I'd be there at 5. I can stop by your office at 4."

"4 o'clock. Got it." There was a smile in her voice. "You know, one of these days you're going to meet a woman who'll mess up that precious schedule of yours."

"One day. Maybe. But not today," I said. "See you at 4."

"We'll see about that." She laughed and hung up.

I merged into the right lane, already recalculating my afternoon. Two miles instead of three for the run. Pool laps tomorrow morning instead of tonight. Still doable.

Harmony's comment lingered for a moment before I dismissed it. My schedule worked perfectly fine as it was.

7

grace

I sat in the G-wagon outside Harmony's office building for a full five minutes, hands still gripping the steering wheel.

This was insane. Letting a stranger—a woman I'd met for all of thirty minutes—pick men for me to date. The control freak in me wanted to reverse out of this parking spot and text my friends a polite "thanks but no thanks."

But I'd already seen the hope in their faces. Already accepted that maybe—just maybe—they had a point.

I checked my reflection in the rearview mirror, smoothed down a flyaway hair, and forced myself out of the car before I could talk myself out of it.

The office building sat on a busy corner in the Outer Richmond, squeezed between residential apartments. Through the glass doors, I spotted a security guard at a desk—older man, gray hair, completely absorbed in whatever was on his phone. He didn't even glance up when I walked past.

Note to self: this building's security is performative at best.

I took the stairs to the third floor, partly for the exercise, mostly to burn off nervous energy. The hallway was narrow, fluorescent-lit, with four office doors. The one Harmony had texted me about had a nameplate that read "Dr. Kellogg, Marriage and Family Therapy."

I checked the address twice. Definitely the right place.

Before I could knock, the door swung open. Harmony's face lit up.

"Grace! Come in, come in." She stepped back, reading my confusion. "I sublet from Dr. Kellogg. Two weekends a month, I get the smaller office. It works for both of us."

Smart. Affordable. I followed her through a compact waiting room—two chairs, a small side table with outdated magazines—and into an office barely larger than my walk-in closet. A modular desk sat against the window, multiple monitors connected to a laptop, folders stacked with color-coded tabs. In the corner, a small table with a second laptop, clearly set up for clients.

Everything was organized with the care of someone who ran their operation on minimal square footage and maximum efficiency.

"It's small, I know." Harmony settled into her desk chair. "But Dr. Kellogg wasn't using this space at all. Now she gets a little extra income, and I get a professional setting without breaking the bank. Win-win." She gestured to the corner table. "I've got a questionnaire pulled up on that laptop for you. Take your time with it—some of the questions are pretty personal, but they're there for a reason. I need to make sure I'm matching you with the right kind of people. Do you need anything?"

"I'm fine, thanks."

I sat down at the client table and I started clicking through.

Standard stuff at first—age, occupation, interests, dealbreakers. Then: *Describe your most significant relationship. What ended it?*

I typed quickly: "Marriage. Lasted 5 years. Ended due to emotional incompatibility and one-sided effort. He was in love with someone else and not me. We share a child together. As long as we manage the topics, we get along fine now. We've learned to coexist."

The next few questions were easier—what I liked to do for fun, what kind of dates appealed to me, whether I wanted kids (already had one, wasn't looking for more).

Then I hit the question that made my fingers freeze over the keyboard:

Have you experienced sexual assault, coercion, or violation of consent? This is asked to ensure your matches understand consent, respect boundaries, and provide emotional safety. You can choose to discuss details in person if you prefer.

I stared at the screen.

My therapist and I had worked through this. I knew, or at least a part of me knew deep down, that what happened wasn't my fault. That Todd was a predator who manipulated a sixteen-year-old girl.

But sitting here, about to check that box, the shame still sat heavy in my chest.

I clicked "Yes" and typed in the text box: *Prefer to discuss in person.*

The rest of the questionnaire blurred together. I finished in about fifteen minutes, giving surface-level answers that were technically honest but revealed nothing.

When I stood up, Harmony glanced at her watch and pressed her lips together—clearly noting I'd rushed through—but said nothing. She gestured to the chair across from her desk.

"Water? Coffee?"

"I'm good." I settled into the chair, hyperaware of the notepad in front of her, the pen in her hand.

Harmony pulled up my questionnaire on one of her monitors, scanning it briefly. When she looked back at me, her expression was kinder if that were even possible.

"I want to start by acknowledging what you shared at the end of the questionnaire. I ask that question because I need to match you with men who understand what consent really means—not just physically, but emotionally. Men who respect your boundaries, your pace, your needs." She paused. "Would you be comfortable talking about it? You don't have to go into detail if you don't want to."

I took a breath. This was why I was here, wasn't it? To stop hiding and actually take a chance on love?

"I was in high school," I said. "I was sixteen. There was this senior—Todd. I had a crush on him, thought if I showed him how much I cared, he'd feel the same." My hands were in my lap now, fingers laced together. "I made him a homemade birthday cake. Brought it to his house."

Harmony's pen moved across her notepad, but her eyes stayed on me.

"He got me alone. Told me afterward it was my fault—for showing up, for wanting his attention. I didn't want him to get in trouble, so I accepted the blame. Told myself that it was my fault, just like he had. And I..." I swallowed. "I believed him."

"For how long?" Harmony's voice was steady, warm.

"Years. I didn't understand what it really was until college. Didn't deal with it until later."

Harmony set down her pen. "And by then, you were already with Evan?"

I blinked. "How did you—"

"You said your marriage lasted five years. Divorced for around eight. You would've been in medical school or right after when you met him."

"Evan and I met after." The pieces were clicking together in my own head even as I said them out loud.

"And Evan was in love with someone else when you met him."

"Yes." My throat felt tight. "I knew that. I knew she'd left him and that he wasn't over her. But I thought... I thought if I never asked for anything, if I was perfect enough—the perfect wife, perfect mother, perfect earner—then he'd choose me. Because asking for too much, wanting too much...that's what got me hurt before."

The realization took over me as the words continued to fall from my lips. "I stayed for five years because I thought that's what love was."

Harmony leaned forward. "You were trying to protect yourself the only way you knew how. But the lesson you learned at sixteen was wrong, Grace. You didn't cause what Todd did. And you don't have to earn love by erasing yourself."

Something in my chest cracked open.

"I know that now," I whispered. "But every relationship since Evan, I've still been doing the same thing. My friends say that I don't want to throw my heart into the ring again, so I look for situations in which I can maintain control of my emotions."

"That's why you're here." Harmony's voice was firm but kind. "This time, you get to be in control but in a healthier way. Which is why this is just a dating experiment. There is nothing to fix. If the vibes don't work, you move on. It's not always on you to do the heavy lifting."

I wiped at my eyes, surprised to find them wet.

"Okay," I said. "Okay."

Harmony smiled. "I actually have a couple of names for you already. Coffee dates—low pressure, public places. Actually, I have one I want you to try out first. He's a physician and has some of your interests."

I tried not to wince at "physician." Another doctor was the last thing I thought I needed.

But Harmony was already describing him and despite myself, I felt a flicker of curiosity.

When I stood to leave, my shoulders felt lighter. Like I'd set down a weight I'd been carrying for decades.

"Thank you," I said, and meant it.

"I'll text you details this week." Harmony walked me to the door. "And Grace? Keep an open mind. You deserve someone who chooses you without you having to convince them you're worth choosing."

I took the elevator down this time, too emotionally wrung out for stairs. When I reached the lobby, the security guard still hadn't looked up from his phone.

I checked my watch. Still time for a run before I started meal prep. My phone buzzed—my mom, texting about some specific brand of hot honey sauce she wanted me to bring to dinner tomorrow.

I was typing a response, digging through my purse for my keys, completely distracted.

I didn't see the man until I'd already walked straight into him.

8

luke

When I pulled into the guest parking at Harmony's building, I was still riding high from my afternoon. I'd hit my workout targets, showered, and caught the second half of the Georgia game. My alma mater would always be Stanford, but SEC football had my heart. Mom was from Louisiana, and some things were just in the blood.

I noticed a black G-wagon two spaces over. Probably someone using one of the other offices. Saturdays brought a different crowd to the building.

My phone rang as I was getting out—Marcus, my former teammate, calling to brag about his son's touchdown for Texas. I'd watched the play, so we were deep into trash talk by the time I walked through the lobby doors.

The security guard didn't even look up. Same as always.

I was mid-sentence, laughing at something Marcus said, when I collided with someone coming out. Hard.

A woman stumbled back, and my phone went flying across the tile floor. I grabbed her arm on instinct—keeping her upright—then realized I was holding on longer than necessary. She looked pointedly at my hand, then at me, and I released her like I'd been burned.

She was tall. Beautiful. Light brown skin, hair swept up, wearing a long blue dress and... Converse sneakers. The contrast was striking.

"I'm so sorry!" She rushed to retrieve my phone from where it had skidded halfway across the lobby.

I watched her crouch down—the dress, the sneakers, the efficiency of her movements. When she walked back and handed me the phone, I took it, but somehow, we ended up with our hands overlapping. Again.

Marcus was still yelling my name through the speaker.

I couldn't look away from her. "I gotta call you back," I said into the phone, eyes locked on hers.

She gently extracted her hand. "Excuse me, let me get that back." Her smile was small, careful. But her eyes stayed on mine.

And that's when I felt it.

What Kyle had described a hundred times. What I'd witnessed when he met Jada. The thing I'd convinced myself I wasn't capable of—that instant recognition, that pull. Like my entire body was recalibrating around this one moment, this one person.

I didn't even know her name.

"Sorry about that." I managed a grin. "I didn't mean to hijack your hand—although you did send my phone airborne."

Her smile widened slightly, and something in my chest shifted.

"Your phone's okay, right?" she asked. "I'd be happy to pay for repairs if it's damaged. This is the second time today I've almost taken out a man who was minding his own business." She laughed, and when she lifted her hand to her forehead, I noticed a fresh-looking tattoo on her wrist. Olympic rings.

"Kind of like a rampage," I said. "I should probably get your name. For identification purposes. In case you have a third victim later."

She raised an eyebrow. "Shouldn't I run away now so you can't identify me? Although eyewitness testimony isn't always reliable."

"I can't imagine anyone misidentifying you." I held her gaze, taking my shot. "What's your name? For my records, of course."

She studied me for a moment, clearly weighing something. "I guess that's safe enough. My name is Grace."

She extended her hand—formal this time, offering a proper handshake.

I took it, and the contact sent that feeling through me again. Stronger this time.

But she let go first. The smile faded from her face, and I caught something in her eyes—uncertainty? Maybe even fear.

Grace looked away. "I don't want to hold you up from wherever you were going."

"Right. My meeting." I leaned slightly, trying to catch her eye again. "I know this is forward, but is there any way I could get your contact information? To follow up about the phone. Or maybe even get a coffee or a drink sometime?"

She straightened to her full height—maybe five-nine, which still put me a good six inches taller. I watched her think it through, saw the internal debate play across her face. She wasn't trying to hide it.

After a moment, she reached into her purse and pulled out a business card. I accepted it gratefully and took a quick look.

Grace Robertson, MD, Gastroenterologist.

A doctor. Smart, beautiful, and standing right in front of me.

"What's your name?" she asked.

"Lucien. But everyone calls me Luke."

9

luke

I took the stairs to Harmony's office. Force of habit—I only used elevators when someone was with me who couldn't handle stairs, like my mother, or wouldn't, like Kyle.

I knocked on Dr. Kellogg's door and walked in when Harmony yelled, "Enter!"

"Hey! Is that how you greet your clients?"

She came around the desk and pulled me into a tight hug. "Is that better?"

"Much better. Though you almost knocked my phone out of my hand. A woman downstairs already did that as I was coming in. I don't understand what you all have against my phone."

Harmony grinned, gesturing broadly at her newly organized office. "Maybe it's all the discarded women whose numbers are probably still in there. We women are trying to band together to protect future women from you."

"I don't discard—I date. And when I'm finished dating, I move on. As for the woman in the lobby, she gave me her card so I could call her."

"Are you going to? If so, heaven help her!" Harmony retorted.

"I am definitely calling her. But that's all you need to know about my business."

I looked around at her rearranged space. "I see you added a whiteboard. For mapping out your strategies to ruin lives long-term?"

She snickered. "Flip the board around. You can get a peek at my new client—the one I was telling you about. I haven't created a full plan for her yet. Honestly, I can't believe she even needs my services—"

As she spoke, she turned the rolling whiteboard around.

My chest tightened.

The woman I'd just met in the lobby. The one whose hand I'd held too long. The one whose business card was currently in my pocket. The one I'd been planning to call tomorrow.

Was Harmony's client.

Dr. Grace Robertson. Two photos pinned to the board—one clearly from today, still wearing that blue dress. The other from what looked like Fisherman's Wharf, laughing with three other women, the Ghirardelli building visible behind them.

"I know, right?" Harmony was watching me. "She is really pretty and a doctor to boot. But her friends signed her up for my services, so here we are."

I couldn't look away from the photos fast enough.

"Stop staring!" She turned the board back around, frowning at me. "Whew, I'm glad you don't know her. You probably would go out with her and mess with her mind."

Tell her.

The thought came immediately. The honest thing would be to say, *"Actually, I just met her downstairs. She gave me her card."*

But if I told her that, I knew exactly what would happen. Harmony would forbid me from calling Grace. She'd probably call Grace herself and warn her off. This conversation would end with me being banned from someone I'd felt an actual *something* with for the first time in years.

Grace gave me her card. That was her choice.

I kept my mouth shut.

"You make me sound like I'm hazardous to women," I said, forcing a lighter tone.

"You have a proven track record of temporary relationships and friendships with women. You've broken quite a few hearts—some that I know personally."

There it was. The same argument we'd been having for years.

"I'm upfront about what I want, Harm. That's more than a lot of men can say."

"Upfront?" She crossed her arms. "Remember Simone? You dated her for a year. A whole year, Luke. And when she brought up the future, you acted like she'd lost her mind."

"I told her from day one I wasn't interested in marriage or kids. She chose not to believe me." The memory still left a bitter taste. "She thought she could change my mind."

"And when she couldn't, it destroyed her."

"That wasn't my fault." But even as I said it, I remembered the tearful phone calls, the desperation in her voice asking what she'd done wrong. The rumors she'd spread afterward, trying to salvage her pride. "I was clear about my intentions."

"You were twenty-six and terrified of becoming Dad."

She wasn't wrong. We'd both watched our father cycle through women after divorcing her mother—leaving behind a trail of slashed tires and broken windows. We'd learned to park our cars around the corner so they wouldn't be mistaken for his.

I'd sworn I'd never do that to anyone. Never let someone build a life around me when I had no intention of staying.

That's why I got the vasectomy right after Simone. Twenty-six years old, and I knew with absolute certainty I never wanted to be like him.

"I'm not Dad," I said quietly. "I don't lie to people. I don't make promises I can't keep."

"No, you just don't make promises at all." Harmony's voice softened. "You haven't reconsidered those intentions at all? At your big age?"

I did. About thirty minutes ago, in the lobby downstairs.

When Grace looked at me with those careful eyes, when she hesitated before giving me her card, when she asked my name—something shifted. For the first time in years, I'd wondered what it would be like to want more than a few months.

But I couldn't tell Harmony that. Not when Grace's picture was on that whiteboard.

"My big age? Funny." I turned toward her mini fridge. "Don't you have bottles of water in this place?"

She tossed me one, clearly not fooled by the subject change. "As always, stay away from my clients. I saw you eyeing her like a snack. That's why I didn't tell you her name." She pointed at me. "You would go looking for her and ruin my project and probably ruin her as well."

Too late.

I already had her name. Her number. Her card in my pocket.

"Give me the preserves and I'm out of here," I said.

Harmony handed over the box of six jars carefully. "Thank you for doing this." She kissed my cheek. "You know I love you, even though you have weird habits. I don't know why any woman would put up with you."

"Love you too, Harm."

I left before she could read anything on my face.

In the stairwell, I pulled out Grace's card again.

Grace Robertson, MD, Gastroenterologist.

I should tell Harmony. It was the right thing to do.

But maybe, it wasn't.

10

grace

I sat in the G-wagon for a full minute before starting the engine, hands resting on the steering wheel, heart still beating faster than it should.

Lucien. Luke.

Tall, handsome, Stanford ring, probably played football. The kind of man I would've talked myself out of five years ago because he was too attractive, too confident, too likely to break my heart.

And I'd given him my card.

I replayed the moment—his hand holding mine too long, the way he'd looked at me, the flutter in my stomach when he'd asked for my information. I'd hesitated, done the mental calculation, and then handed over my business card before I could talk myself out of it.

It wasn't until I was pulling out of the parking lot that I remembered: I'd just signed up with a matchmaker.

Shit.

But Harmony had said the contract could be part-time, right? Trial basis? I hadn't signed away my right to meet people on my own.

And Luke had asked for my information. I hadn't chased him. He'd wanted my number, and I'd given it to him.

That felt different.

Didn't it?

I merged onto Geary, trying to sort through what I was feeling. Harmony's words kept echoing in my head: *You deserve someone who chooses you without you having to convince them you're worth choosing.*

Luke had chosen to ask. I'd chosen to say yes.

For the first time in years, I hadn't picked someone safe. I'd taken a risk.

My phone buzzed at a red light. Mom, asking me again to pick up some specific brand of hot honey sauce for tomorrow's family dinner. Of course. I fired back a quick "I'll try" and made a mental note to stop at a store on the way home.

Family dinner. Stacia would probably be there. I'd need to get my mind right before I walked into that particular minefield.

But right now, I was still thinking about Luke.

About the way his voice had sounded when he said my name. About whether he'd actually call, or if this would turn into another "You're a GI doctor, let me ask you about my stomach issues" situation. That had happened before.

After I got home—hot honey sauce acquired after two stops—I changed into a pair of Juicy Couture sweats and was halfway through meal prep when my phone rang. It was almost eight o'clock my time, so it wasn't Gabe. That call was going to be in the morning.

Autumn.

"Hey! I just wanted to check in with you. You didn't call any of us after your meeting with Harmony. Did everything go okay? Are you really upset with us? Radio silence isn't really your style."

"I'm fine." I put her on speaker while I transferred containers to the fridge. "I met Harmony, we talked. She has some ideas for no-pressure dates for me. It might be fun."

Autumn gasped. "I'm sorry—what?"

"What's the matter with what I said? I'm cooperating. I thought you'd be pleased."

"I am. I'm just shocked. What happened in that session?"

I paused, hands stilling over the Tupperware. "We talked. Really talked. About... patterns. About why I choose the men I choose. About what I actually want from this whole thing."

"Grace." Her voice softened. "That sounds intense."

"It was." I closed the fridge and leaned against the counter. "But good. I think."

"Okay. So, you're actually going to give Harmony's matches a shot?"

"Yeah. And..." I hesitated. "I also met someone. In the lobby after the session."

"You what?"

"I ran into him. Literally. Almost destroyed his phone."

"Grace—"

"I know, I know. You're going to say I should let Harmony handle it."

"I was going to say: tell me everything."

I smiled despite myself. "Six-three, smooth brown skin, really good-looking, nice beard. Probably played football. Went to Stanford. First name Lucien—everyone calls him Luke. Don't know his last. That's all I got."

"Stanford means smart. Probably has a job." Autumn paused. "Sound attractive. Not your typical type right now, which is ugly inside and out."

I winced but didn't argue. She wasn't wrong.

"What are you going to do if he calls?" she asked.

"If he calls." I sat down at my dining room table. "He might not. I destroyed his phone. That might be the only reason he took my card."

"Or maybe he was interested. Did you consider that?"

Had I? The way he'd looked at me suggested yes. But years of choosing wrong had made me doubt my own judgment.

"I don't know," I admitted. "Autumn, what if this is just... another mistake? What if I'm already falling into the same pattern?"

"What pattern? Being attracted to someone? Taking a chance?"

"Choosing someone based on chemistry instead of compatibility."

"Grace." Autumn's voice was firm. "You've spent years choosing men you're NOT attracted to because it felt safer. And how did that work out?"

"Not well."

"Exactly. So maybe—just maybe—feeling something is actually a good sign."

I let that sit for a moment. "I'm scared."

"I know. But you're also brave as hell. You went to that session today. You were honest with Harmony. You gave this man your card even though it terrified you." She paused. "That's not a mistake. That's growth."

My throat tightened. "What if he doesn't call?"

"Then he's an idiot, and you move forward with Harmony's matches. Either way, you tried. You took a risk. That's what matters. I've gotta go. Theo's waiting for me with a present."

I didn't need further information. We were all aware that as Theo had aged, the physical sex had decreased from every day to once a month. Tonight was that night. After we hung up, I finished cleaning the kitchen and got ready for bed.

He probably wouldn't call. Or if he did, it would be to ask about digestive issues. Or to say he'd given it more thought and realized he wasn't interested after all.

But as I turned off the light, I couldn't help wondering.

What if he did call?

What if, for once, I'd made a choice that led somewhere good?

I fell asleep with that question hovering at the edge of my thoughts—equal parts terrifying and hopeful.

11

luke

I arrived at my mother's assisted living facility at five on the dot, preserves in hand. Mom valued when people were punctual, and I'd learned early not to test her patience.

Miss Emilie Merci lived in the Inner Richmond, close enough that I could visit regularly but far enough that she maintained her independence. When she'd sold her house, I'd offered to have her move in with me, but she'd shut that down immediately. "Your house is all the way in the Marina, Luke. I'd be trapped. Here, I have friends. Activities. A life."

Fair point.

I found her in her apartment, looking tired. "We're ordering in tonight," she announced before I could suggest going out.

"Sushi?" I asked, already knowing the answer.

"Akiko's. You know what I like."

We ordered her usual—maki rolls, sashimi deluxe, pork and veggie dumplings—and settled in with cups of tea that may or may not have been spiked with gin. With Mom, you never knew until you took a sip.

She launched into her daily recap: activities at the facility, field trips, gossip about whose dress was too loud at last night's dinner. I was half-listening, nodding at the right moments, but my mind kept drifting.

To Grace's hand in mine. The way she'd hesitated before giving me her card. That flash of uncertainty in her eyes before she'd smiled.

I'd already pulled out her card twice since leaving Harmony's office. Once in the car. Once while waiting for Mom to answer her door.

Grace Robertson, MD, Gastroenterologist.

Should I call tomorrow? Wait a few days? What was the right move here?

"—and Mr. Alfred has been joining me for breakfast."

I blinked. "I'm sorry, what?"

Mom's eyes narrowed. "I said, there's a new gentleman in the building. Mr. Alfred. Seventy-one. We've had breakfast together several times over the past two weeks."

I sat up straighter. "Who is this Mr. Alfred?"

She took a deliberate sip of tea. "He's my new boyfriend. And no, you can't investigate him. I'm not giving you his information so you can try to run him off."

"Mom—"

"Don't 'Mom' me. You're not the only one allowed to have a social life." She set down her cup and studied me with that look that always saw too much. "Speaking of which, what's going on with you? You've been distracted since you walked in. Checking your phone. Not listening to my stories."

"I'm listening."

"You are not. What's her name?"

I should've known better than to think I could hide anything from her. "What makes you think there's a 'her'?"

"Because you've got that look. The same one your father used to get." She paused. "But different. Better, maybe. Who is she?"

I leaned back in my chair, debating how much to say. "I might have met someone today. That's all. I literally ran into her and got her business card."

Mom's face lit up. "Oh my. Tell me about her."

"I don't know that much yet."

She harrumphed. "You could've kept that to yourself 'til you knew more." She took another sip of tea, eyeing me over the rim. "But you mentioned her anyway. Which means something. So—how do you say it—I want the *tea*."

Before I could answer, the phone rang. Food delivery downstairs.

I took the stairs down to grab it, grateful for the escape. Took my time coming back up, too.

Mom fussed at me about making her wait, but when I set out the food, she picked right back up. "So. This woman. You're going to call her?"

"Maybe."

"Lucien Benoit. You're forty-four years old. How long are you going to keep doing this? Dating women for a few months, then moving on when they want more?"

"I'm honest about what I want, Mom. That's more than Dad ever was."

Her expression tightened. I shouldn't have brought him up.

"Your father made a lot of mistakes," she said quietly. "But you're so busy not being him that you won't let yourself have anything real."

"I have a good life."

"You have a beautiful house that's empty. A schedule that runs like clockwork. Women who come and go." She reached across the table, placing her hand over mine. "When was the last time you felt something that scared you?"

Today. In a lobby. When a woman in a blue dress looked at me like she was trying to decide whether I was worth the risk.

"This one's different," I heard myself say.

Mom's eyebrows rose. "Different how?"

"I don't know yet." I pulled out Grace's card, set it on the table between us. "But I think I want to find out."

She picked it up, read it. "A doctor. Smart. And you're actually nervous about calling her." She smiled—the first genuine one all evening. "Good. You should be nervous. Means it matters."

"What if she's looking for something serious? Marriage, kids, the whole thing?"

"Are you?"

Was I? Two hours ago, I would've said absolutely not. But standing in that lobby, holding Grace's hand, something had shifted. Like a door I'd kept locked for years had cracked open just enough to let in light.

"I don't know," I admitted. "But I'm going to call her and see."

We finished dinner with Mom telling me more about Alfred—how they'd met at the facility's movie night, how he'd been a jazz musician in his younger years, how he made her laugh.

When she brought up my dating life again, I countered with more questions about Alfred. We ended in our usual stalemate, but this time felt different.

This time, I had Grace's card in my pocket and a plan to call her tomorrow.

When I left, Mom kissed my cheek at the door. "Call her, Luke. Don't overthink it."

"Yes, ma'am."

"And bring her to meet me. If she's worth calling, she's worth introducing."

I drove home thinking about what Mom had said. About not being so afraid of turning into my father that I never let myself have anything real.

About Grace's smile when she'd handed me her card. The way she'd asked my name.

Tomorrow. I'd call her tomorrow.

For the first time in years, the thought of "more" didn't make me want to run.

It made me want to know what came next.

12

grace

I woke up at 4 a.m. Pacific time and immediately checked my phone.

No missed calls. No texts from unknown numbers.

Of course not. It's Sunday morning. He's probably still asleep.

Or he'd decided not to call at all. That was also possible.

I pushed the thought away and FaceTimed Gabe. He answered on the second ring, looking way too alert for someone who should still be half-asleep.

"Hi Momma!"

"Hi, baby! How are you? I missed you!"

"I miss you too, Mom."

We fell into our usual rhythm—practice updates, how his classes were going, whether his father was micromanaging again (yes, always). Evan couldn't help himself. He'd trained for the Olympics his whole life, and now he was trying to relive it through Gabe and Alex.

"At least the coaches are getting paid to deal with it," I said gently. "But listen to your dad when it makes sense. He knows what he's talking about, even if he's a little intense."

"Yeah, I guess." Gabe shifted, and I could tell something else was on his mind. "Mom, Alex is still dating that Skylar person."

I smiled. "Is that a problem? Are you jealous?"

"Jealous? No. But sometimes she comes over and wants to watch kissy-face movies." He made exaggerated kissing noises. "And I miss my friend. Like, he's always with her now."

My heart squeezed. "One day that'll be you with some lovely young lady. But here's the thing, Gabe—talk to Alex. Tell him you miss hanging out. Set up time for just the two of you. He's your brother now. No one can come between that if you don't let them."

Even as I said it, I thought about Celeste. About how we'd let distance and hurt feelings create a canyon between us. About Vic, stuck in a marriage with someone who actively worked to isolate him from the family.

Do better than we did, baby.

"Thanks, Mom. That makes me feel better. I gotta go. Love you!"

He was gone before I could respond. Growing up too fast.

I spent the rest of the morning going through the dating profile drafts Harmony had sent, trying not to check my phone every ten minutes. By the time I pulled into my parents' driveway in Berkeley at 1 p.m., I'd convinced myself Luke wasn't going to call.

Fine. That's fine.

The thought didn't make me feel better.

No sign of Vic and Stacia's SUV yet. Small mercies.

Dad was waiting in the doorway, tall and handsome despite the slight stoop age had given him. He pulled me into a hug and kissed my cheek.

"Good afternoon, Gracie. I see you found the sauce for your mother."

"Barely. Three stores. What's she doing with hot honey anyway?"

He chuckled, leading me inside. "Charcuterie board. You know your mother—always trying something new." He paused in the foyer. "How's my grandson?"

"Good. Really good. Swimming's going well, grades are solid. Evan's being Evan."

"Micromanaging?"

"Constantly."

"That man." Dad shook his head. "At least he's consistent. Your mother still thinks you should've stayed in Miami with Gabe."

"Dad—"

"I know, I know. You have a life here. Your practice. But she worries you're lonely."

I thought about Luke's hand holding mine. About giving him my card. About lying awake last night wondering if I'd made a mistake or finally done something right.

"I'm working on that," I said.

Mom intercepted us in the foyer and took the hot honey bag from me. "I hear you complaining about my sauce choices. Then I expect you won't be eating any of it."

"Mom—"

She was already heading to the kitchen. I followed, finding her arranging an elaborate charcuterie spread. The hot honey was going on a board that actually looked incredible.

"Okay, I take it back. This looks amazing."

"Mm-hmm." She handed me a knife. "Make yourself useful. And don't eat everything before it gets to the tray."

The doorbell rang. Vic let himself and Stacia in—she'd rung the bell despite having a key. Still playing guest after four years of marriage.

Stacia mumbled a greeting and headed straight outside. I rolled my eyes and focused on the food.

Vic entered the kitchen, stealing some salami immediately. "Hey, Gracie! Oh, that's sweet salami. That's good."

"Right? None of this is making it to the tray."

Mom kissed Vic's cheek, then looked toward the deck where Stacia had planted herself outside, staring at her phone. "Should I go speak to her?"

"She's in one of her moods." Vic's voice was flat. "I need to talk to Dad. Where is he?"

Mom touched his face gently. "Garage. Have you two talked about counseling again?"

He shook his head and walked away.

I watched him go, chest tight. "There's no fixing this, Mom. She tied her tubes. She's made it clear what she wants, and it's not him."

"Grace—"

"I know. I just hate watching him stay in something that's killing him." *I know what that feels like.*

Mom shifted topics. "Speaking of staying or going—how's Gabriel really doing? You haven't mentioned my grandbaby once. How is he doing in Miami?"

We talked about Gabe while I kept stealing from the board. She asked about my visit in two weeks, whether she and Dad could come (work conflict, maybe next time). Then she pivoted.

"How was brunch yesterday?" She had always been a little nosy, and these family meals were her chance to offer her advice about the happenings in my life. So, I gave in and told her about Harmony, leaving out some of the more personal details.

"I've heard of those," Mom said. "We had some teaching cases involving dating coaches back at Berkeley. If you don't take it too seriously, it could be fun. You really need to get out there and enjoy yourself more." She paused. "You've been different since the divorce. Especially since Evan remarried. I know it's hard, but you need to get on with your life."

She wasn't wrong.

Dinner was tense but manageable. Stacia barely spoke. Vic looked miserable. Mom and Dad kept conversation flowing. I checked my phone twice under the table.

Nothing.

After dinner, my phone rang. Harmony.

"Hi!" I glanced at Vic, who was trying to leave. Stacia was pulling him toward the door, but I held up a finger. *Wait.*

"Are you in a hurry?" Harmony asked.

"My brother's about to leave, but I can talk. What's up?"

"I wanted to set up a speed coffee date for you. Tuesday at lunch. That physician I mentioned? He's excited to meet you."

Tuesday. Two days away.

Two days for Luke to call. Or not.

"I have patients until one. I could do two?"

"Perfect. I'll text you details. It's just twenty or thirty minutes—cursory get-to-know-you. Low pressure. You might like him. If not, we'll try other options."

"Where would we meet?" I asked hurriedly.

"You gave me the address of your clinic yesterday afternoon. There's a coffee shop nearby that would be perfect since you both have to get back to the office. There's no chance of running out of conversation topics."

"Sounds...fun," I murmured. "Could you text that to me so I can put it in my calendar? I'm interested to see how this works."

"Perfect! I'll speak to you after the speed date!"

"Okay. Yeah. Thank you."

We hung up, and I headed toward Vic before Stacia could drag him out. She saw me coming and literally growled. "You know she doesn't like me. Why would you let her badmouth me?"

I rolled my eyes. I wasn't the most religious person, but I asked God to give me strength at that moment not to curse that woman out again.

"Could I talk to you for a minute?" I guided Vic through the back glass doors, down to the second deck where Stacia couldn't hover.

The view was beautiful—a vibrant sunset over the bay. I turned to face my brother, straightening to my full height.

"I'm not trying to get in your business, but your wife was rude to Mom again. You're unhappy. She's changing all the terms of your relationship. What are you going to do?"

"Shhh!" He looked around. "I contacted an attorney. But I wanted to try counseling first. It was... worse than you can imagine. So, it is what it is."

"What it is, is over. She wasn't sweet, Vic. Not from the beginning. Remember her first dinner here? She's been showing you who she is. You just didn't want to see it." I softened. "Once she tied her tubes, you should've known. She's trying to position herself for alimony by quitting her job before you file. Get out now."

"Four years. Have I been that blind?"

"We all are when we want something to work." *I stayed with Evan for five.* "But we got you—Mom, Dad, me, even Celeste. We want you happy and healthy. This isn't it. She's not good for you, and she doesn't want to help you. You need to take care of yourself."

I kissed his cheek. "This is the end of my TED talk. But I'll keep bringing it up until you deal with it. I love you."

"You can be nice. Contrary to what everyone says."

"Keep talking wild and find out how not nice I can be."

He laughed, punched my shoulder gently.

We headed back up, pausing to look at the view, feeling a little optimistic.

Despite my reservations, today had been a good day.

I hadn't cursed out Stacia. We had a pleasant meal. I had a speed date on Tuesday.

And somewhere out there, Luke either would or wouldn't call.

The day had been almost perfect.

But I was still checking my phone.

13

luke

Sunday was supposed to be simple: football, research, maybe order some food. Rest and recharge.

Instead, I spent the entire day staring at Grace's business card.

I'd pulled it out of my wallet three times by noon. Propped it against my laptop while I pretended to read journal articles about our company's latest device trials. Set it on the coffee table while I watched the Niners game, except I couldn't tell you the score.

Just call her.

But every time I picked up my phone, I talked myself out of it.

She was Harmony's client. My sister had specifically told me to stay away from her clients. Especially this one. "She's been through a lot. Don't you dare."

Too late. I was already planning to dare.

By 3 p.m., I'd abandoned any pretense of productivity. I paced my living room, phone in hand, Grace's card in the other.

She gave you her card. That means she wanted you to call.

Or she was being polite after nearly destroying my phone.

Call her.

I pulled up her number. Stared at it. My thumb hovered over the call button.

What if she said no? What if Harmony had already warned her off? What if—

I hung up before it could ring.

"This is ridiculous." I was forty-four years old, talking to myself in an empty house about calling a woman.

But I hadn't felt like this in years. Maybe ever. That pull in the lobby—like my entire world had transformed after one moment, after meeting one person.

Kyle called it lightning bolts. I'd always thought he was being dramatic.

I wasn't so sure anymore.

By 4 p.m., I'd made a decision. I'd call. Keep it simple. Ask her to coffee or dinner. See if what I felt was real or just adrenaline from a collision.

And if Harmony found out?

I'd deal with that later.

I dialed before I could overthink it again.

It rang twice. Three times.

She's not going to answer.

"Hello?"

Her voice hit me in the chest. I'd forgotten how it sounded—warm, cautious, curious.

"Uh, hi. Dr. Grace Robertson? This is Luke Sloane. From the collision yesterday?" *Smooth, Luke. Real smooth.* "I hope I'm not interrupting anything."

A pause. Long enough that my heart rate kicked up.

"Oh yeah! The immovable object?" There was a smile in her voice. "How are you doing? Better yet, how's your phone?"

I exhaled. "It's working—unfortunately. I was hoping to use it as a reason to see you again."

She laughed, and something in my chest loosened.

"But I see now that would be a weak opening line."

"Do you have a better one?" The way she said it—playful, a little flirtatious—made me grin.

"Not really. Just the truth. I know you don't know anything about me, but I'd love to take you out. Dinner, lunch, coffee. Whatever you're comfortable with."

"Well, why don't you tell me something about yourself before I answer? I only know your first name and that your phone doesn't have wings."

I laughed. "Fair. Luke Sloane, Stanford graduate, former NFL player, current business owner."

"Stanford? Boo!" She was joking, I could tell. "I went to UC Berkeley."

"I can let that slide."

"Let it slide, huh? Okay, I hear you. What do you do for a living with that Stanford degree?"

"I'm a biomedical engineer. My college roommate and best friend and I own Sloane-Wash—"

A small gasp. "You're *that* Luke Sloane? I've heard of your company. I read about the prototype you're studying—the one that could make gastric by-pass surgery less invasive? That's incredible. Wow. I didn't know I'd run into high-powered medical royalty."

I felt heat creep up my neck. "I don't know about royalty. But hopefully we're making a difference."

She knew about the company. Which meant she probably knew about my net worth. That information usually came out eventually—better to get it out there sooner as opposed to later. But she didn't bring it up.

"Are you not comfortable talking about your work?"

"I don't want to bore you with technical stuff up front. At least not until I get to wow you with my charm."

I could practically feel her smile through the phone.

"That's reasonable. Are you a native Californian?"

"Born and bred. I can tell you are too."

"I'm not going to ask how you know that. It's true, but I don't know if I want to know how you came to that conclusion."

"It's not anything bad. Native Californians carry themselves a certain way." I paused, realizing the conversation was flowing easily. Too easily. The nervous energy from earlier had settled into something warm, comfortable.

Terrifying.

"So," she said quietly, "what type of date did you have in mind?"

"I'd like to take you out for a meal, but not just a meal. You look like you're in great shape—are you able to walk around easily?"

"I was on the track team in college, and I just started running again. But what of it?"

"A scavenger hunt. With dinner after."

"Scavenger hunt?" She sounded incredulous. "Are *you* going to hide things for me to find?"

"Of course not. There are organized scavenger hunts all over the city. The one I want to try is on Fisherman's Wharf. It's outside, explores that part of town.

We can eat before or after." I held my breath, half expecting her to laugh and hang up.

"A scavenger hunt!" She sounded genuinely delighted. "That sounds like fun. And different. I love it."

Relief flooded through me. "Are you sure? I wanted a date where we could talk and get to know each other."

"That's always a nice way to plan a date. Have you done a scavenger hunt before?"

"I have, but not this one. I've got season passes—don't laugh." I could hear her trying not to. "But I haven't done the Fisherman's Wharf one. So, we'd both be going in blind."

"Okay. This would be better during the day, right?"

"The outdoor hunts work best with light. Are you able to do something during the day? Don't you have patients to see?"

"I have more flexibility. I set up my schedule years ago to accommodate my son's activities."

My hand tightened on the phone. "Your son? Tell me about him."

I didn't hate kids. I just didn't want biological ones. This could actually work in my favor.

"He's thirteen. A swimmer. I arranged my work schedule so I could take him to coaching sessions and meets. His father—my ex-husband—has a busier practice, so it was harder for him to be as flexible."

Ex-husband. A kid. She'd been married before.

"Do we need to schedule around his practice?"

"Oh no. Gabriel's in Miami at a swim academy. He's hoping for the Olympics one day. My weird schedule is just for me now." She paused. "But enough about schedules. Back to our date—I'm really curious about this scavenger hunt. My afternoon tomorrow is free. I didn't ask about your schedule."

"I make my own schedule. There are a couple things I need to do in the office this week, but they don't have to be done tomorrow." I swallowed. "If you must know, I really want to see you. I'd move things around if I had to."

Silence settled between us. Not uncomfortable. Weighted.

"What time do you want to meet?"

We settled on 4 p.m. Monday, Fisherman's Wharf. I would pick her up at her office.

After we hung up, I sat on my couch, phone still in my hand.

I had a date.

With Grace Robertson.

Tomorrow.

Grace Robertson, who was currently Harmony's client.

Grace Robertson, who I should have told my sister about and didn't.

I should call Harmony. Come clean. Tell her I'd met Grace before I saw her picture on that whiteboard.

But if I did that, Harmony would shut this down. She'd call Grace, tell her I was emotionally unavailable, and would break her heart.

And maybe she'd be right.

Except this felt different. Grace felt different.

For the first time in years, the thought of "more" didn't make me want to run.

I'd deal with Harmony later.

Right now, I had a scavenger hunt date to plan.

14

grace

Monday morning, I woke up with butterflies in my stomach.

I had a date. Today. With Luke.

And tomorrow, I had a speed coffee date with Harmony's match.

Two dates in two days. When was the last time I'd gone on two dates in two *months*?

I got to the clinic early for the 7 a.m. epidemiology presentation. Free breakfast, continuing education credits, and a distraction from checking my phone every five minutes to see if Luke had texted me to cancel.

He hadn't.

The presentation was fine—straightforward case studies on GI disorders—but I couldn't tell you a single thing the fellow said. My mind was elsewhere.

After it wrapped, I headed to my office to prepare for my half-day clinic schedule. Violet, my clinic nurse, intercepted me in the hallway with my patient charts and a massive bouquet of flowers.

Pink carnations, tulips, peonies, roses.

"Dr. Robertson, you look very nice today." Violet's eyes sparkled with mischief. "These came for you this morning."

I raised my eyebrows. "So, I generally don't look nice?"

She turned beet red. "Oh, I'm sorry! That's not what I meant, and you know it. But you do look extra nice. And I don't know who these are from, but they're beautiful."

I took the vase from her, feeling heat creep up my neck. I'd taken more care with my appearance today—floor-length royal blue skirt with a slit in the back, same color knit top that could slide off-shoulder for the scavenger hunt, hair curly and loose instead of scraped back in my usual bun. Of course, Violet noticed.

"Let me ask," Violet continued, "do you have plans after clinic?"

I set the flowers on my desk and pulled out the envelope. It was larger than a standard florist card. "If you must know, I have a date."

"With whom?"

Yvonne, the clinic manager, appeared in my doorway like she had radar. "You have a date? Is he employed?"

The office staff knew about my dating disasters. All of them.

"Yes, he's employed. He owns his own company. I literally ran into him Saturday and knocked his phone across the floor."

I opened the envelope and pulled out a card—heavy cardstock, the size of a prescription pad. Luke's handwriting was neat, neater than mine:

Grace,

I couldn't stop thinking about our conversation. Thought you might like these while you're saving lives today. Looking forward to our scavenger hunt.

— Luke

Something in my chest squeezed.

He'd sent flowers. The morning after we talked. He'd put thought, effort into this. It had been so long since someone had done something like this for me.

And that sounded sad...

Yvonne read over my shoulder and harrumphed. "Well, I hope he merits your enthusiasm. You seem thrilled today. Your face card?" She waved her hand at my face, gave a chef's kiss, and disappeared into her office.

I smiled despite myself.

My morning patients were all routine—follow-ups for chronic conditions, post-procedure check-ins. Nothing complicated. Which was good, because my mind kept drifting to Luke's voice on the phone yesterday. By 12:45, I was finishing up with my last patient—a woman I'd been seeing for years, since my fellowship. We chatted about her grandkids, about Gabe, about life. When I walked her out to schedule her next colonoscopy, it was just after 1 p.m.

I had three hours.

Back in my office, I ate my salad while finishing patient notes, keeping one eye on the clock. At 3:15, Violet appeared in my doorway.

"Time's up. You still look great, just freshen up your lipstick. What are you two doing anyway?"

I stood, organizing the stack of charts on my desk. "Scavenger hunt at Fisherman's Wharf."

"Oh, that's different! I hope you have a good time."

"Me too. He seems nice. And cute."

In the bathroom, I reapplied lip gloss and checked my reflection. Forty-two looked nice on me to say the least. My skin was holding up well—it likely helped that Autumn stayed on me about skincare. I touched up with powder and fluffed my hair.

Dating in your forties is different. Relax. Stop worrying.

Luke thought I was attractive enough to ask out. Interesting enough to send flowers to.

I could do this.

I grabbed my purse and headed out.

Standing on the sidewalk, I realized I didn't know what kind of car Luke drove. I'd relented on driving myself and agreed to let him pick me up—mostly because I'd Googled him after our call and confirmed he was who he said he was. Also, I was pretty sure Autumn had hidden an AirTag in this purse she'd given me for my birthday last month. She'd never admit it, but I knew.

It didn't matter that I didn't know his car, because when I saw him sitting on the hood of a BMW in the fire lane, my breath caught.

He stood when he spotted me, and I nearly stopped walking.

He looked incredible. Beige fitted t-shirt showing off his build, brown jeans, leather boots, tan denim jacket. Trimmed beard. And his eyes screamed one word.

Hopeful.

Oh dear. I might be in trouble.

I walked toward him, heart hammering, and when I stopped in front of him, the air between us felt electric.

"Hi," I managed.

"Hi," he replied with a smile.

This was happening. I was doing this.

And for the first time in years, I wasn't trying to control where it would go.

15

luke

When Grace slid into the passenger seat, the air in the car shifted.

She smiled at me, a little breathless, and I forgot how to speak for a second. Up close, she was even more beautiful than I remembered—curls framing her face, that off-shoulder top showing smooth skin, Converse peeking out from under her long skirt.

"You look amazing," I said.

"Thank you." She blushed slightly, tucking a curl behind her ear.

I closed her door and jogged around to the driver's side, pulse racing. When I got in, she was looking around the interior with interest.

"Is this the electric BMW? I haven't seen many of these in the wild. How does it drive?"

I pulled out of the fire lane, grateful for something to focus on besides the way she smelled—something floral and clean. "I'll let you be the judge of that."

The drive to Fisherman's Wharf was only about fifteen minutes, but I wanted to make it count. I'd queued up zydeco music—my go-to for when I needed to settle my nerves—and Grace noticed immediately.

"Is this zydeco?"

"Yeah. My mom's from Louisiana. I grew up on this stuff. Is it too much?"

"No, I like it. It's different." She tilted her head, listening. "I'm not a car person, but I'm considering getting a different car soon. My G-Wagon is too big for me since my son is in Miami. I mean, it was probably too big before he left. You can ask me, you know?"

"What?"

"Ask me. You're dying to know why my son is in Miami and I'm not."

"I didn't want to pry."

Her whole face softened. "He's there for swimming. He got accepted to this elite academy—the kind of place that produces Olympic athletes. His coach thinks he has real potential." She looked out the window, and I caught the flicker of emotion. "It's been an adjustment. He's only been gone since August."

"How old is he again?"

"Thirteen."

"That must be hard. Being away from him."

"It is." Her voice was quiet. "I'm in the middle of my contract—my out kicks in at the end of this year. But he's with his father and stepmother, so he's not alone. And I fly down to see him as much as I can. Financially, it would have been challenging for me to move this summer. It's not ideal, but it's what we have."

I glanced at her. "You're a good mom. I can tell."

She smiled, but it was bittersweet. "I'm trying. Some days I wonder if I made the right call, letting him go. But Evan—my ex—had already planned to move down there. And Gabe wanted it so badly. How do you tell your kid no when it's his dream?"

You don't. Because you love him more than anything.

And that's when I felt it. The first crack in whatever foundation I was trying to build here.

She was a mother. Not just in title, but in every fiber of her being. The way she talked about Gabe—the pride, the ache, the fierce protectiveness—it was who she was.

And I'd had a vasectomy at twenty-six.

"How old was he when you and your ex split?" I asked, pushing the thought away.

"Almost five. We'd been married five years, together for seven. Evan and I... we tried to make it work. But some things can't be fixed." She shifted in her seat. "Gabe handled it better than I expected. Kids are resilient. And honestly, Evan and I are better co-parents than we ever were spouses."

"That's good. For Gabe."

"Yeah." She was quiet for a moment. "What about you? Ever been married?"

"No. The topic came up for discussion once, but it didn't work out."

"How close were you?"

I merged onto the Embarcadero, buying myself a few seconds. "Close enough to know it wasn't right. She wanted things I couldn't give her. Wouldn't give her."

Grace didn't press, which I appreciated. Instead, she shifted topics. "So, this scavenger hunt. You really do these regularly?"

"I do have season passes," I admitted. "Don't judge me."

She laughed. "I'm not judging. I think it's kind of great that you have something you're genuinely into. Most people our age just... I don't know. Golf?"

"I'm not a golf guy."

"Good. Golf is boring."

I grinned. "Agreed."

The conversation flowed easily after that—trading stories about bad dates, favorite spots in the city, whether Stanford or Berkeley had better food. She was quick, funny, self-deprecating in a way that made me want to know everything about her.

But underneath it all, my mind was working.

She might move to Miami next year.

She'd never said it out loud, but I heard it for what it was: her entire life could shift in less than twelve months. She'd uproot everything to be with her son.

As she should. That's what good parents did.

And me? My whole life was here. The company, my house, my mother, Harmony, Kyle. I couldn't just pick up and move even if I wanted to. I'd planted my feet in this city for reasons I wasn't even sure of anymore.

"You got quiet," Grace said, pulling me out of my head.

"Sorry. Just thinking about parking. Fisherman's Wharf on a Monday afternoon can be a nightmare."

It wasn't a complete lie. But it wasn't the truth either.

The truth was that I was already doing the math. Already seeing the expiration date on whatever this was.

She was a mother who might move across the country. I was a man who'd made sure he could never have biological children.

Even if this worked—even if we clicked as much in person as we did on the phone—there was likely a ceiling. A limit.

I should tell her. Right now. Before we even started the scavenger hunt.

I can't have kids. I had a vasectomy when I was twenty-six because I watched my father destroy women and I swore I'd never do that. I don't want biological children. I never have.

But when I looked at her, saw the way she was smiling at something outside the window, the way the afternoon light caught in her curls, I couldn't say it.

Not yet.

Maybe she didn't want more kids. Maybe Miami wouldn't happen. Maybe I was overthinking all of this.

Or maybe I just wanted a few more hours before reality set in.

"There," she said, pointing. "Is that a spot?"

I pulled into the parking space, killed the engine, and turned to look at her.

She was already unbuckling her seatbelt, excited, ready to go. And God, she was beautiful.

"Ready?" she asked.

"Yeah," I said. "Let's do this."

But as we walked toward the starting point for the scavenger hunt, I couldn't shake the feeling that I was setting myself up for something I'd already decided couldn't last.

Even if I wanted to see if it could.

16

grace

The check-in location was on Hyde Street Pier, right at the water's edge. Luke pulled up the scavenger hunt app while I looked around, taking in the afternoon sun, the smell of salt water and fried food, the sound of sea lions barking in the distance.

"Okay," Luke said, studying his phone. "How familiar are you with this area?"

"I know Ghirardelli's. I visited a lot when I was pregnant with Gabe. But I didn't really explore beyond ice cream, so I don't know much about the history or landmarks."

"Perfect. We're both going in semi-blind." He grinned. "First task: Find a ferry and take a selfie with it."

I looked around. "That seems... easy?"

"They get harder. Trust me."

He wasn't wrong.

Over the next two hours, we worked our way through the list: the Fisherman's Wharf sign, the Fountain, the SkyStar Big Wheel, a decommissioned submarine, a specific game inside the Musée Mécanique. We had to clap with the sea lion colony, take a picture with a street performer, find something obscure at Ripley's Believe It or Not, pose with wax figures at Madame Tussauds.

What surprised me was how competitive I got.

"No, wait—the clue said *north* side of the fountain," I said, pulling Luke back before he could take the photo.

"Does it matter?"

"Yes! We have to do it right."

He laughed. "You're really into this."

"I didn't come all the way to Fisherman's Wharf to lose a scavenger hunt."

"We're not competing against anyone."

"We're competing against the app. And I'm winning."

His smile was warm. "Okay, Dr. Robertson. North side it is."

I liked the way we moved together—him reading the clues, me spotting the landmarks. When I got stuck on a riddle, he'd think through it methodically. When he overthought something, I'd see the obvious answer. We balanced each other.

At the Musée Mécanique, we had to find a specific vintage game and play it. The place was dim, packed with old arcade machines and mechanical wonders. Luke spotted it first—a 1920s fortune-teller machine in the back corner.

"There!" He grabbed my hand without thinking, pulling me through the crowd.

I didn't let go when we got there.

We fed the machine a quarter and watched it whir to life, the mechanical fortune teller's hands moving over cards. Our fortunes were printed out on tiny slips of paper.

"What does yours say?" I asked.

He read it, then looked at me with an unreadable expression. "A new path awaits. Trust your instincts."

"That's very... vague."

"What's yours?"

I unfolded mine. "The journey is better than the destination."

We stood there for a moment, hands still linked, the noise of the arcade around us fading into background static. His thumb brushed across my knuckles, and heat flooded through me.

"Grace—" he started.

But someone bumped into us from behind, breaking the moment. We laughed it off and headed back outside.

The sun was starting to set by the time we finished most of the clues. My feet hurt from walking in Converse for two hours, but I didn't care. I couldn't remember the last time I'd had this much fun on a date.

Or any date, honestly.

"Are you hungry?" Luke asked as we uploaded the last photo.

"Starving."

"Seafood okay? I should've asked earlier—"

"I love seafood. I have reflux, so I'm careful with spicy things, but as long as I take my medication, I'm fine." I paused, looking around. "I'd love to go to Scoma's, but I know you need a reservation. We can do that another night."

The words were out before I could stop them.

My eyes went wide. "I—I mean, if you want to. I'm not assuming—" Heat flooded my face.

Luke gently pulled my hand away from where I'd covered my face. "Why? I like that you said what you want. What are you doing tomorrow evening?"

My heart jumped. "What do you have in mind?"

"We can discuss that over lobster rolls," he said, nodding toward Broad Street Oyster Co.

We ordered food and beer, then kept walking, knocking out a few more clues while we ate. The lobster rolls were perfect—buttery, fresh, exactly what I needed. The beer helped calm my nerves.

"I hope you don't think I'm a bad date because I didn't take you to a sit-down dinner," Luke said as we headed toward Ghirardelli.

"This was perfect. An urban hike. I would've been surprised if we'd switched gears and gone somewhere fancy. I'm not dressed for fancy." I gestured at my outfit. "No stress, no pressure. Just good vibes."

"Just good vibes?" He stopped walking, turning to face me. "I was hoping the vibes were way more than good."

My breath caught. We were standing under a streetlight, the Ghirardelli sign glowing in the distance. Tourists moved around us, but I barely noticed.

"All I know," I said quietly, "is that these are some crazy hot vibes I'm not ready to let go of yet. But I don't always make great relationship decisions when I get blinded by attraction."

Something shifted in his expression. He stepped closer, and I could feel the heat coming off him, smell his cologne mixed with ocean air. The space between us felt more charged than it had been in the car, if that were even possible.

For a moment, I thought he was going to kiss me.

For a moment, I *wanted* him to kiss me.

But instead, he took my hand, his fingers threading through mine.

"Grace." His voice was low. "I really like you. But I think... before this goes any further, I need you to know some things about me."

The air between us was still thick with want, with possibility. But something in his tone made me pause.

"Okay," I said carefully.

"I don't always make great relationship decisions when I get blinded by attraction either," he said, echoing my words from earlier. "I rarely make relationship decisions at all."

I blinked. "What does that mean?"

He looked toward Ghirardelli, then back at me. "Can we get ice cream? And talk?"

I nodded, even as my heart started to pound for entirely different reasons.

We walked hand in hand toward the ice cream shop, the tension between us shifting from heat to something more fragile.

Whatever he was about to tell me felt big.

And I wasn't sure if I was ready to hear it.

17

luke

We ordered our cones—sea salt caramel for her, dark chocolate for me—and found a table near the window. For a few minutes, we just ate in silence, the cold sweetness a sharp contrast to the heat still coursing through my body.

Grace broke first. "So. What did you mean—you rarely make relationship decisions?"

Here it was. The moment where she'd either understand or walk away.

"I know you've been married before."

"Yes. For five years."

"Right." I took a breath. "Well, I haven't."

"Engaged?"

"Nope. Longest relationship was one year."

She tilted her head, studying me. Not judging. Just... listening.

"I told her up front," I continued, "that I didn't want to get married and didn't want children." I watched Grace's face carefully. "Once we hit the one-year mark, she thought I'd change my mind. I didn't. She even tried to get pregnant anyway. It was a mess."

Grace's eyes widened slightly. "Tried to get pregnant? As in..."

"She stopped taking birth control without telling me. Then turned on all the big guns to get me into bed. Thought if it just happened, I'd come around."

"That's... that's a violation."

"Yeah." I appreciated that she saw it that way. Not everyone did. "It didn't work, obviously. Because I'd already made sure it couldn't happen."

She blinked. "What do you mean?"

"I got a vasectomy when I was twenty-six."

Her cone paused halfway to her mouth.

I pressed on before I lost my nerve. "I watched my father cycle through women my whole life. Leaving destruction everywhere he went. I swore I'd never risk bringing a child into the world unless I was absolutely certain I could be the kind of father they deserved." I looked down at my hands. "I wasn't certain I could then. I'm still not certain now about many things. So, I made sure it couldn't happen accidentally."

Grace set down her cone carefully. "That's... very definitive." She didn't say anything else for a long moment.

"Why are you so against marriage?" she asked finally, her tone genuinely curious. No disgust. No 'I can change his mind' expression I'd seen on other women's faces.

"My parents divorced when I was fourteen. My father was a serial cheater and pretty cruel about it. In the football world—both college and pros—most of the relationships I saw were transactional or unhappy. Made everyone around them miserable." I paused. "It doesn't help that I don't think I've ever been in love before."

We sat in silence, the sounds of the ice cream shop filling the space between us.

I waited for her to get up. To thank me for a nice evening and say this wasn't going to work.

Instead, she reached across the table and covered my hand with hers.

"I have been in love before," she said softly. "And I'm not sure I can recommend it."

Something in my chest relaxed. "So, we're both..."

"Damaged?" She gave me a small, sad smile. "Maybe. Or just realistic."

I looked at our hands—hers on mine, her thumb brushing across my knuckles. "I need to clarify something. I said I didn't want children. That's not entirely accurate."

She tilted her head, waiting.

"I don't want biological children. But I do want to be a father. Just... differently." I took a breath. "I want to adopt. Specifically, I want to foster and adopt older kids from the system. Preteens, teenagers. The ones everyone else passes over. Kyle and I also created a mentoring foundation for older foster kids."

Her mouth opened slightly. "That's... Luke, that's incredible."

"I have already been certified as a foster parent. Took all the classes, passed all the background checks. But before I actually accepted a placement, I had to think about whether it was fair. I travel a lot for work. Would it be right to bring a high-risk kid who really needs stability into my home, only to leave them with hired help when I'm on the road? The agency had the same concerns." I shook my head. "It didn't seem fair to any child."

"That's very thoughtful," Grace said quietly.

"And that feeds into the marriage thing, too. If I had a partner, we could do it together. Share the responsibility, the caregiving. But I wouldn't want to marry someone just to check a box so I could adopt. That seems..." I searched for the word.

"Unfair to everyone involved," she finished.

"Exactly."

She was quiet for a moment, processing. Then: "Maybe you'll meet someone you want to marry for the right reasons. Someone who also wants to foster and adopt. They don't have to be the causation for each other—marriage and adoption."

"True." I looked at her, this woman who somehow got it. Who wasn't running. "Your turn. When are you going to tell me about your marriage?"

She sighed, then met my eyes. "Okay. Here it goes."

18

grace

His words had thrown me off.

Luke was completely different from everything I'd expected on this date. Fascinating. Complex. And he seemed genuinely interested in what I was saying, actually listening.

I had to keep my wits about me. I could easily fall deep into those gorgeous brown eyes and come out battered and broken again. But he'd been so honest with me. About the vasectomy, about his father, about wanting to foster kids. The least I could do was be honest back.

"Okay," I said. "Here it goes. I married another resident during my residency. My damage is that I knew he was still in love with his med school sweetheart, but I thought I could change his mind." I forced myself to keep looking at Luke. "He loved me as a friend but wasn't in love with me. I tolerated it way longer than I should have. Once we had our son, I realized it wasn't healthy. I deserved better. So, I asked for a divorce."

"That sounds painful," he said, shaking his head slightly. "Can I ask you something? It might be personal, so you can say no."

I took a long lick of my cone, considering. "We're being pretty open today. Go for it."

"How do you think you ended up in that situation? You're gorgeous—if it's okay that I say that. You don't seem crazy, you're obviously brilliant. How did you end up with someone who was wrapped up with someone else?"

I gave him a half shrug. "My therapist has a new yacht from trying to decipher that one." Luke laughed, and I felt some of the tension ease. "All I can figure is that I had a high opinion of myself and my ability to fix things. A little perfectionism—if I work hard enough, I can keep the bad things from happening. And I couldn't." I paused. "And that's all I'll say right now."

I could feel tears pricking the back of my eyes. I dropped my chin, trying to shield them.

"I'm sorry," Luke said quietly. "It sounds like there was a lot more to that. Your therapist earned that yacht."

I couldn't help but laugh again, even as I wiped at my eyes.

"So, falling in love—wouldn't recommend, huh?" He reached across the table, hooking his finger under my chin and bringing me to eye level. "I don't know about that. I think I'd need to find out for myself."

My breath caught. "You sound like you have falling in love on your list of things to do."

I tried to sound lighthearted, but the look in his eyes stopped me cold. I knew that look.

Hunger.

After a moment, he reached for a napkin to wipe his fingers, easing back into the conversation. "Do you want to get married again? Have more kids?"

"I'm ambivalent about marriage," I said carefully. "And honestly? After my marriage to Evan? I'm not sure I believe in the fairy tale anymore. As for kids, I almost died having my son. So, giving birth to another child is not on my agenda."

Suddenly, I felt exposed. We were working through deeply private thoughts on our first date. It usually took months before I'd broach these subjects.

Luke must have sensed my shift because he tried to lighten things. "I'm kind of glad I'm not a woman. That having a baby stuff is for the birds."

I gritted my teeth. "I have to agree. And I wouldn't wish it on birds either."

Luke looked at me a little sheepishly. "Maybe that didn't come out right."

I laughed at the look on his face. "I appreciate the walk-back. Let's pretend that last exchange didn't happen."

We sat in comfortable silence for a moment. I could tell he wanted to say something so I waited until he was ready.

He grabbed both my hands and leaned forward. "You were honest with me so I will be honest with you. I have no intention of hurting you or making your life difficult. There's no trail of women following me around. Women won't be coming up to you in the grocery store trying to slash your tires because you were with their man."

I gave him a side-eye. "That's oddly specific."

"I have football stories!" Luke held his hands up in mock protest.

"When you were nineteen, twenty years old, were you enjoying your fame with women? I mean, you don't look that different now," I smirked, a blush spreading across my face. "I was on the track team at Berkeley—I might have made a play for you myself if I'd met you back then."

He laughed. "I looked younger, I'll admit. When I first got to Stanford, I was at my final height but not my final weight. The coaches gave me a weightlifting regimen and made sure I ate at the training table."

"Oh, the training table! We track stars didn't get quite the love that the football players did, but it was available for us too."

"I gained so much muscle from that! But you have to remember I was also a biomedical engineer. I couldn't hang out all the time. I had labs. And there was little belief I'd make it to the pros. The women interested in me were future doctors and engineers. The girls looking for rich athletes didn't think that's what I'd be."

"More fool them."

He tilted his head as he chuckled. "I haven't heard that phrase in a really long time!"

"I had a fascination with the Brits as a kid. Watched British TV reruns—Benny Hill, Are You Being Served?, Monty Python. My mother hated it."

"I love it. Did it make you foul-mouthed?"

"Yeah, a little. My mother hated that, too. And as the oldest, my siblings followed my lead." I grinned. "I find Europe interesting. I even spent this summer trying to learn Spanish curse words. I had a plan!"

"You with your Monty Python and me with my scavenger hunts. Our parents didn't know what they had on their hands!"

We sat giggling for a minute.

Ironically, we didn't know what we had on our hands either.

At ten, the shops on the Wharf started shutting down. We walked back to his car holding hands. It was getting chilly, so he draped his light jacket over my shoulders.

When we reached his BMW, he turned to face me, his back against the passenger door.

"Grace."

I stepped closer. We'd spent hours together—walking, talking, laughing, getting vulnerable in an ice cream shop. And through all of it, the pull between us had only gotten stronger. I could feel it across every inch of my body. It was almost like just *being* around him was doing something to me.

"Yeah?"

"I know this is complicated," he said quietly. "I know we both have damage. I know I can't offer you everything a normal relationship would look like."

"Normal is overrated."

"I'm serious. I don't know where this goes. I don't know if I can be what you need."

I reached up, cupping his face. "I don't need you to have all the answers. I just need you to be honest. Which you have been."

"Then can I be honest about something else?"

I nodded. "Anything."

"I really want to kiss you," he whispered.

"Then kiss me."

He did.

It was soft at first, as if he were asking me for permission to enter my space. Then deeper, his hands finding my waist and pulling me closer. I wrapped my arms around his neck, pressing into him. My hands found the back of his neck, fingers threading through his hair. He tasted like beer and ice cream. When his tongue swept against mine, I made a sound I didn't recognize.

He pulled me tighter, and I could feel every inch of him pressed against me. Could feel exactly how much he wanted this. Wanted *me*.

When we finally broke apart, both breathing hard, he rested his forehead against mine.

"Go on another date with me. Scoma's tomorrow?" he asked.

"Six o'clock work?"

"I'll pick you up."

"It's a date."

I kissed him once more, then let him open the car door for me.

As he drove me back to my office, our hands linked across the console, I thought about Harmony's speed date tomorrow at two.

I should cancel it.

But something held me back. Maybe it was self-preservation. Maybe it was the voice in my head reminding me that Luke had said he'd never been in love, that he didn't do relationships, maybe this had an expiration date.

Deep down, I knew it was just me, being Grace, keeping one foot out the door.

19

luke

I woke up Tuesday morning unusually happy.

I'm normally even-keeled, but this morning I felt giddy. Like a teenager who'd just had his first kiss instead of a forty-four-year-old man who should know better.

The date with Grace had been perfect. The scavenger hunt, the conversation, the way she'd opened up about her marriage, the kiss by the car. I'd come home and told Fitz all about it while giving him treats, then had dreams about her that were equal parts sweet and filthy.

Not a bad night at all.

Of course, there was a voice in the back of my mind whispering that I needed to tell her about Harmony.

Grace hadn't mentioned she was using a matchmaker. Maybe she'd decided not to go through with it after our date. Maybe she'd had such a great time she'd quit the whole thing, and I'd never have to tell her at all.

I shoved that voice deeper.

I'd find the right time to tell her. Just not yet. Not when things were going this well.

Downstairs, I let Fitz out and poured myself coffee in a travel mug. My housekeeper Gail wouldn't be here until later, so it was just me and my dog for our morning walk. Fitz waited patiently by the door—all that training finally paying off after years of battles with various trainers.

We took our usual route through the neighborhood. Depending on the path, we could watch boats in the bay. After ten minutes, Fitz did his business while I waited, bags ready.

That's when I called Grace.

"Hi." She sounded groggy but warm.

"Hi." Like two kids shyly saying hello. "I hope I didn't call too early."

"No, I'm awake. Not out of bed yet, but awake. About to get dressed to see patients. Trying to get my mind right for work. Thanks to you."

My chest tightened in the best way. "I should be thanking you. You were the first thing on my mind this morning. And not for the reason you might think. Although I will cop to some sexy thoughts involving nakedness."

"I'm blushing now. And afraid to ask what you were thinking. Just hoping I was a very good girl in whatever you were imagining." She almost purred that last sentence.

I nearly dropped my coffee. My mind went straight to the gutter—and this journey was not tame at all. "Well, um, okay. I have a plan—um—for dinner—for tonight. Hold on. Let me get my mind right here."

I took a deep breath. Fitz looked at me like I was losing it.

"Okay," I continued. "I know we discussed going to Scoma's, but I thought of something else. So, we can stick with the current plan, or I'll continue with my new idea. Basically, I'd like to see the sunrise and sunset with you."

"Is that another way of saying 'spend the day with me'?" She sounded amused. "I have questions. However, given how well you did last night, I'll give you the benefit of the doubt. Plan away."

"No pressure, huh? Are you off tomorrow? No patients, no obligations?"

"Yes. Do I need to bring a change of clothes?"

"It probably would be for the best. That's all you get for now." I smiled. "I just wanted to hear your voice. I'll pick you up at six if you're okay with my coming to your home."

"Surprisingly, I'm okay with that," She giggled. "I'm going to have to watch myself with you."

"Seriously though," I replied. "If at any point if you don't feel comfortable, let me know. I want you to always feel safe. I'll see you tonight."

"Tonight."

I hung up, grinning like an idiot.

Fitz gave me a look that clearly said, *You're pathetic.*

"I know," I told him.

Back at the house, my phone buzzed. A text from Harmony.

Harmony: *Remember my client? Well, I've done it again! This time it's a coffee date and I am so excited (and proud of myself!) Fingers crossed!*

My stomach dropped.

So, she was still doing it.

Which meant I really should tell her. Right now. Before this got more complicated.

I stared at my phone, thumb hovering over Grace's contact.

Just tell her. "Hey, funny story—my sister is your matchmaker. Small world, right?"

Except it wasn't a small world. It was a deliberate omission. I'd seen Grace's picture on Harmony's whiteboard and said nothing. Had asked Grace out anyway, knowing my sister would lose her mind if she found out.

If I told Grace now, she'd feel blindsided. Might think I'd been playing some game. Might wonder what else I wasn't telling her.

And Harmony would kill me. Actually kill me. She'd specifically told me to stay away from her clients, especially Grace.

But if I didn't tell her and she found out later...

My phone buzzed again.

Harmony: *Also, have you thought about what I said? About meeting someone who might change your mind about relationships?*

I closed the messages without responding.

My house sitter and occasional dog sitter, Jamal arrived almost twenty minutes later. The kid was applying to college now, had come so far from the withdrawn, angry boy Kyle and I had met years ago through a foster care mentorship program. When we met Jamal, he was a silent, resentful child. He had been in foster care for several years but had been bounced around from home to home through no fault of his own. Jamal was smart, but with no one to push him and no person he could trust, he wasn't going to put himself out there for ridicule or disappointment.

Jamal also was the reason I'd first applied to be a foster parent—before the agency told me I couldn't do it alone because of my schedule. After meeting him, Kyle and I also started our own small mentoring program connecting older foster kids to businessmen in the community. But work had been so busy that neither of us had focused on it like we needed to. I wanted to change that at some point.

"I'm taking Fitz to Mr. Kyle's and then to the park," Jamal said. "It's been a couple days since the labs have seen each other. They probably have some energy to burn off." Jamal also watched Kyle's yellow lab Deuce, one of Fitz's sisters. Kyle and I hoped that Jamal would be able to continue with this even when he went to college.

"Sounds good. How's the college application going?"

"Just waiting on Mr. Kyle's recommendation letter. I'm looking forward to the challenge."

I smiled. "You're going to do great. And remember, you can work for us as long as you want. Even after you start school."

"I don't know what would've happened to me if you and Mr. Kyle hadn't taken an interest. I don't know if I can ever repay you."

"You're repaying me now. Just seeing you go after your goals." I paused. "How's that young lady you mentioned?"

"We went out a couple times. Having a good time getting to know her. You know how that is."

I definitely did.

After Jamal left with Fitz, I got ready for the office—gray plaid suit, white shirt, no tie. Something I could wear to dinner with Grace tonight.

My phone sat on the bathroom counter, Harmony's messages still unread.

I should tell Grace. The right thing, the honest thing, would be to call her back right now and come clean.

But I liked her. Really liked her. And I was selfish enough to want a few more days before everything got complicated.

Just until after tonight. After our second date. Then I'd tell her.

Probably.

I grabbed my phone and headed out, shoving down the guilt that was already starting to build in my chest.

20

grace

Running had been my thing in college—middle distance, every single day. I'd maintained it through med school, but residency killed that routine completely. Adding Gabe and his schedule made it even more difficult to maintain.

Now that I was in my forties, I couldn't just eat like I used to. I'd finally started running again—three miles a day to start. If training went well, I wanted to compete in a 10K by the holidays. Maybe work up to a marathon next year.

After my run and shower, I stood in front of my closet trying to decide what to wear.

I needed something appropriate for clinic. Something that worked for a coffee date at two. Something I could change into for dinner with Luke at six. Plus, an overnight bag for whatever mystery activity he had planned.

"What the fuck am I getting into today?" I muttered.

I settled on professional-casual for work and the coffee date, packed a nicer outfit for dinner, and threw in an extra change of clothes just in case I needed to hitchhike out of wherever Luke was taking me.

As I got in my car, Claudia called.

We used to catch up during the morning commute all the time when Gabe was home. That had fallen away over the past couple of months since my routine changed. But given that I'd hired a matchmaker and Autumn had definitely blabbed about me meeting Luke, I should have expected this call.

"Good morning, Claudia. How are you?"

"Doing well. Just dropped the kids at school. You heading to work?"

"Yes. Before you ask, I have a coffee date set up by Harmony this afternoon."

"Well, I heard you met a guy on your own over the weekend."

Of course. Autumn couldn't keep her mouth shut for anything. "True." I considered what to say and decided to keep the details to myself for now. There had been only one date – nothing to tell. "Still waiting for him to call..."

Technically true...

"Who is this guy?"

I gave her the condensed version—Luke, biomedical engineer, former NFL player, owns Sloane-Wash Sciences.

"Are you sure that's who this is?"

I rolled my eyes at the dashboard. "Yes, I've Googled him. His picture matches. His history checks out. He's not trying to scam me. And I still have that AirTag Autumn implanted in my purse for when - if – we go out. Don't act like you don't know."

"W-what? Autumn did that? I-I had no idea." Claudia was the worst liar.

"Anyway, I'm almost at my office. We need lunch this weekend. My life is suddenly blowing up."

"In a good way, right? You're okay?"

"Yeah, I'm okay. Thanks for checking on me. I miss our morning calls. I know my life changed when Gabe left, but I still need my friends."

Claudia was quiet for a second. "I'm sorry. I felt like I'd be rubbing it in, talking about my kids when I know you weren't excited about Gabe leaving. I didn't think not calling might make you sad too. I'll do better."

"I need updates on your badass kids anyway. Makes me feel stronger in my resolution not to have any more."

"Bitch! Before the twins, I wasn't planning on more either."

"Lies! Talk to you later. Have a great day."

We disconnected as I pulled into the clinic parking lot.

The morning went smoothly, that is until around ten when Harmony texted me.

Harmony: *Your date! Everett Garfield, MD. Sending photo so you don't end up with a random stranger. Have fun!*

A photo popped up. Nice-looking in a boyish way. Same height as me, played golf, enjoyed the arts and football. No kids.

Well, it shouldn't be boring.

I stared at the photo for a long moment.

I should text Luke. Tell him about the matchmaker, about this coffee date in four hours.

It would be the honest thing to do.

But we'd only had one date. And Luke had been clear—he didn't do relationships, he'd never been in love, he got a vasectomy specifically to avoid complications.

This wasn't serious. Not yet. Maybe not ever.

So, what was the harm in keeping my options open?

I put my phone away and went to see my next patient, shoving down the guilt that was starting to build in my chest.

How the hell was I going to manage this?

21

luke

Kyle called while I was driving to work.

"You ready for the meeting?"

Before every investor meeting, I got this nervous check-in call. It had started when we were college students with Kyle pitching our first prototype. The only reason Kyle didn't call before our initial investment meeting almost twenty-five years ago was because I was on a football field and couldn't be reached.

"Yes. Are you?"

"Of course. Though I don't know what we need more investors for when we're already sitting on enough money."

"So, you and your team can keep creating innovations that make everyone's lives better. Besides, these investors want us to focus on underdeveloped countries. That's rare. I want to hear what they have to say."

"Great point. This is so much more than we thought it would be when we were in college, isn't it?"

"We were pretty innocent then. Just thinking we'd make enough money to go out to eat when we wanted. Impress a girl or two." We both laughed.

"Anyway, I know we're ready. I just needed to hear it again. I don't think I could do this without you, Luke. You keep me sane." Kyle paused. "Palate cleanser—your date. You haven't mentioned anything. No call last night. Was it bad?"

I took a deep breath. I was about to say something I'd never said to him about any date. Ever.

"It was the best date I've ever been on."

Silence.

"What?" When Kyle finally replied, he sounded stunned. "Was it because there was sex?"

He had a point. Good dates for me usually ended in sex – even if there was no next date forthcoming. Maybe Harmony was right about my relationship issues.

"There was no sex. Very little kissing."

"Okay. And that didn't add up to 'no next date'? No microscopic issues that bug you, but you feel bad bringing up? No 'I'm too busy, she's nice, but I didn't feel it, no need to drag this out'?" Kyle's voice rose. "What kind of sorcery did this woman put on you?"

"Don't get me started. I can't get lost in it right now—I need to stay focused on the presentation. Let's just say we're having dinner tonight."

"What?" Kyle repeated. "Man, you gotta stop dropping bombshells on me like this. Wait until I tell Jada. She might just drop dead."

I had to admit, I couldn't blame him for the incredulous comments. I was pretty shocked myself. Grace had inserted herself into my life after only one date.

"See you at the office in twenty," I said, disconnecting before he could ask more questions.

⚗

The investor meeting went well. Better than well, but I was never the type to jinx things. Kyle's presentation wowed the room—potential uses for our current medical devices and developmental prototypes that could significantly improve lives worldwide. These ambassadors were interested in technology built for the realities of life in developing countries, not Western assumptions. After they left for another engagement, Kyle walked over carrying two bottles of expensive apple cider. He twisted off both caps and handed me one.

"To not screwing up a three-billion-dollar opportunity." He clinked his bottle against mine.

"To keeping you from having a nervous breakdown before every pitch." I took a sip. The cider was perfect.

Kyle settled into the chair across from me with *that* look on his face. The one that meant he was about to dig.

"So. Tonight."

"Tonight," I echoed, keeping my expression neutral.

"This mystery woman. Where are you taking her?"

"Dinner."

"Where?"

"A place."

Kyle narrowed his eyes. "You're being weird. You're never weird about dates. Usually, you give me way too much information about—"

"We might go to a winery," I interrupted. "Not the one we have shares in. One in San Luis Obispo. Maybe see the sun rise."

"Might?" Kyle leaned forward. "Since when do you 'might' anything? You have color-coded calendars, Luke. You plan bathroom breaks."

I took another drink, saying nothing.

"Oh my God." Kyle's eyes widened. "You're being cagey. You never get cagey. This woman really has you wound up."

"I'm not wound up."

"You're being cagey about being wound up, which means you're incredibly wound up." He was grinning now. "What's her name?"

My stomach tightened. "Why do you need to know her name?"

"So, I can Google her. See what kind of sorcery she's using on my best friend."

"There's no *sorcery*."

"Lies. You just admitted to the best date of your life, you're taking her on an overnight trip for date two, and you won't even tell me her name." Kyle set down his bottle. "I'm claiming dibs right now—I'm going to be your best man, right? This woman has you acting different. She's going to be the first Mrs. Sloane."

"Don't get ahead of yourself. Let's see how date two goes."

The name hit me harder than I expected.

Mrs. Sloane.

Kyle didn't know what that meant. Nobody did, really, except my mother and Harmony.

I'd taken that name—Sloane—when I was fourteen. Changed it from Zambo, my father's name, to my mother's maiden name. My father had finally asked for a divorce after years of affairs and after getting another woman pregnant. The woman he'd marry. Harmony's mother.

I'd been furious. More upset than my own mother, who'd been civilized about the whole thing.

But not me. I rejected everything about him including his name.

Sloane was my choice. My mother's name. A promise to myself that I wouldn't be like him.

The vasectomy at twenty-six was part of that same promise. Never accidentally create a child. Never trap someone.

Never become him.

And now Kyle was joking about "the first Mrs. Sloane."

Except I was already keeping secrets from Grace. Lying by omission about Harmony. Planning this elaborate date while knowing my sister had set her up with someone else today.

Am I becoming him after all?

"Earth to Luke." Kyle waved a hand in front of my face. "Where'd you go?"

"Sorry. Just thinking about tonight."

"Well, don't screw it up. I want to meet this mystery woman who's got you acting like a human being with feelings."

I forced a laugh, but the weight sat heavy in my chest.

I should tell Grace. Today. Before this elaborate overnight date. Before things got deeper.

My phone buzzed. A text from the train company confirming our Coast Starlight reservations. Private car, sunrise breakfast at the winery, sunset dinner.

I'd spent two hours this morning coordinating everything—the train, the car service to meet us in San Luis Obispo, the winery reservations, making sure they'd have Grace's favorite wine available. The one she told me about last night.

The kind of effort I'd never put into a date before.

Because Grace was different.

Which was exactly why I should tell her about Harmony.

I stared at my phone, at Grace's contact entry.

After tonight, I decided. *After the winery. After I know this is real.*

I shoved the guilt down and headed to my next meeting, my father's ghost following me like a shadow.

22

grace

At 12:30, I headed to The Roasted Cup, the coffee shop across from my office. The coffee wasn't bad, and they had nice Danishes most mornings. It was a popular spot among the doctors and medical staff in the clinic building.

I scanned the shop as I entered. No sign of my speed date yet, so I waited to order. Didn't want to give the wrong impression.

At 12:45, Everett hurried in—white coat, stethoscope around his neck, phone in hand. He was more handsome in person than in his photo. He scanned the coffee shop, holding up his phone, comparing each woman to the picture.

I could have stood up and waved. But watching his search was rather entertaining.

Finally, he spotted me in the back corner and hurried over.

"I'm so sorry for being late. My last patient had questions. Lots of them!" He looked genuinely apologetic. "Did you order already? I can get something for both of us."

"No, I waited. I'll take a chai with 2% milk, please. Thank you." I reached for my wallet, but he waved me off.

When he joined me at the table with a numbered tag, I asked, "Have you done this before? Speed dating?"

"Yes. Once or twice. I'm so busy that finding time to date is almost impossible. So, I met Harmony. Funny story—someone actually tried to fix us up at first."

My mouth dropped open. "Really?"

"Yeah. That friend had no concerns about the age difference. Didn't give me a heads up either. This was a couple years ago, so she was in her late-twenties and I was pushing forty. Smartly, Harmony took the date intending to match me with someone she knew."

"Well, I guess she was always on the grind."

"It was for the best. She introduced me to some lovely women. Age-appropriate, similar interests. Nothing long-term came of any of it, but I had fun."

"So why are you back?"

"Just got out of a one-year relationship. Decided to dip my toes back in. Speed dating's a good way to do that. What about you?"

"My friends decided my dating exploits after my divorce have been questionable, if not downright sad. They want to wipe my slate clean." I laughed.

"Great friends!" He joined in.

The server brought my chai, his black coffee, and a croissant sandwich.

"So, what made you go into medicine?" I asked, wrapping my hands around the warm chai.

"Honestly? Rebellion." He grinned. "My entire family is in law. My father's a judge, my mother's a corporate attorney, both my brothers are at big firms. Every Sunday dinner was Supreme Court cases and precedent arguments."

I laughed. "That sounds exhausting."

"It was. When I was sixteen, my grandmother had a stroke. I watched the ER team save her life, and I just... knew. Medicine was what I wanted." He took a bite of his croissant. "My parents were horrified. Still are, a little. What about you?"

"Both my parents are in law too, actually. My dad was a part of administration at Berkeley Law, and my mom taught there before she retired. Very academic household. But I wanted to do something tangible, you know? Help people."

"Berkeley," Everett said thoughtfully. "What's your dad's name?"

"Vincent Billings, Sr."

His face lit up. "Wait—Vincent Billings? Dean of Academic Planning?"

"That's him."

"My father knows him! They've been on panels together. Judge Harold Garfield?"

My mouth dropped open slightly. "Your dad is Judge Garfield? My parents definitely know him. They went to some NAACP fundraiser with him last year."

"Small world," Everett said, shaking his head. "Bay Area Black professional circles."

"Incredibly small." I made a mental note to ask my parents about the Garfields later. They'd want to know about this.

Then it turned out he knew Zay, Claudia's husband. And more oddly, Evan.

When he connected our shared last name, I had to admit Evan was my ex-husband.

"You know I played golf at a charity tournament with both Evan and Zay. I heard Evan moved to Miami. Something about his son and swimming."

I nodded. "Our son. He's at a swimming academy there. Evan and his wife live there now for support during training."

"That must be exciting. Is he aiming for the Olympics?"

"That's the dream. We'll see if he has what it takes." I took a sip of my chai. "The training is intense. Six days a week, sometimes twice a day. He's only thirteen, so we're trying to balance pushing him and not burning him out."

"That's a tough balance. I don't have kids myself, but my ex—the woman I was with last year—she had a son. Seven years old, played soccer and baseball." Everett's expression softened. "I got pretty involved, actually. Coached his rec league team for a few months."

"Really? That's sweet."

"It was fun. Until it wasn't." He cleared his throat. "When we broke up, I lost him too, you know? One day I'm at every game, helping with homework, the next I'm just... gone from his life. That was harder than I expected."

I nodded slowly. "That's one of the hardest parts of dating as a parent. My son gets attached to people. I have to be really careful about who I bring into his life."

"Smart. I didn't think about that going in. Thought I was just dating her. Didn't realize I was signing up for both of them." He smiled wryly. "Learned that lesson the hard way."

"At least you cared enough to show up for him while you were there. A lot of men wouldn't."

"Yeah, well. Kid deserved better than me disappearing without explanation. But that's what happens when the relationship ends." He finished his coffee. "Is that something you worry about? With the matchmaking thing?"

I thought about Luke. About how careful I was going to be about mentioning him to Gabe.

"All the time," I admitted as the conversation merged into other topics.

He was nice to talk to.

And I compared him to Luke the entire time.

When we finally said goodbye, we both agreed to keep things in the friend zone.

A smart decision. Because I wasn't being fair. Wasn't being impartial.

Not while Luke was getting under my skin.

It had been a long time since I'd gotten this caught up in someone after one date.

Red Flag #1

23

grace

On my way home, I called Harmony to report back.

"Oh! I'm glad you called! Been anxiously waiting. I know this is your first experience with my services. How did it go?"

I gave her my honest opinion: nice guy, knew my ex-husband, we agreed to be friends.

Harmony made an agreeable noise. "As I expected. I didn't select him for your first date thinking you'd have fireworks. I think he's potentially a good friend, but not a boyfriend. I wanted to get your feet wet with someone comfortable and friendly. Someone who wouldn't have your brain short-circuiting because of chemistry."

"That was your strategy? How did you know there wouldn't be scorching heat?"

"I'm pretty good at this!" She laughed. "One, Everett's not a scorching heat kind of guy. Two, it was a coffee date during a workday—less likelihood of that mindset. And three, he's not your typical type based on your past relationships and what you wrote on your intake form."

"You considered all of that? Maybe you were listening to me."

Her reasoning made sense. Maybe she had strategies I could use. Which was weird, because I'd been dating almost as long as she'd been alive.

Based on my results, though? It was quite possible I'd been doing it wrong.

"I'd like you to keep a dating journal." Harmony broke into my train of thought.

"I don't journal."

"Well, that was definitive. Given where you are, maybe you should."

That shut me up for a minute. "Okay. What do I need to put in it?"

"Your thoughts. Write about your feelings each day. In general, and about each date. What you think about him, what you notice. You'll start to see patterns, weak points, things you should know."

I exhaled loudly. I'd resisted when my therapist asked me to journal—probably why my shit was still a struggle.

"Okay. I'll stop and buy a pretty one that might encourage me to keep doing it. I think I need a little space before the next date."

"Right. Write it down, and we can talk about next steps."

We disconnected.

Maybe this journaling thing wouldn't be so bad. I had so many feelings right now—mostly about Luke—that were overwhelming in a way I hadn't felt since Evan.

And that was dangerous.

Maybe writing it down would help me manage, help me not get swept away and make another terrible mistake.

As I pulled into my garage, Vic called.

"Hey, Vic."

"Gracie... I did it."

I walked to my bedroom, staring at my closet. I'd changed my mind again about what to wear tonight. "Did you talk to the lawyer Dad introduced you to?"

"Yes. I'd already talked to him. I just didn't tell anyone yet. I filed yesterday."

I sat on the bed. "Hallelujah! Where are you right now? When is she getting served?"

"I'm at home. Stacia went to a bodybuilding competition. She'll be back tomorrow." He paused. "She might get served today."

"Damn, little bro. That's a little gangster—serving her at the competition. Where will you be?"

"Gangster? That's weird hearing you use that word. Anyway, hopefully I'll be at your place. Can I crash in your guest room for a day or two? I'd change the locks at the house, but legally I can't just lock her out. I want to give her a chance to gather her stuff and leave."

I laughed. "You think she's leaving willingly? You know you can crash here for a few days. We'd kill each other if it went on much longer though."

"True. I'll go stay with Mom and Dad if she balks. I just need to get on with it."

"You haven't lost your key, have you? I'm going out tonight."

"What? I'm not coming until tomorrow. You're not going to be there? I thought we could sit and eat popcorn and ice cream and talk about the suck that is marriage." His voice went weird. "You aren't bringing your date back to the house, are you? Don't answer. I don't want to know."

"Stupid! I have to get dressed. Let yourself in. There's food in the fridge if you need it. Take care of yourself. I don't trust Stacia."

"Don't worry. I'm okay."

After disconnecting, I went back and stared into my closet with trepidation. Picking up my phone, I dialed Luke.

He answered on the first ring. "Grace."

My belly lurched when he said my name in that smooth baritone. I needed to get this under control.

"Hi! What do I need to wear?"

"You're stressing about this, aren't you?" He chuckled. "Okay, I'll make it easy. Whatever you wear needs to be comfortable—you have plenty of clothes that would work. I don't even have to look in your closet to know that."

I grunted.

He laughed again. "And tomorrow, be ready for walking. Do you like wine?"

"Are we going to a winery?"

When he didn't respond, I continued. "Where am I sleeping tonight? You keep hinting I'll be comfortable, but I like to know what I'm walking into. Surprises are nice, but can you give me a little more? I rarely do this so quickly. We just met."

I heard the words coming out of my mouth, knowing I'd jump him in a minute. The sex devil on my shoulder wanted to yell into the phone, *Fuck me! Fuck me now!*

I quickly muted my phone to make sure I didn't mumble that where he could hear it.

"Oh, you might not be sleeping at all. And not for the reasons your mind may be jumping to. I'm a gentleman—for now. I'll see you at six."

I laid out a long, form-fitting knit dress and my Timberland boots—they'd double for walking tomorrow. Packed essentials and a wrinkle-proof jumpsuit into my AirTagged day bag.

In the shower, I made sure there were no errant hairs—just in case. Even though I'd had electrolysis everywhere after med school, occasionally I had to clean up. I had no intention of anyone seeing anything today, but I needed to repeat that as a mantra when I looked into those eyes.

At six on the dot, Luke rang my bell.

He looked amazing in that gray checked suit with a crisp white shirt. And boots.

Hmmmm...

He spun me around to get a full view of my dress, which clung to my hips and ass and cascaded to the floor. Eggshell, could pass as dressy or casual. I owned this dress in three colors—it got a lot of wear.

After applying moisturizer, I'd fluffed out my hair and finger-curled a few strands for definition. I'd added a bonnet to my bag.

"As expected, I'm not disappointed. You're absolutely stunning!" He pulled me into a hug with a gentle kiss on the lips. Just enough pressure to make my knees buckle. He then grabbed my hand and led me to a chauffeur-driven BMW SUV. "Come on, let's go. We have a schedule to keep."

I stopped. "A chauffeur? Where are we going?"

He climbed in and helped me in. "The chauffeur's name is Todd—a former foster kid I hired after he graduated high school. We're going to dinner first." He placed my day bag on the row behind us, next to his overnight bag. "By the Amtrak station. Because we have a train to catch."

"A train? To where?"

My AirTag better work if I ended up buried behind a Giant Sequoia.

"We're taking the Coast Starlight—the luxury Amtrak—to San Luis Obispo. There's a gorgeous ranch and winery where we're having breakfast at sunrise and dinner at sunset. Then a ride back. You'll be back in SF around six Thursday morning." He tipped my chin toward him.

My mouth fell open.

This was the most elaborate date I'd been on in years. And it was the second date!

Luke gently closed my mouth with his index finger.

"Do you create these big dates for all the women you date?" I ducked my head.

"There haven't been that many women. And no, I've never done anything like this before. This is all for you."

I looked up at him, searching his face for any sign of a lie.

All I saw was honesty. And want. And something that looked a lot like hope.

"Okay," I said softly. "Let's go catch a train."

As Todd pulled away from my house, Luke's hand found mine across the seat.

And I tried very hard not to think about the fact that I was catching feelings for a man who'd said he'd never been in love.

Or that I still hadn't told him about Harmony.

24

luke

"You okay?" I asked. Grace's hand was warm in mine as Todd drove us toward Emeryville.

She turned to look at me, something vulnerable in her expression. "My dating life recently has been me hoping the guy remembers to order DoorDash for dinner." She laughed softly. "I'm not used to this. Someone being this attentive, this thoughtful. Planning something this elaborate. It's a little overwhelming, you know?"

My chest tightened. "I'm sorry. Am I coming on too strong? We can scale back—"

"No." She squeezed my hand. "Don't apologize. I'm just... adjusting. This is a good thing. A really good thing. I'm just not used to good things."

I lifted her hand to my lips, kissed her knuckles. "Then let me be clear about my intentions. I plan to erase the memory of every guy who didn't appreciate what he had. From your mind, heart, and soul." I held her gaze. "Even if this doesn't go any further than tonight, I want you to understand that I think you're exquisite. That you deserve all of this and more."

Her eyes went soft. "I think about you all the time."

"Yeah?"

"Yeah." She ducked her head, smiling. "It's kind of terrifying, actually."

I pulled her closer, and she leaned her head on my shoulder for the rest of the ride.

The Townhouse restaurant was exactly what I'd hoped for—laid-back atmosphere, good food, close enough to the Amtrak station that we wouldn't have to rush. The restaurant had been a speakeasy, a country-western bar, a political hangout. Now it was just a solid neighborhood spot with history in its bones.

Grace ordered seared ahi tuna salad. I got the salmon tagliatelle. We shared a bottle of wine.

"Tell me about growing up," she said, leaning forward. "You mentioned your mom's in San Francisco?"

"Yeah. Assisted living complex in Inner Richmond. She's doing well—still sharp, still bossy." I smiled. "Despite everything with my parents' marriage, I had a pretty happy childhood. My mom made sure of that."

"What was she like? As a mom?"

I thought about it. "Warm. Present. She worked, but she always made time. Always had kids at our house—neighbors, my friends, kids who needed a place to crash when things got hard at home. My father hated it, said if she wanted more kids she should have another baby. But she couldn't." I paused. "So, he eventually went out and had one. My half-sister was born when I was fourteen."

Grace's eyes lit up. "You have a sister? Are you close?"

"We're getting closer now that we're adults. I babysat for her, watched out for her growing up. But there's a big age gap—by the time she could talk and really annoy me, I was in college. We never lived in the same house." I took a sip of wine, knowing that I was getting too close to my lie. "What about you? Loud childhood in Berkeley?"

She laughed. "So loud. My dad's a professor, my mom was too. Very academic household, lots of debate at the dinner table. I have two siblings—Celeste is in Korea, Vic is here. We fought constantly growing up but we were close." Her expression softened. "I sometimes wish Gabe had that growing up. Siblings. But it wasn't meant to be."

"You almost died having him."

"Yeah." She took a sip of wine. "Evan wanted more kids. I couldn't give him that. It was one of the many ways I wasn't enough."

I reached across the table, covered her hand with mine. "You were enough. He was the problem."

She looked at our hands, then at me. "You're very good at saying the right thing."

"I'm just saying what's true."

The server brought dessert—chocolate lava cake to share. Grace took the first bite, closed her eyes.

"Good?" I asked.

"Obscene." She opened her eyes, grinned. "You're watching me eat cake like it's pornography."

"You make it look like pornography."

She laughed, the sound filling something in my chest I hadn't realized was empty.

We finished the wine, the cake, talked about college and careers and how we both ended up in the Bay Area. She told me about track, about choosing medicine over academia. I told her about football, about starting the company with Kyle, about how everything happened at once and how my head was spinning most of the time.

"You never felt overwhelmed?" she asked. "NFL draft and a startup?"

"Constantly. But Kyle kept me grounded. And my mom." I paused. "And honestly, football gave me an out. When the business stuff got too intense, I had practice. When football got too intense, I had the lab. I could switch gears."

"That's smart. I did something similar with running and school. When my brain was fried from studying, I'd run. When my body was exhausted, I'd study." She smiled. "We're more alike than I thought."

"I noticed."

By the time we paid and walked out hand in hand, it was nearly 9 p.m. The air was cool, the night clear.

Todd dropped us at the Emeryville Amtrak station, and I confirmed pickup details for tomorrow night. Grace watched him drive away, then turned to me.

"This is really happening. We're getting on a train."

"We are. With two reserved sleeper cars."

She smiled at my admission and continued. "For sunrise breakfast at a winery."

"And sunset dinner."

She stepped closer, looked up at me. "Luke Sloane, you're either the best thing that's happened to me in years or you're going to break my heart so badly I'll never recover."

I cupped her face in my hands. "I vote for option one."

"Me too," she whispered.

I kissed her then, right there in the parking lot. Soft at first, then deeper when her hands fisted in my jacket and she pulled me closer. She tasted like chocolate and wine and something uniquely her that I was already addicted to.

When we finally broke apart, we were both breathing hard.

"We should check in," I said.

"Yeah," she agreed, but neither of us moved.

Finally, I forced myself to step back and took her hand. The station didn't have a lounge, so we sat in the back corner of the waiting room.

"Unfortunately, this station doesn't have a lounge," I said. "Which I apologize for."

"You won't find me complaining." Grace smiled. "I need to go to the restroom. I'll be right back."

I watched her walk away, marveling at how five days ago I didn't know she existed. Now I couldn't imagine not knowing her.

By 9:45, we were settled in one of the sleeper cars. Grace stepped inside, looking around with wide eyes.

"This is like Murder on the Orient Express," she said.

"I was thinking Trading Places."

She looked at me and laughed, the tension breaking. "Of course you would! This train has a dining car and a lounge, right? Where you can watch the scenery?"

"It does. We can see from here too, but the other car gives you a fuller view."

We both moved to the window. I stepped up behind her, close enough to smell her hair—coconut and something floral. My hands found her waist. She leaned back into me slightly with a soft yawn.

The train lurched forward and she fell against me completely. My body responded immediately. If she felt my erection against her, she didn't say anything.

"Come on," I said, voice rough. "Let's explore before you fall asleep on your feet."

We visited each car then had wine in the dining car, watched the dark scenery in the lounge. By the time we got back to the sleeper car, she'd been yawning for the past twenty minutes.

"Do you want to set up the other sleeper? You can nap there."

"I didn't think I'd be this tired." She stretched, and I tried not to stare at the way her dress pulled across her body. "Why aren't you exhausted? You called me early this morning."

"Adrenaline."

She turned to face me. "I don't want to go to the separate car. I feel like I'm going to miss something. I'm on a luxury train!" She yawned again. "I'm not ready for the evening to end."

I grabbed a blanket from the top bunk, spread it on the seat. "Sit with me then."

We exchanged a look—acknowledgment of what we both wanted, what we weren't doing yet. Then she sat down, untied her boots, curled up, and carefully placed her head on my shoulder.

I wrapped my arm around her, pulled her close.

She tried to keep talking—about the scenery, about dinner, about tomorrow. But within minutes she was mumbling, then softly snoring.

I adjusted the blanket over her legs, leaned my head back, and let myself feel this. Grace Robertson asleep on my shoulder, trusting me, soft and warm and perfect.

The car was quiet except for the train and her breathing.

I thought about the text from Harmony. About Grace's coffee date with Everett.

About how she hadn't told me about the matchmaker.

About how I hadn't told her who my sister was.

We were both liars now.

But as I looked down at her sleeping face, I couldn't bring myself to care. Tomorrow we'd watch the sunrise together. She'd see how much I wanted this to work.

And maybe by then, none of the secrets would matter.

25

grace

I woke up around 3:30 a.m., my head still on Luke's shoulder.

It was remarkable that I'd been comfortable enough to fall asleep—soundly asleep—with a man I'd known less than a week. But he had to be uncomfortable, his shoulder in that awkward position for hours.

I sat up gently. The cabin was dark except for a night light.

I took the opportunity to study him while he slept. He looked peaceful. I was jealous of those thick lashes, the perfect line of his jaw. His lips looked so inviting I almost couldn't resist—I leaned over but stopped short of kissing him.

He stirred but didn't wake.

I retreated, pleased that he didn't snore.

Then I cringed, remembering I'd been told I sometimes did snore. Hopefully he hadn't noticed. Not at this stage.

I thought about yesterday. About sitting across from Everett at 1 p.m., making pleasant conversation while thinking about Luke. About getting Harmony's text with the coffee date details and almost canceling. About going through with it anyway because I was hedging my bets, keeping my options open, protecting myself.

About how Luke had picked me up at 6 p.m. and I hadn't said a word about spending my lunch hour on a date with another man.

The guilt sat heavy in my chest.

I should tell him. Eventually. When we were more solid. When it wouldn't sound like I was playing games.

I snuggled back into the space between his shoulder and chest, breathing in his scent.

I could stay here for a long time, I thought as I drifted off.

"Hey, Sunshine. Time to wake up."

Luke's voice pulled me from sleep. I stretched and stood up.

"Sunshine? Is that my nickname?"

"I know it sounds corny. I can skip it if it bothers you." He smiled. "I do have another nickname for you that I'll try later."

"It doesn't bother me. No one's ever confused me with sunshine before. I kind of like it." I stretched my neck and shoulders. "How's your shoulder? I shouldn't have kept you in that position all night."

He rolled his shoulders and stood up. "It wasn't bad."

"Liar."

"We're almost at San Luis Obispo. We'll take a car to the ranch for our sunrise breakfast."

"So, we can watch the sunrise together." I tilted my head up. "This is very romantic. You really don't do this for all the girls?"

"No." He wrapped his arms around my waist and pulled me close. "Or any of the girls. Only one gorgeous, smart woman who tried to knock me out four days ago gets this treatment."

I ducked my head. "I tried to forget about that."

"I think it was fate." His voice went soft. "You're walking all over my heart in those Timberlands. I'm still adjusting."

My breath caught. "Luke—"

A knock on the door. "Ten minutes to the station!"

We pulled apart. I grabbed my day bag and checked my reflection. My hair was a mess, I probably had sleep in my eyes.

And I'd never felt more beautiful.

At the station, a driver stood with a sign that said "Sloane."

"That's us," Luke said.

"Hello, Mr. and Mrs. Sloane. My name is Adam. I'll be your driver."

The words hit me like a physical thing. *Mrs. Sloane.*

"Oh no, I'm not his wife." I heard myself say it flirtatiously. "We're on a date. Our second one, actually. He's very kind to take me to such nice places."

Luke kissed my cheek and we followed Adam to the car.

But as I settled into the backseat, I couldn't stop thinking about it. *Mrs. Sloane.* How easily Adam had assumed it. How Luke hadn't really corrected him either.

How good it had sounded.

How scared that made me.

La Lomita was stunning—historic buildings, peaceful grounds, mostly empty since there were no events going on currently. After checking into our rooms for the day, we splashed water on our faces and headed straight to breakfast.

The server led us to a patio under some trees. The buffet was elaborate—charcuterie, meats, cheeses, breads, fruits. A chef ready to make anything. Mimosa and sangria bar, local wines.

"How many people are eating with us?" I asked, stunned.

"Just us." Luke stood behind me, close enough that I felt the heat of him. "I wanted you to have choices."

"You've been spoiling me for three days straight." I picked up a piece of bacon, smiled at him. "But I do appreciate it."

He gave me a smile that made my knees weak and my underwear damp.

The sun was rising through the trees, painting the sky in oranges and yellows.

"We're eating a lot of food this morning. Is there a gym here? I will need to run some *miles* today after all this." I bit into a chocolate croissant. "You could have warned me to bring running clothes."

Luke grinned, pulled out his phone. "I can order you workout clothes. Which brand of shoes do you like?"

My eyes went wide. "Don't you dare! I was kidding—"

He was laughing. The servers were laughing too.

"Don't be mean." I threw a piece of pineapple at him. "Okay, how about this—you run too, right? Order me something if you order yourself something and we go together." Another piece of pineapple. "I see you thinking about it."

"That's tempting. You ran track at Berkeley, right? What was your distance?"

"800 and 1500. Middle distance. At Berkeley." I emphasized it playfully.

"Should have been at Stanford. Were you any good?"

"I placed in the PAC-12 championships each year. Good enough for college." I frowned as he started texting. "What are you doing?"

He put down his phone. "Ordering us running gear."

"You're serious?"

"You challenged me. I don't back down."

"OK. We'll see how that goes for you," I snarked as I moved my chair to his side of the table—better view of the sunrise, but also, I wanted to be closer to him. The sun created cascades of color across the sky and distracted me from our potential running challenge.

"This is beautiful," I said softly.

"Yeah," Luke agreed, but when I looked over, he was staring at me.

Heat flooded through me.

This was risky. This feeling.

But I didn't want it to stop.

After breakfast, the attendant led us back to our rooms. Luke had reserved two—mine was first in the hallway.

I kicked off my shoes, set down my day bag, then knocked on Luke's door next door.

"Who is it?" he yelled, but before I could answer, he opened the door and kissed me, pulling me inside.

I melted into him as he teased my mouth open with his tongue. I could taste sangria and something uniquely him. His hands explored my back—one tangling in my hair, the other cupping my ass and pulling me closer.

I slid my hands under his jacket, grabbed his butt, drew him closer. Still not close enough.

He released my mouth, whispered in my ear, "Are you sure?"

I nodded breathlessly. No words were necessary.

Luke swirled his tongue around my ear and my knees got weak—

Knock, knock. "Mr. Sloane, I have your delivery. Since it was a rush, you have to sign for it."

Luke pulled back, not letting go of me completely. "I'm sorry. I forgot I ordered the running clothes," he whispered to me, leaning his forehead against mine. "Be right there!" he then yelled to the delivery person.

He kissed me once more, then went to the door.

I moved to the window, trying to regain my composure. The room had classic Mexican furnishings, WiFi, linen bedding, a kitchenette. It felt intimate despite the open layout.

I fanned myself. Just a kiss and I was ready to combust.

Luke came back with a large box. He took off his jacket, and I could see the flex of his chest and biceps through his shirt. Football physiques were ridiculously sexy—I'd crushed on several Berkeley Bears in college. But none of them had looked like this.

I looked away before I embarrassed myself.

"What did you get me?" I asked, trying not to stare.

"Come look."

Inside were two pairs of running shoes and several workout items for me. For him, one warm-up suit.

"You didn't have to do this," I said. "I don't want to look like I'm only here for what you can buy."

"I don't think you are." Luke stood up. "I have a lot of money, but I don't spend like this. I rarely flex my cash that way. I wanted to see how it felt." He paused. "Is it too much?"

I studied him. "Not tacky. Just not used to this during a date. And don't get me wrong, I could get used to it."

That devastating smile again.

"How did it feel? Flexing a little?" I asked.

"Like grocery shopping with rush shipping. Besides real estate, I haven't spent much of the Sloane-Wash money. I made some money from the NFL and endorsements, but Kyle and my mother make fun of my general frugality." He smiled at me. "You made me want to splurge."

I sat on the bed, offered my hand. "Well, a girl likes to be pampered." I moved further back, sitting on my knees. "Hey, let me rub your shoulder. The one I slept on all night."

"That would be great." He slipped off his shirt.

I involuntarily gasped.

Six-pack. Beautiful pecs. A tattoo of an African shield on his back. His gorgeous back.

I was going to need my vibrator if I planned to abstain much longer.

"Are you okay?" He turned around, placed his hand on my knee. "You look flushed." He caressed my face. "Yeah, you're warm."

I leaned into his hand instinctively. Wrong move. I was flushed and drenched.

I slid back. "Do we have massage oil? Let me check the bathroom!"

I could hear him chuckling as I escaped.

In the bathroom, I splashed water on my face. I shouldn't have suggested a shoulder rub. I was trying to be smooth and outsmarting myself.

"Hey! Are you okay? Did you find any oil?"

Quick look around. "No. Sorry."

I inspected myself in the mirror. There was a hickey on my neck. When had that happened?

I took deep breaths, fluffed my hair, anything to buy time.

When I came back out, Luke was asleep on the bed.

Relief flooded through me.

I found a blanket, laid it across him. Got my running clothes from the box and brought them to my room to try on. Everything fit perfectly—including the shoes.

I didn't want to run without him, so I took a quick bath and crawled into bed for a nap.

26

luke

I woke to the front desk calling about our winery tour.

I felt refreshed—must have needed that nap. I looked around but Grace wasn't there. She must have gone back to her room.

I called her. She answered on the first ring and was ready in eight minutes.

She was wearing a clingy off-white jumpsuit that emphasized every curve. I twirled her around, noting we had twenty minutes to get to the meeting point.

We arrived a couple of minutes late, but the guide seemed unbothered.

The wine tasting—they called it a Wine Sensory Experience—lasted ninety minutes. We sampled several bottles from La Lomita's range.

First, the Hospitality Room, where the guide explained aromas, winemaking procedures, aromatic families, and grape varietals. I didn't know most of this, and Grace asked a lot of questions.

I should know more about winemaking since Kyle and I own part of a Napa winery. I tried to remember everything so I could apply it to our investment.

After the tasting, we went on an Immersive Vineyard Picnic. The guide took us to Islay Hill Vineyard—a pergola overlooking the Edna Valley. We ate luxurious charcuterie and tasted red varietal wines.

We sat sipping wine, comparing which we liked best, deciding which to order for home.

After a while, we were both getting tipsy. Grace was getting looser with her words.

She went straight to sex talk.

"It's getting very difficult not to sit on your face. Oh, you do that, don't you?" She turned in her chair to face me. "Am I being too forward? I'm a little drunk."

"You're cute when you're drunk. But as much as I would love to savor every part of you until you wondered how you ever lived without it or me, right now's probably not the right time. And as this is our second date, I'm willing to wait."

"Why?"

"Because when I first met you, I felt like there could be something great here. And so far, I haven't been wrong."

She pulled back slightly. "You're right. I'm talking big game because I'm nervous."

"Scared?"

She smiled, ducked her head. "How'd you know? We've known each other five days. I could easily ignore caution and enjoy everything you have to offer—and I mean everything. But then reason pokes its head out. I don't know what you want from me. Really want. And why me?"

"But I already know what I want from you. Everything. It's fast, I know. But when I met you, I felt it."

She searched my face. "Felt what?"

"You're going to think I'm weird."

She shook her head. "Tell me."

"Lightning bolts. I felt like I'd met you before. That we'd lived this life before. That you were who I'd been looking for." I paused. "Kyle jokes about this. I was there when he met his wife. He called it being struck by lightning. He knew immediately. I always wondered what that felt like. Then I met you. So, I know what I want."

"But I can't give you everything—not yet. I can't make that commitment. I'm not sure I can ever do that because the last time I handed my heart over, it took years and a yacht's worth of therapy to put it back together."

"I get that. And I'm not in a hurry. I know we've been in this less than a week. I'm on your timetable. I'll accept whatever you offer whenever you're ready. No pressure." I leaned over and kissed her gently. "We have time. Plus, if you decide you need to use me for sex, I'll accept that too."

Grace snickered. "Only you would switch gears that quickly. Obviously, I wasn't planning to use you in this outfit."

I let my eyes travel up and down her body. "I see that. You've dressed to impress, but there's no skin showing or obvious zippers."

"Yeah. It's a pull-on one-piece. You can't take any of it off without taking the entire outfit off. Not good for clandestine activities."

She laughed and jumped up to display her jumpsuit, demonstrating how difficult it would be to remove. Chuckling, I pulled her down onto my lap.

We looked into each other's eyes. She gently put her hands on either side of my face, leaned in, softly kissed my forehead, then my nose. As she moved to my mouth, I leaned in and captured her lower lip with my teeth.

She grinned and dove in. We kissed hungrily, tongues battling. Two forty-somethings making out fully clothed under a pergola in a vineyard.

It was oddly fun. Not orgasm-inducing but satisfying. We were acting like teenagers, trying to maintain decorum when other visitors walked by, smoothing our clothes while giggling.

Like the track star making out with the football player under the bleachers after the game.

We were learning each other as younger versions of ourselves.

After the picnic ended, we traveled back to freshen up for sunset dinner.

We were taken to the other side of the property for a better sunset view. The waitstaff gave us menus.

"I'm sorry. I can't handle a big meal. I'm still full of wine and meat and cheese." Grace looked at the menu. "Maybe an appetizer? Or salad?"

"I could have some chicken. But you don't have to order anything. We can just enjoy the sunset."

"That might be the play for me."

Watching the sunset sounded perfect. I'd always liked sunsets better than sunrises. The colors—oranges, reds, pinks spreading across the sky—seemed to tell a story.

I looked at Grace in the fading light, which bathed her in a glow that fascinated me.

Sunshine.

I knew now why that nickname had popped into my head. She burst into my life like a ray of sunshine—unexpected but totally welcome, brightening everything in her path.

Adam picked us up after we checked out. Grace had more clothes and shoes now than would fit in her day bag, so she got the box from my room and packed everything back in. I carried it out to the car.

"Hello, Mr. Sloane and ma'am. I hope you had a relaxing day. This place is very popular for quick getaways."

"I can see why." Grace settled into the car. "We might have to come back sometime."

She looked at me, waiting for a reaction. When I didn't comment, she smiled.

At the San Luis Obispo station, we waited until 9 p.m. for the train. This time we didn't watch the scenery. We went straight to the sleeper car and fell asleep immediately, arms wrapped around each other.

27

luke

Todd was waiting at the Emeryville Station well before the sun came up Thursday morning.

"Mr. Sloane, did you go anywhere else in San Luis Obispo? I've gone hiking at Pismo Preserve. Fabulous water views. If you go back, try that trail." He opened the door. "Did you enjoy your trip?"

"Yes, we did," I said.

"It was lovely. And thanks for the recommendation." Grace added. "If we go back, we'll keep that in mind."

We rode to her house in comfortable silence, holding hands. I thought about everything we'd learned about each other over the past thirty-six hours. I needed to rein in my emotions—I didn't want to love-bomb her, frighten her off.

Maybe it was better I didn't have a history of falling in love. Otherwise, I would have accomplished nothing in life. Or maybe I was acting like a teenager because I didn't get this out of my system as a kid.

Either way, I needed some self-control.

When we pulled up to her house, there was an SUV in the driveway that wasn't her G-Wagon.

Todd hopped out to give us privacy and get Grace's bag and box from the trunk.

I looked at her—she didn't seem concerned about the car.

Grace caught my expression. "Oh, I forgot. I told my brother he could stay with me for a couple days. I got distracted." She side-eyed me mischievously.

"Everything okay with him?"

"He just served his wife with divorce papers. When she was out of town. We thought it best he not be home when she returns."

"Won't she know to come here?"

"She knows not to come to my house. We don't get along." She paused. "I would introduce you to Vic, except he's kind of a mess right now. Let him get himself together first."

"So, you're going to introduce me to your family?" I smiled. "I like that."

"If I introduce you to Celeste, my sister in Korea, you'll know you've made it."

Before I could reply, my phone rang. Kyle.

"Kyle, it's early. What's wrong?"

Kyle never called this early unless there was a problem.

"Yeah, I know. I'm sorry. I gotta make this quick." His voice was strained. "Remember I was going to Seattle for a client meeting, then staying for the game with the kids? Well, my father is very sick. He's in the hospital. We're all flying to Chicago today. It's pretty bad, Luke."

There was a hitch in his voice. Kyle was close to his father, his only surviving parent.

Grace looked at me with concern. I held up a finger—hold on. She sat back, put her hand on my knee.

"Oh man. Papa Washington. I'm sorry. What do you need?"

"Can you take the Seattle meeting? I know you hadn't planned to leave town again, but—"

"Say no more. You'll need to brief me quickly. I need to read through everything before Friday."

"Yes. I'll courier it over. You can call with questions. This is up your alley—you did the prelim research a while back. So, it shouldn't be too hard."

"Hey, if your dad is that sick, I want to fly to Chicago after the meeting."

"I wanted to ask but didn't want to be presumptuous. You might have had plans."

"You know better than that. Papa Washington was there for me when my own dad wasn't or couldn't be. I'm coming." My voice was firm. "I want to pay my respects and offer support."

"Thanks, man. Let me get packed. I'll call with more details."

I disconnected, turned to Grace. "I guess you heard. Kyle's dad is ill—it must be bad for him to fly the whole family out. I'm covering his meeting on Friday in Seattle, then flying to Chicago. We'll have to delay our next date."

"I guess so," she said softly. "I'm sorry about your friend's father. He sounds really important to you both."

I kissed her forehead. "He helped me during college when my father wasn't able to. Especially when I wasn't talking to my dad." I tilted her head up, gently kissed her lips. "I have to go. I wish I had more time to say goodbye properly. Or is it good morning?" I attempted a joke.

She groaned.

"But I have a lot to do—rearrange things, get ready. I want to thank you for a really lovely extended date. We'll go out again when I get back."

"I look forward to that. Have a safe trip. I hope Papa Washington gets better."

"Thank you. I'll call you." I kissed her again, deeper this time.

Grace got out of the car and waved goodbye. Todd had placed her bag and box at her front door.

As we drove away, I looked back. She was standing there watching me leave.

My phone buzzed. A text from Harmony.

Harmony: *My client's coffee date went so well! Everett said friend zone, but he really liked her. Told you she was great! Want to grab lunch this week and talk about YOUR dating traumas?*

I stared at the text.

Grace was standing in her driveway, watching me leave.

Harmony wanted to have lunch and talk about my inability to commit.

The two most important women in my life, and neither knew about the connections between the three of us.

The weight of it was getting oppressive.

But I was in too deep now. Way too deep.

I'd tell them eventually. When the timing was right. I had more pressing matters to consider right now.

I deleted the text and told Todd to take me home.

28

grace

I watched Luke drive away, already missing him.

It was 7 a.m. I had less than two hours to get ready for clinic.

I raced inside and upstairs, shed the jumpsuit - laughing as I remembered how it had constrained us at the winery. I hadn't made out with anyone in so long I hadn't even noticed this outfit was a one-piece contortion punisher.

In my closet, I found a brown sweater dress that didn't need ironing. After a quick shower, I stood in front of the mirror to do my makeup and put my hair in a bun.

There were now three hickeys on my neck, which were incredibly noticeable.

I rifled through my makeup drawer for concealer. I'd never hear the end of it at the office.

By the time I got downstairs, Vic was awake, stumbling around my kitchen. He hadn't seen my arrival with Luke - thankfully avoiding the ribbing I'd have gotten.

My kitchen was already a disaster from his breakfast efforts. The baby of the family, spoiled by four "parents" who never let him do anything for himself. Then he went out into the world, and women wanted to do everything for him too! Somehow, he'd still ended up with Stacia, who did nothing for him and made his life miserable.

Vic looked up as I walked in. Tan cargo pants, navy button-up, eating my last croissant with salmon, scrambled eggs, and a smoothie.

"I heard you come in this morning. Why didn't you tell me you weren't going to be here last night?"

"I was on a date. He surprised me by taking me to San Luis Obispo. A winery. We had a great time." I grabbed a cereal bar from the cabinet.

"You're only eating that?"

"You ate my croissant." I exhaled dramatically. "Let somebody crash at your place and they eat all the good stuff."

"I'll split it with you." He broke it in half, handed me part.

I accepted gratefully, poured coffee into my Berkeley mug. "Thanks. Hey, have you heard from your wife?"

"Got a voicemail before I woke up. I'm not answering - per my attorney. She should be back today." He sipped his smoothie, eyeing me. "She might come here."

I rolled my eyes. "She won't. She doesn't know if I have a gun, and she doesn't want to find out the hard way."

"You do, right? Or did Evan take it?"

"Evan has his own. Mine's in my safe." I turned toward the garage.

"Hang on, let me move my car!" Vic followed me out.

I had three colonoscopies scheduled that afternoon and only two patients in the morning, so I spent the rest of the morning catching up on paperwork.

Violet had many questions about my activities. I didn't tell her specifics, just that I'd gone on an extended date.

That still created a stir. Violet had seen Luke Monday - nosy ass - so when I went out Tuesday, she was suspicious it was the same guy. I'm sure she'd gossiped around the office. But without details, I could hold the rumor mill at bay.

My procedures went smoothly. After, I shut myself in my office to complete notes.

I had no dinner plans tonight and it threw me into a funk. Last year I'd have been planning for two, rushing to Gabe's practice or a lesson. I missed my kid.

And I was confident Vic hadn't left me much in my fridge. I'd have to pick up something on the way home.

My cell phone rang. I clawed it out of my scrubs pocket.

Harmony.

My stomach dropped. But I still answered the call.

"Hi Dr. Grace. Are you busy?"

"Just finishing notes. I'll be heading home soon. My brother's staying with me, so I have to pick up dinner. What's up?"

"Do you have time tomorrow for another speed date? Same philosophy - just a meet and greet. I have a dentist who just became available. Or we can schedule for next week."

I opened my mouth to say no.

The word sat right there. *No. I can't. I'm seeing someone.*

But if I said that, she'd ask who. And I'd have to tell her about Luke. And then I'd have to explain that I went on Everett's date four hours before Luke picked me up for our romantic overnight trip.

And she'd know I'd been lying. And didn't give her program a shot. Maybe ruining her shot at building her business...

And Luke would find out I had a matchmaker.

My hand hovered over my phone, finger ready to end the call, make an excuse.

"Let's schedule for Monday," I heard myself say. "After my morning clinic. Then I need to take a break. I'm leaving town to see my son next weekend, and my sister's visiting from Korea the week after. My brother's in crisis."

And I may have already met the man of my dreams and I'm lying to everyone about it.

"My life has gotten really hectic all of a sudden," I finished. *Shame on me...*

I could hear disappointment in her voice, but she tried to cover it. "Well, yes. You need to handle your business. Have the date Monday, then let me know how it goes. You can contact me in a couple weeks. I should have some potentials lined up to keep you busy during the holidays."

After we hung up, I dropped my head on my desk.

One more date. Monday with Keith, the dentist.

Then I'd tell Luke about the matchmaker. After Monday.

Except that was what I'd said before Everett.

The guilt sat in my chest, heavy and sharp.

I pulled up Amazon, searched for journals. Found one with a pretty cover. Added it to cart.

Maybe writing this down would help me figure out what the hell I was doing.

My mother called as I was leaving.

"Hi, Mom."

"I just spoke to Victor. He served that woman. I'm concerned for his safety."

"She's not going to hurt him. He spent last night at my place. You know he can stay as long as he needs." I unlocked my car. "He'll need to grocery shop if he stays much longer though. He ate all my food."

Mom laughed. "Girl, you're fine. Just make sure that woman doesn't get near my boy."

"If you didn't live so far out of his way, I'd send him to you."

"Oh, my Gracie. I love you very much. By the way, your sister is coming to town early. In two weeks. The kids are coming later."

My expression soured – fortunately, my mom couldn't see that. "Why? Why so early?"

"She has business here."

"Her business is convincing you to leave. That's the only reason."

Mom tsk-tsked me. But before she could respond, my phone beeped.

"Sorry, Mom. I have another call. Talk later?"

I switched over, grateful for the escape.

It was Luke.

My heart jumped, then immediately sank.

I should tell him. Right now.

"Hey," I said, voice coming out softer than intended.

"Hey yourself. Just wanted to hear your voice. How was your day?"

"Long. Good. I miss you already."

"I miss you too." He paused. "I'm sending you something tomorrow. Don't let Violet steal it."

I laughed despite the guilt churning in my stomach. "More flowers?"

"Maybe."

We talked for a few more minutes - him updating me on Papa Washington, me telling him about my procedures. Normal couple conversation.

Except we weren't normal. We were built on secrets.

After we hung up, I sat in my car in the parking lot, staring at my phone.

Monday. One more date. Then I'd tell him everything.

I had to. If I wanted to build this thing between us right.

29

luke

I never really got used to urgent changes in business plans. I liked time to study data, answer questions fluently. Fortunately, I'd done most of the original research on this client, created the PowerPoint that first got them in the door. Kyle had taken over when it moved to his division - device design and licensing.

This meeting was to discuss project parameters.

I'd have to finish reviewing everything on the plane. I also needed to make sure nothing urgent was happening at the SF office. If we kept growing at this pace, we'd need to hire additional upper-level people. Kyle and I liked handling initial client interactions, but we'd probably need to let that go too.

Sloane-Wash had one private jet. I was using it for this trip. Kyle and his family were chartering to Chicago - they needed to get Corie and Adrian sorted with their private school and get Deuce settled in doggie daycare. Jamal would watch both dogs and check on both of our homes this weekend.

Upon arrival at the airport, we were told we couldn't take off until afternoon, which gave me time to check on my mother.

I called her while following up on office deadlines. She answered on the second ring.

"Lucien! Calling to check up on me? Keep Mr. Alfred out of my room?"

"Hell, Mother. I just called to say hi. Now I need therapy. Thanks." *Why did she have to wake up and choose violence today?*

"You know I have to get my freak on. Isn't that how you young people say it? Your father acted like I wasn't sexy enough because I couldn't have more kids. I was glad when he asked for a divorce. I loved being free."

If this continued, I'd lose my breakfast. "Mom, back to Mr. Alfred. Are you sneaking him into your room?"

"Wouldn't you like to know?"

I tried to change subjects. Knowing your mother was a sexual being was one thing. Hearing her talk about it was different. I told her I was leaving town for work and to visit Papa Washington.

"Oh dear. I hope he gets better. Send him my love. He's a very sweet man. When am I seeing you again?"

I tried to visit weekly, but that wouldn't happen this week. "I won't be back until next week, depending on Papa Washington. Would you like Harmony to visit? Maybe she can bring her mother."

"I would like that. Maybe I could go to their house and bake something for Mr. Alfred."

She cackled. My mother was much freer now than when she was with my dad.

🔬

I planned to call Harmony on the way to the airport.

My phone buzzed before I could dial. A text from her.

Harmony: *Lunch this week? I want to hear about your mystery woman! Aunt Merci just called and let it slip. Said you've been smiling more. I NEED DE-TAILS.*

My stomach dropped. I knew I shouldn't have mentioned Grace to my mom. I can't believe she remembered and blabbed to Harmony... at least she didn't mention a name.

I stared at the text. Typed a response. Deleted it. Typed another.

Me: *Crazy week. Seattle today, Chicago after. Papa Washington is really sick. Rain check?*

Harmony: *Oh no! Sending prayers. Yes of course. But when you're back, you're telling me EVERYTHING. I can't remember the last time you tried to be happy. She must be special.*

I put my phone down, a sinking sensation coming over me.

She was right. Grace was special.

Which made this so much worse.

I should just tell Harmony. *Hey, funny story - remember Grace Robertson? Your client? Yeah, I'm dating her.*

Except it wasn't funny. It was a disaster waiting to happen.

And the longer I waited, the worse it got.

I called Harmony back anyway, steered the conversation to safe territory.

"Can you take Jackie to visit my mom? I'm going to be gone a few days."

"Sure! Aunt Merci just called asking us to come over – at your request, I guess. When doesn't matter, right?"

"Mom wants to bake something for Mr. Alfred, her new boyfriend. She doesn't have an oven in her room."

Harmony got excited. "Mom would love that! I'll call your mom and set it up. This is perfect - I was feeling down because one of my clients is slow-walking my process. Ugh. I don't want to talk about it."

My heart stopped. *Grace?*

"I'm sorry," I said carefully. "I need to get through security. Thanks for helping with Mom."

"No problem. Tell Kyle, Jada, and the kids I'm praying for his father."

After we hung up, I sat in my car, staring at nothing.

Was she talking about Grace? Was Grace pulling back from the matchmaking?

I should be relieved. Should feel vindicated - see, she's choosing me.

Instead, I just felt sick.

Because if she was pulling back, it meant she was falling for me as hard as I was falling for her.

Which meant when the truth came out, it would hurt her even more.

By 8 p.m., I was in my Seattle hotel room. I'd reviewed Kyle's documents, felt ready for tomorrow's 8:30 a.m. meeting.

Before bed, I ordered flowers for Grace. Another bouquet to her clinic. I wanted her to know I was thinking about her.

Each romantic gesture made the lie bigger.

I knew that. Did it anyway.

Then I called her. She sounded sleepy, like she'd been dozing on the couch. I appreciated her trying to stay awake for me.

"This time last week we didn't know each other," I said. "It's amazing how much things change in a few days. I miss you. Hopefully we'll really talk tomorrow. Good night."

After I hung up, I lay in bed staring at the ceiling.

I was in love with her.

I knew that now. Fully. Completely.

And I was lying to her every single day.

Friday's meeting went well. The clients wanted to move to the next step with our designers and researchers. While our scientists gave them a tour, I went to make calls.

Kyle and I discussed inviting them to our Heavenly retreat next month. This deal was worth tens of millions short-term, possibly hundreds of millions over time. Inviting them seemed smart.

Kyle thought it was promising. Our travel coordinator Cherie got the request out within an hour. They accepted before any of us left the warehouse.

I left at the same time as the clients.

The flight to Chicago took four hours. I slept the entire way.

We landed at O'Hare and I went straight to Mount Sinai Hospital. Papa Washington had severe pneumonia and a kidney infection - could've been avoided if he hadn't been so stubborn about seeing a doctor. He'd hidden how he felt from Kyle, who was busy in San Francisco and missed the signs.

Kyle was guilt-ridden. After visiting Papa Washington on a ventilator, I sat with Kyle and let him vent about his father's situation. If his dad survived, Kyle was going to bring him to San Francisco.

"I can help you look for places," I offered. "I have connections from when I was looking for my mom."

Kyle accepted the offer gratefully but quickly slid back into present worries.

I spent Friday at the hospital. Papa could only have one visitor at a time for short periods. I worked and made sure Kyle's family ate, fielding any issues that came across either of our desks. It was unclear how long this would go on. I hoped Papa just needed intensive treatment with a definite endpoint.

Things were happening at our offices. Both of us couldn't be out long.

And I needed to check on my mom. Harmony and Jackie were visiting tomorrow, but I was worried about her "freedom" and Mr. Alfred. And her sudden burst of clarity about my social life.

Plus, I truly missed Grace. We talked and texted, but that wasn't enough.

I was considering flying home Sunday to see her. I could afford the plane fuel.

My phone buzzed. Another text from Harmony.

Harmony: *My client has another speed date Monday! He's a dentist, really nice guy. I think this one might have potential. Keeping my fingers crossed!*

I stared at the text.

So, she was still doing it. Still going on dates Harmony set up.

While I was sending her flowers. While we were falling in love.

While I was lying to my sister about who I was dating.

While Grace was lying to me about having a matchmaker.

We were both trapped in this now.

And I had no idea how to get out without losing everything.

I deleted the text and went back to the waiting room, the weight in my chest getting heavier.

30

grace

Friday morning started beautifully.

Luke sent another vase of gorgeous flowers. Violet had placed them on my desk before I arrived. Another card shaped like a prescription pad.

Grace,

Still thinking about the sunrise. And the sunset. And everything in between. Can't wait to see you again.

— Luke

My chest squeezed.

Then the guilt hit like a wave.

Monday. I had a date with Keith on Monday.

I pulled out my phone, stared at Harmony's text with Keith's information. Nice-looking, dentist, enjoyed hiking and live music.

I should cancel.

My finger hovered over the call button.

But if I canceled, Harmony would ask why. And I'd have to tell her about Luke. And then she'd know I'd been lying to her. Going on dates with Luke while she was setting me up with other men. And she had asked me to be honest about any outside dates.

I put my phone away.

Monday. One more date. Then I'd figure this out.

I had two colonoscopies scheduled for the afternoon. I hated Friday procedures, but that was the short straw I drew when I reorganized my schedule for Gabe.

Vic decided to spend the weekend with our parents. Stacia had planted herself at their house, refusing to leave. She thought she could force a confrontation, change his mind.

The house was in Vic's name only - he'd owned it before meeting her. She'd refused to put her name on the mortgage. Didn't want to be responsible for bills. Fortunate now.

Now she wanted the house, but Vic's lawyer was offering a lump sum - two years of half the mortgage - even though she'd never paid any. No kids, she made more money than Vic, so no child support or alimony. Not going according to plan for her.

On Saturday morning, I went to the Ferry Market early. Didn't want to see Curtis again.

After shopping, I went for a run in the new shoes Luke bought. Then Autumn called, invited me to lunch at Brenda's French Soul Food.

"Is it just us, or are Claudia and Zoe coming?"

"Just Claudia. Zoe's still throwing up everywhere. Not good around food." Autumn cleared her throat. "We expect an update on your matchmaking efforts. Or any other efforts. We're all living vicariously through you. We always wanted to but your dating stories were so sad..."

I groaned. "We'll see. What time?"

"Noon."

"Great. I can take a bath - I just ran three miles."

"It's too early for running. And yes, thank you for bathing," Autumn said, laughing.

I hung up on her smart ass.

By noon, I was seated under Autumn's reservation. She arrived a minute later.

"Damn. You know I can't abide when you get here before me." She air-kissed both my cheeks. "You look great. I love that dress and the color."

Royal blue sweater dress, brown boots. My hair in a bun because I hadn't had time to wash it.

Claudia appeared five minutes later, looking like she'd run the whole way. "The four-year-olds are killing me. I don't remember my oldest being this difficult. These kids are into everything, way more destructive. I'm too old for this." She gave us a weary smile. "Have you gone on any dates with Harmony?"

I explained Harmony's philosophy - practice speed dates, low pressure. I'd done one with Everett, had another Monday.

"The one I did was nice for chatting. No chemistry. He knew Zay and Evan."

"Oh my God. Really? You need someone none of us know." The server came for drink and appetizer orders.

"Agreed. How are you feeling about the process so far?"

"Right now? Ambivalent. At least the dates are screened, so I feel safer."

I was tempted - so tempted - to tell them about my dates with Luke. About the scavenger hunt, the train ride, the winery, the lightning bolts confession. About how I couldn't stop thinking about him.

But I couldn't.

Because I'd have to explain that I'd gone on Harmony's date four hours before Luke picked me up. And they'd know I'd been lying to everyone. And they would have doubts – because of my track record. I didn't want to hear any of that right now.

"That's all you got?" Autumn asked skeptically. "Do we need to talk to Harmony? I thought there'd be details, gossip, man news."

Claudia agreed. "We need more! I thought we'd finally get the single-woman chronicles. Sex and the City with Black folks - you as the star."

I exhaled. "I'll be sure to get on that. In more ways than one."

"Now that's what I'm talking about. I like hearing about new dick," Autumn said, sipping her mimosa.

Claudia shook her head, laughing. "After all this time with a classy rich dude, you're still just as messy."

"What? Theo ain't that classy. He likes when I talk about dick."

I forced myself to laugh along.

But inside, I was screaming.

Because I had someone. Someone incredible. Someone I was falling for so hard it terrified me.

And I couldn't tell my best friends. Yet.

Autumn studied me across the table. "You're different."

My heart skipped a beat. "What?"

"You're glowing. Like, actually glowing." She leaned forward. "What aren't you telling us?"

"Nothing! I'm just... trying to be more open. Like you said."

"Mm-hmm." Autumn didn't look convinced. "You've checked your phone three times since we sat down. You waiting for someone to call?"

Luke. I'm waiting for Luke to call.

"Just Vic. He's dealing with the divorce."

Claudia reached over, squeezed my hand. "We're here for you, you know. Whatever's going on. You can tell us."

The weight in my chest got heavier.

"I know," I said softly. "I know."

But I didn't tell them.

I couldn't.

Not yet.

Luke called Saturday afternoon. "What are you doing tomorrow?"

I frowned. "Nothing specific. Getting meals ready for the week. Hanging around the house. Vic's staying with my parents."

"Would you like some company?"

My heart jumped. "Whatever do you mean?"

"I want to come home for a day before flying to Boston for business. Papa Washington's still not doing well, so I'm taking more meetings for Kyle. But I need to check on my dog and the woman I'm dating. If she'll have me."

"I would love to see you. But I'm not up for big productions. I was just planning to stay home."

"That sounds perfect. I want to eat wings and watch football. Read research. Play with my dog."

"What kind of dog do you have?"

"Fitz. He's a labrador retriever. Very happy about new places. I'd have to bring him over in short exposure bursts or he'd destroy your house."

I laughed. "So what time are you coming over?"

"Football starts early on the West Coast. Sundays are about the NFL."

"I'll be here. Maybe with snacks."

After we hung up, I sat on my couch, staring at nothing.

Tomorrow, I'd see him. We'd have a normal, domestic day. Just us.

And I had another matchmaker date scheduled for Monday.

The journal I'd ordered sat on my coffee table, still in its packaging. I hadn't written a single word.

I opened it to the first page, stared at the blank lines.

What am I doing?

I closed it again.

31

luke

Our pilot team was going to need raises and more vacation after this stretch. San Francisco to Seattle to Chicago and back to San Francisco and then to Boston. To spare them, I might charter to Boston or fly commercial.

I'd gotten spoiled. Really spoiled.

But my favorite pilot was rested and available to fly me back Sunday. Since I was only there one day, I wasn't going commercial. I wanted to spend as much time as possible with Grace.

I was looking forward to hanging out with her - no pressure, no schedule beyond football start times, not having to dress up. You could learn a lot about people that way.

We landed at 7 a.m. I rented a hotel room so my pilots could sleep. I called my mother, but she was sleeping, didn't want to talk. She'd had a long day baking with Harmony and Jackie, and a long night doing something I wanted no information about.

I used a rideshare to get home. Jamal had brought both dogs over for a visit. I missed Fitz. Both pups were happy to see me. We rolled around on the floor for half an hour.

Jamal gathered the dogs, took them back to his place. I called Grace to confirm I was still coming.

"Hi! And yes. I even made charcuterie since you like it so much. Whatcha bringing?"

"Wine, chocolate movie theater candy, unpopped popcorn, and flowers. Does that work?"

"Sounds great! Did you get Crunch bars?"

"No, but I will. Do you know how to pop popcorn properly? Need butter or oil?"

"What do you think I am?" She burst out laughing. "Of course I can pop popcorn. On the stovetop. I'll show you."

"I look forward to that. Be there soon."

Stopping by a grocery store, I picked up flowers, wine, movie theater candy, and unpopped popcorn. Pulling up to Grace's house, I had a quick pang of nerves. This was a date that resembled real life. I hadn't done many of those. I was great at grand gestures, expensive shows. But days where you just sat around and spent time together? Nothing else to distract you? Just the two of you?

Not familiar with that.

Even in my one actual relationship, I spent most of the year playing football. Out of town or at camp for much of the time. Every actual date was splashy.

Let's see how this goes.

Grace opened the door as soon as I stepped onto the stoop. I could hear 90s R&B in the background.

"Hi!" She smiled at me. "I'm glad to see you! Come on in."

"I brought what I said I would. And these flowers are for you." I handed them over, got a good look at her. She didn't dress up but still looked amazing - jean shorts hugging all the right places, white fitted t-shirt with the 49ers logo. Not wearing much makeup but glowing.

"Thank you!" She sniffed the bouquet. "They're beautiful! You're good with flowers. Do you like my shirt? I'm supporting the home team." She headed to the kitchen.

I followed, watching her. Had to redirect my attention before I got in trouble.

Pictures of her family throughout the house. I stopped at one of her with a young man who probably her son. "This is your son?"

"Yeah, that's Gabe. He's taller now. Taller than me. That picture's a couple years old." She pointed to the island. "Here are the snacks. And my tray." She swayed to the music.

I put everything down, tasted items from the tray. "Excellent choices." I looked at her. "I haven't greeted you appropriately. Can I give you a hug?"

She beamed. "I wondered what was taking you so long."

She walked into my arms, snuggled against me. When I let her go, I spun her out to the beat.

"Are you a dancer?" she asked, eyebrow arched.

"I've done my share." I spun her back against me.

"You'll have to show me later," she said, grabbing my hand.

She led me to the family room. The TV was already on. Using the remote, she turned down the music so we could hear the game.

Before she could sit, I stole a quick kiss.

She eyed me. "That's all I get?"

We kissed again and fell onto the couch, both bursting into giggles. She'd placed a smaller snack tray on the coffee table. We settled to watch the game. The announcers notified us that the starting quarterback and the star defensive lineman for the 49ers were both out this week. My expectations for this game plummeted.

The first play from scrimmage was a scoop and score for the other team. Grace made a wiseass comment about lack of scoring both on screen and in this house.

I responded by pulling her on top of me, kissing her hungrily, hands on her ass. I promised her there'd be additional scoring before I left.

We stopped, stared into each other's eyes.

"Promises, promises. You also promised me a good game today."

"Unlike the 49ers, I keep my promises." I kissed her lightly, sat up, and turned back to the game.

Grace settled beside me, close enough that our thighs touched. On screen, the back-up 49ers quarterback dropped back for a pass.

"Oh, he's gonna get sacked," Grace said.

"No way, he's got time—"

The opposing linebacker came through untouched, flattened him.

"Told you." She grabbed a piece of cheese. "Their offensive line is trash this season. Can't give him more than two seconds in the pocket."

I looked at her. "You know football?"

"I went to Cal during the Aaron Rodgers era. You pick things up." She gestured at the screen. "Plus, my dad has season tickets. I've been watching the Niners disappoint me periodically since I was five."

"Aaron Rodgers era," I repeated. "So, you witnessed greatness and decided to stay loyal to this? You didn't follow him to the Packers?" I pointed at the screen where the 49ers were now down by fourteen.

"Don't start. At least we have Super Bowl rings this century."

"Ouch."

"What? I'm just saying - when's the last time Carolina won anything?"

"We're not talking about Carolina right now."

"Because you know I'm right." She grinned, took a sip of wine. "Face it, Sloane. Your team's mediocre."

"Your team is losing. Right now. On your TV."

"Difference is, I have hope for the future. You have Cam Newton's concussions and nothing else."

I laughed, pulled her closer. "You really do know how to hurt a man."

On screen, the 49ers fumbled.

"Oh, come ON!" Grace yelled at the TV. "What are you doing? That's basic ball security! They teach that in Pop Warner!"

"Pop Warner, huh?"

"My son plays— played— youth football before he switched to swimming. I sat through enough practices to know that's inexcusable." She pointed at the replay. "Look at that. Linebacker didn't even hit the ball, the running back just dropped it. That's mental errors. That's coaching."

"Now you're a coaching expert?"

"I'm a pattern recognition expert. I'm a doctor. I see the same mistakes over and over." She turned to me. "You played. Tell me I'm wrong."

I couldn't. "You're not wrong."

"Thank you." She sat back, satisfied. "The shirt's from Autumn's birthday party three years ago. She made us all wear team gear. I'm not actually a huge fan, but I know enough to know when they're playing like garbage."

The 49ers threw an interception.

"GARBAGE!" Grace yelled.

I was laughing so hard I had to put down my wine.

"What?" She looked at me. "What's funny?"

"You. You're funny." I kissed her temple. "And I love it."

Her expression softened. "Yeah?"

"Yeah."

We turned back to the game, her head on my shoulder, and I realized I'd never been happier watching football in my life.

By halftime, we ordered wings and fries. They didn't arrive until the end of the game - which the 49ers lost in ridiculous fashion. By then we'd eaten popcorn, charcuterie, chocolate.

When the second block of games came on, we were sprawled on the couch, full of junk food, laughing at everything on screen.

Best way to keep sexual tension under control.

The front door opened. A man yelled, "Who ordered wings? And whose car is in the driveway? I didn't have anywhere to park."

A man I recognized from pictures walked in carrying wings and fries and what looked like cheesecake.

I jumped up as Grace groaned. "If you told someone you were coming back, maybe you'd have a space." She stood to hug her brother. "What are you doing here? I thought you were at Mom and Dad's."

She hugged him. "Vic, this is Lucien Sloane. Luke, this is my uninvited brother."

I shook his hand. He eyed me suspiciously.

"Am I interrupting a date? I'm sorry. Is this the extended date from earlier this week?"

Grace rolled her eyes, took the food, walked to the kitchen.

Vic turned to me, apologized. "Sorry, man. I guess I'm interrupting. I hope I'm not cock-blocking - and that hurt me to say."

I snickered. "We were watching football. I have to leave soon anyway. Flying to Boston."

"You seem busy, Luke. Wait a minute. Lucien, Luke Sloane? That name..." He searched for context. Suddenly he snapped his fingers. "Stanford! You played for Stanford and the Carolina Panthers!"

"If you're staying, baby brother, come get your food. Don't harass my friend." We went to the kitchen. Grace was drinking wine.

"Friend, huh?" Vic grabbed wings and water, headed toward a part of the house I hadn't seen. "Forget I'm here. I'll watch in the guest room. Nice to meet you, Luke. I suspect I'll see you around."

He disappeared.

"He seems cool," I said. "Doesn't look stressed about his wife."

"He had a break from her calling while at our parents'. She likes to act like they don't matter because she knows they don't like her. She won't call there." She paused. "I'm sorry about him bursting in. I thought he was staying with our parents. He never said he was coming back."

"That's okay. I do have to leave soon. Your brother's an added incentive to keep my hands in my pockets." I leaned closer, breathed in her scent. I needed to find out what perfume she wore. It was intoxicating.

"Oh, I think you have some time... He's going to stay in his room. Anyway, you were going to give me something to think about."

I looked at her face, bit my lip.

This moment. Right here. Domestic and perfect and real.

But tomorrow she had a date with Keith the dentist. Harmony had set it up.

And I knew. Had known all week.

And said nothing.

"Luke?" She touched my face. "You okay?"

I should just say it. Right now. *Grace, I need to tell you something. My sister is Harmony. I've known you were her client this whole time.*

"Yeah," I said instead. "Just thinking about how much I'm going to miss you when I leave."

She smiled, pulled me closer. "Then stop thinking and kiss me."

So, I did.

And I buried the guilt a little deeper.

32

grace

I picked up the almost empty charcuterie tray and took it into the kitchen. I could hear the music come back on - D'Angelo's "Lady" - and Luke came up behind me, wrapped his arms around my waist, kissed my neck.

"When exactly do you have to leave? How is Kyle's father?" I asked, leaning back against him.

"He's not great. But at least he's stable. Jada and the kids are still in Chicago. If Papa Washington gets better, he'll have to move out here. Which will be a big production."

"Like assisted living?"

"Probably rehab at first? Maybe nursing care? All of us will have to adjust. I guess I shouldn't jump ahead though. Let's get him well first." He kissed my neck again as we swayed to the music.

It had been a lovely day. Non-flashy, just us. I felt completely content in this moment.

Luke reached around me to move the tray over, clearing space on the island. "What are you doing?" I asked with a smile as he spun me around.

"All day, we've been dancing around what we really wanted to be doing. Am I right?"

"Yeah. Trying to be mature. Take the high road."

He kissed the skin behind my ear. "And we watched football together. You know that kind of compatibility is important to me. As a former ball player." Kisses to the other side. "You watching with me means a lot. Supplying the food. I want to show my appreciation for everything today - especially since I have to leave town again. I want to leave you," a kiss on the lips, "with something to think about while I'm away."

I arched my neck back. He kissed my neck, drew circles on my skin with his tongue. I gasped at the sensations traveling down my body.

"Would you like that?" he whispered, lightly nibbling my neck.

I moaned. Hell yeah. But I couldn't speak, just nodded.

"That's my Gimbiya," he growled into my hair.

I wrapped my arms around his neck. Shoving the charcuterie tray further aside, he lifted me by my waist and set me on the marble countertop.

He leaned forward, hands still on my waist, and softly said, "You're my lady." Almost in tune with the song.

And I felt the ache - in my chest and in my belly. I felt like his lady. In this moment, I wasn't scared. I felt secure in his arms. I didn't know how long that feeling would last, but I wanted to enjoy any moments of feeling cared for and protected.

Luke tipped my chin up and kissed me, teasing my lips apart with his tongue, our breaths mingling. I felt his hands sliding under my shirt. His left hand unclasped my bra, freeing my breasts. But he left my shirt on - just slid his hands underneath. His large hands encircled my ribcage, thumbs brushing my nipples. I gasped into his mouth as he caressed the sensitive tips.

"I want to taste you. Is that okay?" he growled. "I made you a promise. I do want you to think about me while I'm out of town. But I want something to think about too - how good your pussy tastes, how you look when you come, how wet you get. If you want me to stop, let me know."

I looked at him in a haze of arousal and nodded.

"You want me to stop?" he asked.

I realized I'd answered the wrong question and shook my head quickly. "Don't you dare fucking stop!"

He grinned like he was about to sample a seven-course meal. Left a trail of kisses and bites down my neck. Kissed and sucked my nipple through the cotton of my shirt.

He slid my ass toward him until I was snug against his crotch. My jean shorts were suddenly unsnapped, being pulled down my hips.

"I-I-I can't be naked in the k-kitchen," I panted out as he slid his hand into my thong, pulling it down too.

"You aren't naked in the kitchen. You have on a 49ers shirt. Not naked." He pushed me back against the countertop, slipped my shorts and thong all the way off. He spread my legs to admire my core, drenched and glistening.

"Such a pretty pussy. And so wet - just for me." Luke licked his lips. "I think I may have found a new favorite thing..."

Luke leaned in and licked the length of my slit - I almost jumped off the counter.

He chuckled. "Oh, I'm just getting started. Don't go anywhere."

His tongue performed beautiful work on my clit - licking, sucking, pressing. I felt the pleasure building from my center. *Jesus.* I felt like I was going to explode from the inside.

When he slid two fingers inside me, into my contracting core, and pressed against my front wall, finding that spot that drove me crazy... the explosion of sensations ricocheting throughout my body, wave after wave crashing sent me into another realm. I saw stars. At some point I'd grabbed his head but didn't remember when. I called out Luke's name and God's name and probably a few curse words as my orgasm roared through me.

Luke just watched me writhing on the countertop, grinning and sucking his fingers clean.

Did he really just eat me out in the kitchen? I was on my back, feeling the cool marble on my overheated skin. My thong was ruined on the floor, and I could feel my release pooling between my legs. It had been so long since I'd had a non-toy assisted orgasm. But that was the hardest I'd come in years...

Once my breathing regulated somewhat, he kissed me gently - I could taste myself on his lips. Luke then scooped me up in his arms and carried me back to the couch.

"You are so beautiful," he kept murmuring as he placed his hand on my cheek and lay down next to me. Covered us both with the throw blanket from the back of the couch. I was still vibrating.

"I'm sorry. I don't know what came over me. I feel like I just used you." I felt a little embarrassed but spent. I tried to reach for his belt buckle. "It's not fair."

"Hey, I'm good. And as for using me, I loved every minute of it. Use me whenever you need or want to, Gimbiya."

"What does that mean?" I asked dreamily.

"Princess. My father was from Cameroon. He used to call my mother that when they were getting along." He nuzzled my neck. "Besides, I have a ratio I like to live by. You need to come three to four times more often than I do. You just needed a little head start because the next time we see each other—"

With his words, I shivered as we lay intertwined on the couch as he murmured endearments into my ear and gently ran his hand up and down my leg.

He looked at his watch. "I have to go. I wanted to leave you with something to think about." He leaned over to kiss me softly. "Don't feel bad. Just think about how good that felt and how much better it will feel when we actually fuck."

I watched him walk through the door with a dazed look.

Better? Holy shit...

After the door closed, I sat on the couch for a long moment, still trembling slightly.

Then reality crashed in.

Tomorrow. I had Keith's date tomorrow at 2 p.m.

I grabbed my phone, pulled up Harmony's contact.

I should cancel. Right now. Just text her - *I can't make it tomorrow. Actually, I need to pause the matchmaking indefinitely.*

My finger hovered over the keyboard.

But if I canceled, she'd ask why. And then I'd have to explain everything – Luke, the romantic train trip, the winery, meeting him at her office building the same day she signed me up.

And she'd know I'd been lying to her.

And Luke would find out I had gone out with other men as we were trying to figure us out.

I put my phone down.

It was just coffee. Thirty minutes. Then I'd tell Harmony I needed a break. That would be it. Final date.

Then I'd tell Luke everything. After Miami. After I had time to figure out how to explain this without it sounding as bad as it was.

I got up from the couch, put my shorts back on, started cleaning up the kitchen. Loaded the dishwasher. Wiped down the counter.

The same counter where Luke had just...

I stopped, stared at the marble.

You're my lady.

The words echoed in my head.

And tomorrow I was having coffee with another man.

The guilt sat in my chest like a stone.

But I didn't cancel the date.

33

grace

I walked into clinic Monday morning still thinking about Sunday's encounter. Should I think he was just cocky or was he giving me a heads up about how well we'd work together?

Either way, all the feelings in my head and heart bewildered me. This was what I was afraid of. One orgasm - no matter how I got there - and I was wide open.

And I was supposed to meet Keith after clinic.

He was going to see the "I just had a mind-bending orgasm without you - why are you here?" look. This wasn't fair to anyone.

I was glad I'd told Harmony I was taking a break to deal with family after this. My brother was rolling into my house without an invitation. Celeste was coming to town in two weeks. Next weekend I was going to Miami to see Gabe.

If I kept my mind there, I could get through this date.

After clinic ended, I had a quick phone call with Luke. We didn't get into our explosive encounter. He wanted me to check on his mother. I agreed to do it tomorrow, although Miss Merci didn't know me from Santa Claus.

Then I finally walked across the street to The Roasted Cup to meet Keith.

One of my patients came into my clinic earlier with bad gastroenteritis. Because she was severely dehydrated, I had to either send her to the ER or try to directly admit her to the hospital. Getting that accomplished from a clinic was always a challenge. The moving pieces, insurance approval, paperwork almost required an act of Congress.

Doing it while seeing other patients took coordination. Violet and other clinicians had to manage the patient's immediate situation to prevent spread of infection and manage her dehydration. Because she was so ill, I had to make choices about her care. She wasn't from San Francisco, and she didn't want to stay here, so I tried to arrange admission to a hospital closer to her home.

All this made me later than planned. I contacted Keith to reschedule since I was running half an hour late. But he was very nice, offered to wait.

Sure enough, Keith was waiting quietly at a table in the back corner. Reading what looked like a medical journal, sipping coffee. He was handsome like Everett - Harmony got points for that.

I should turn around. Walk out. Text Harmony that I couldn't do this.

Instead, I walked over. "Good afternoon! Sorry to keep you waiting."

Keith stood, pulled out my chair. About an inch taller than me, thin. "That's okay. I know patients' emergencies interrupt the best laid plans." He sat back down. "Did you have lunch, or do you want something to drink?"

I shook my head. "I was eating lunch while trying to transfer my patient. She wanted to be admitted closer to her home in Hayward, where I don't have hospital privileges."

"She came all the way here to see you?"

"She used to be a patient when she lived in San Fran. She moved to Hayward, but her son remained here. She was visiting and called my office. But she was dehydrated from gastroenteritis. Given her kidney problems, I thought it best to get her into an ER. She wanted to go back home. So, there we are."

"That sounds like a busy morning!"

"It was. I might have coffee now that you mention it. I'm pretty worn out. I need a nap."

He chuckled. "Some days are like that! Let me get you that coffee."

We had a pleasant conversation. Keith had a ten-year-old son, so much of it was about kid stories. I got the feeling he was more interested in continuing our connection than I was. Nothing wrong with him. He just wasn't my physical type.

And he wasn't Luke.

I kept thinking about Luke's hands. Luke's mouth. Luke calling me "my lady" and "Gimbiya."

This was unfair to Keith. He was nice. He deserved someone actually present.

I received a phone call - cable sales agent - which I used as an excuse to leave.

"This was a lot of fun. Maybe we can get together again soon." Keith held out his hand.

"It was. Maybe at some point. Life's about to get really busy - trip to Miami, time with my son, my sister visiting from Korea. I won't have much free time for a couple weeks." I released his hand. "I'll keep Harmony updated so she can let you know what's going on."

I wasn't giving him my number. He seemed the type who'd call for a proper date.

After leaving, I returned to the office to make sure my patient was on her way to Hayward.

Violet saw me walk in. "Your patient is in an ambulance on the road. How was your coffee date?"

I stopped in my tracks. "Thank you for the update. How do you know I was on a date?"

Violet smiled sheepishly. "I saw it on your calendar. You've been on a lot of dates lately. I'm still waiting for news about the good-looking one with the BMW."

I rolled my eyes, stomped into my office. Violet was like my office mother - I couldn't fire her. But now I knew to guard my calendar more carefully.

Once home, I almost made the decision.

I pulled up Harmony's contact info. Typed a message.

Hey, can we talk about—

I deleted it.

Tried again.

I need to pause the matchmaking for—

Deleted that too.

What would I say? *I met someone at your office building the same day you signed me up and although I promised to keep you updated, I didn't?*

I put my phone down.

After Miami. After Celeste's visit. After I figured out how to tell Luke about all of this.

Then I'd deal with Harmony.

I went for a run in the shoes Luke bought me, trying to outrun the regret.

It didn't work.

34

luke

I didn't want to leave Grace's place Sunday evening. After our encounter on the counter, I wanted to spend the night making her give me those sexy moans. Only louder - her brother's presence be damned.

But there's a time and place for everything. And my friend needed me to handle things a little longer.

Kyle called as I headed to Boston. His father's vitals were looking better. By Tuesday, they might try him off the ventilator with breathing assistance. I didn't know the names of all the assisted breathing technologies, but I knew this stepdown was progress.

We discussed logistics for the Boston meeting. I was meeting researchers doing a study with a medical device we were considering buying. We wanted their impression of current and potential uses, especially overseas. Kyle was supposed to do this - people underestimated him, let their guard down. He'd negotiated beneficial deals that way.

This trip, we'd make do with me.

I also called my mother to see how her visit with Harmony and Jackie went.

"Hello, son." She sounded tired - probably her bedtime.

"Mom. How are you?"

"I haven't talked to you in a long time."

"I spoke to you earlier today."

"No, you didn't," she insisted.

She complained for a few minutes because I hadn't called this morning. Then told me about her day. "We baked chocolate chip muffins and strawberry muffins. It was nice to hang out with them. Thank you for sending them to spend time with your old mother."

"I'm sorry, Momma. Kyle's father is sick, and I've been helping him with business."

"Kyle's sick? He needs some of my muffins."

"Momma, no. It's not Kyle. It's his father. Are you okay?"

"I'm fine. Just tired. I'm going to bed, son. I love you. Are you coming to visit tomorrow?"

I explained again I'd be out of town. Added that I might have another friend come visit to keep her company.

After hanging up, I contacted the in-house clinic. My mother seemed confused - could they check on her and do an exam? The on-call nurse said they'd check in the morning.

I didn't love that answer. We were paying enough for more immediate service.

I wondered if I could ask Grace to visit her. She seemed confused. While Grace was a GI doc, maybe she could tell if my mother needed another doctor besides the in-house team.

At that moment, I felt stretched thin. Both our surviving parents ill. Covering urgent business. Trying to start an actual relationship.

And I hadn't told Grace my sister was her matchmaker.

The thought hit me as I was thinking about asking her to check on my mom.

I was about to integrate Grace into my family. Have her meet my mother. A huge relationship step.

And I was still lying to her.

The irony wasn't lost on me.

But I picked up my phone anyway. Texted Grace the address, clinic number, my mother's cell. Asked if she could check on her tomorrow.

She texted back immediately: *Of course. Don't worry. I'll let you know something ASAP.*

I stared at the text.

She was meeting my mother tomorrow.

After her coffee date with Keith.

The coffee date I knew about and hadn't mentioned.

My heart felt heavy.

But not heavy enough to tell her the truth.

Monday's interviews finished without a hitch. I hadn't heard from the in-house clinic yet. I texted Grace to let her know. She texted back not to worry, she'd let me know something ASAP. I accepted that and tried to keep my concern under control.

Tuesday morning, I had two more people to talk to, then I was flying back to Chicago.

I anxiously awaited Grace's call during interviews. She didn't call until around 6 p.m. my time, after I'd landed at O'Hare and taken a car to my hotel. I went to the gym to work off nerves. Stopped the treadmill when I saw her number.

"Hey, Gimbiya. Did my mother fuss too much?"

"Oh no! She was as sweet as she could be. The nurses were all helpful. I still can't believe you asked me to meet your mother. She seemed to know who I was. Have you mentioned me to her before?"

I blushed, thinking back to the first night I met Grace. "I'm embarrassed to say yes, I have. And that's all I'm going to say about that." I laughed, then got serious. "What did you find out? Is it something serious?"

"I have good, uncomfortable and bad, uncomfortable news. The good news is I was right about what I suspected. She had a UTI - urinary tract infection. She's on antibiotics now. We took her to the ER for her first dose by IV. She'll be on antibiotics for a week to ten days."

"Thank you!" I felt tremendous relief and gratitude. "I owe you for helping my mom."

"Oh, before you get too happy, I have the bad, uncomfortable news..."

"What do you mean?"

"Mr. Alfred. He's the culprit. I know this will be difficult to hear. But your mother has been sexually active with Mr. Alfred. UTIs can be common in active older women."

With each word, I felt like my head was going to pop off. I didn't want to think about my mother that way. I groaned, asked her to stop talking. I couldn't handle more details.

Grace was giggling. "Sorry. I won't even give you the full story. I sadly had to hear details. Be glad I spared you that!"

"I owe you!"

"Don't worry - I will collect."

After we hung up, I sat in my hotel room, staring at nothing.

Grace had met my mother. Had taken her to the ER. Had handled a family crisis for me.

It would serve me right if this blew up in my face.

35

grace

He truly did owe me.

I didn't have the heart to tell him right then that there was a rash of UTIs going around the assisted living facility. Mr. Alfred was "active" with a lot of folks. I suspected Luke would lose his mind with that information.

Luke and I chatted for a few minutes as I watched my brother walk into my house again. This was getting out of hand. Then he went to the front door and peeked out the window.

"Luke. My brother's in my house again. I need to talk to him to figure out how long this will last."

"He's still there? He's probably trying to cockblock his big sister."

"Do you think he heard us in the kitchen?" I could feel heat across my face. And heat building in my core. I was getting turned on just remembering Sunday.

"Are you blushing?" Luke laughed. "I'll say again, you have nothing to be ashamed of."

"I know..." I was about to say something sexy, but I looked up and my brother was standing in front of me. "I'm sorry. The intruder wants something. Can I call you later?"

We disconnected.

"And what do you want?" I asked Vic. "And why are you standing in front of me? Why are you looking out the window? Who's out there?"

Vic swallowed hard. "I think Stacia's out there."

I jumped up. "Why? Why do you bring your drama to my house?"

"I wasn't trying to. I don't want to call the police on her. She just wants to talk."

He followed me as I went to peek out my window. Sure enough, Stacia was sitting in her car across the street.

"Is she dangerous? You haven't talked to her since you had her served? Has your attorney? Why is she here?"

"She left a message. She doesn't want a divorce. If it's so important, she'll have a baby."

I snorted. That child would be doomed if its mother was having it just to make someone else happy. Besides, she'd had her tubes tied.

He rolled his eyes. "She won't quit her job. Blah, blah, blah. It changes nothing because her attitude and behavior affected how I feel about her. I want out. You were right all along."

I looked at him. "You knew?"

"Yeah, none of you liked her. I knew that. Now it's unanimous. I don't like her either."

I broke down laughing. "Finally."

Then the doorbell rang. Stacia.

I looked at Vic, who indicated I should open the door. Which I did.

She stood there looking the most contrite I'd ever seen. "Hi, Grace." She moved forward to give me a hug, but I stood stiffly while she wrapped her arms around me. She stepped back when she realized I wasn't hugging back.

"Stacia, why are you here?" I asked quietly.

"I'd like to speak with my husband for a few minutes. If that's okay."

She was being respectful for the first time ever.

"Vic, Stacia. Stacia, Vic. I'm not leaving, so keep it down."

I went to my room. To my surprise, there were no raised voices. I could hear mumbling but couldn't understand what was being said.

I wasn't working tomorrow. Too bad Luke wasn't around.

Wait. Could I not get through a couple days without seeing him?

I kicked myself. I needed to get my mind right. I was going to pack for my flight to Miami Thursday morning.

But first, I thought about this morning. Meeting Miss Merci.

She'd been sweet. Charming. A little confused from the UTI but brightening up once the antibiotics kicked in.

And she'd talked about Luke the entire time. How proud she was of him. How he visited weekly. How he'd changed his name to hers when his father left.

"He's a good boy," she'd said, patting my hand. "Takes care of me. Takes care of everyone."

She'd looked at me with knowing eyes. "You're special to him. I can tell. He doesn't bring just anyone to meet his mama."

My chest had tightened.

Because she was right. This was a big step. Meeting his mother. Being trusted with his family.

And the day before, I'd been on a coffee date with another man.

I felt guilty about it all day.

Vic knocked on my bedroom door after Stacia left.

I felt so sad looking at his face. I didn't ask what they discussed. That wasn't my business. But he looked so disappointed and dejected I almost wished he and Stacia could work things out.

Almost.

But looking at my brother's pain, I thought about Luke. About the lies between us.

About how I was setting us up for exactly this kind of ending.

And I still didn't know why I didn't just put a stop to it.

36

grace

As the sun crept over the horizon Wednesday morning, I was at the beginning of a sex dream with Luke as the star performer. The way he moved his hands all over my body... the way he licked and sucked my nipples...the way he—

The alarm jolted me awake violently.

And that's how I felt—violent and angry. My alarm was just out of reach, so I had to open my eyes and scoot to the other side of the bed to shut off the annoying sound.

Fuck! I was spread-eagle on my back on top of the bedcovers—turned on and wet as hell. Before I could open my drawer to get my vibrator out to finish this, there was a knock on my door.

"WHAT!" I yelled out of frustration. "I'm still in bed. What do you need?"

"Celeste is on the phone," Vic stated, knocking again.

Fuck, fuck, fuck... Could she call at a worse time? I slid under the covers and invited Vic in. He handed me his cell phone, and instantly, I was transported back to childhood battles with Celeste. All day, every day.

I was frustrated before I even uttered a word.

"Grace! Sis! How are you?" Celeste always started conversations as if she were excited to talk to you. Maybe she was. But once you didn't give her what she wanted, she went into fight mode.

"Hey, Celeste. How are you?"

"Doing well. Starting to pack. You know I'm coming back earlier without the kids this time. They'll be in the US for Thanksgiving. I know you'll be surprised how much they've grown. I guess Gabe won't be there?"

"Oh no, Gabe's coming home for Thanksgiving," I interjected quickly.

"Oh! I didn't know. No one said anything about his coming. That should be fun, right?"

Celeste's happiness dropped about 50%.

"It'll be nice for all the cousins to see each other." I knew why she was deflated. Gabe being at the house would ruin her argument to Mom about not seeing any grandchildren except hers. If Mom came to Korea, she could see grandbabies every day. My mother saw Gabe too, but my sister acted like that didn't happen.

I'd suggested that if she wanted our parents around so much, she and the family could move back to the US. Her husband Liam had even suggested it. But she resisted. Half-the-year then. Still resisted. Having this argument at least once a month with me—God knows how often with our parents—everyone was tired. We had to bring this to a conclusion. My mother would never go no-contact, but it wore on her.

"That's true. But I really wanted to talk to you about Mom and Dad. Since Gabe moved to Miami, why are you so against them moving to where their grandkids are?"

"So, since Gabe moved, he forfeited his rights as a grandchild? If I used your logic, you already forfeited those rights by hauling everyone off to Korea. It would make more sense for everyone to move to Miami."

Celeste exhaled angrily. "You won't try to see things my way. I'm here all alone. I—my kids—we all miss Mom and Dad. You had your time with them. Why won't you stop being greedy?"

I sank back on my bed. "You know, it would be fucking nice if you called just to talk sometimes. Every conversation turns into this. And it would be fucking nice if you recognized your parents don't want to live in Korea. They don't want to move! There are ways to get around this. Your husband says your family can move back to the US... the kids would love to live here. Why is this such a fight?"

"I hoped you'd matured about this—"

"Me matured? If that isn't ironic! If that's all you called to talk about, I have things to do. Like sleeping or sitting in the bathtub. Or going to see our mother and father and not treating them like chess pieces to move across a board. Treating them like more than puppets in your game to best me and Victor. Damn. I was having such a pleasant morning until you called."

"I don't know why I try—"

"To piss me off? Me either. Bye." I hung up and dropped the phone on the bed. Then I picked up one of my decorative pillows and threw it at the wall.

Vic heard the thud. "You'd better not be throwing my phone. Although I understand after talking to Celie." I pointed at his phone on the bed as he spoke.

He came in and picked it up. "I have to go to work. I don't know why you keep talking to her about this." His voice got louder as he went downstairs. "Why do you think I gave the phone to you?"

After my discussion with Celeste, I was mentally exhausted. That's the effect she had on most of our family except Dad. That she couldn't wear him down with constant speculation and logical fallacies was the main reason our parents still resided in the house they bought and lovingly refurnished. If it were up to Mom, they'd be in Korea and unhappy as hell. It was ironic because whenever they visited Celeste, Mom was on the phone complaining about missing her home, her friends, us.

But let Celeste talk to her, and suddenly she believed living there was the next best thing to the Rapture. It frustrated me and Vic—like Celeste had Mom in a mind meld, and we had to reboot her system. Maybe Mom felt guilty about Celeste being a middle child. Maybe there was neglect I was unaware of.

Celeste avoided those tactics with me because she'd get cussed out, as happened today. I was the more proper sister, but I cussed a lot. I'd learned new curse words in Spanish from Gabe—words I'd love to use in person if she kept this shit up.

She wasn't ready for that barrage. Now she'd call Mom and tell her I was mean. *And I was, so?*

I still believed Celeste wanted Mom in Korea because she was the middle child. She wanted Mom to choose her over the oldest and youngest. I suspected that having our mother there would lose its luster when Mom became a clinger, because she didn't know the language or anyone other than her grandchildren and her son-in-law. Liam, kind man that he is, even tried to help Celeste realize that her parents' moving there would change her lifestyle.

But the middle child in her wouldn't let that go. That attitude had driven a wedge between the three of us. Vic and I bonded against her, and that extended to other areas of our lives.

I'd talked this out with my therapist years ago. I couldn't get Celeste to take part then or at any point. I'd love to have a cordial sisterly relationship with her, but that was going to be on her at this point.

I spent the rest of the day running errands—dry cleaning, oil change. I called Harmony and left a message about my last speed date.

Last speed date.

The words sat heavily.

I should tell her I was done. No more matchmaking. I'd met someone.

But I didn't say that in the message. Just that Keith was nice, I was taking a break for family stuff.

Still lying. Still keeping secrets.

My journal that I'd finally ordered still sat on the table, and I hadn't written a word yet. I spent a torturous hour writing my feelings down on paper—including those about Luke. There's a reason I don't enjoy journaling or haven't become a writer. It was like pulling teeth without anesthesia.

At least my packing for Miami was quick. I was arriving mid-afternoon Thursday to see some of the interclub races Gabe and Alex would compete in.

There was supposed to be a dinner with the kids on Thursday, or at least we would be allowed to take them out. I wasn't sure what the plans were for other days, but MacKenzie had been tight-lipped, communicating only by brief text. With her new practice and everything else, she was probably exhausted.

Friday was Halloween, but again there was no word about the festivities. This shouldn't be a surprise. They were newlyweds, wrapped up in each other, shutting the rest of the world out.

I could only dream of that feeling... but maybe it was closer than I thought.

By evening, I was packed, checked in, and had my airport gear laid out. Vic had finally gone back to his own house for the night. Which made no sense. I wouldn't be home for days—this would be the time to use my soaker tub and hide from his wife.

But Vic and Stacia probably discussed housing arrangements last night. Hopefully, things would stay calm while I was away.

Wednesday evening, Mom finally called. Celeste had called her crying, and Mom asked me to be nicer to my sister because she was struggling. I wasn't in the mood to argue, but the topic made me angry. I'd put this out of my mind, thinking more about my trip and seeing my son, and Mom brought both it and my sister back up before bedtime.

I looked at my watch—too late to call Gabe. I missed him fiercely, but I'd see him tomorrow. All my girls, except Autumn, were tending to children. Autumn's rule was don't call late unless she called first. Besides, I never knew what freaky stuff she and Theo might be up to. After I accidentally wandered into the middle of some of it one day, it scared me, and I became cautious about after-hours visits or calls.

Plus, I'd started the morning on edge anyway. To calm both my body and mind, I'd scheduled a night with my vibrator. I knew Luke had flown back to Chicago and was probably dealing with business. An earlier text noted Kyle's father was doing better, off the ventilator.

As I crawled into bed with my favorite pink rabbit vibrator that worked both the clit and G-spot, I tried to clear my mind and get ready for endorphins. This vibrator guaranteed a full-blown double orgasm.

As I tried to get in the right mindset, my phone vibrated.

A video call.

Luke.

I tried to fluff my hair and straighten my t-shirt. Too late to spruce myself up. Oh well.

"Hey there."

"Hi. I'm so glad to hear your voice. See that beautiful face." He sounded weary.

"Bad day?"

"Yeah. A lot of phone calls—for both branches of Sloane-Wash. Kyle is a god for handling so much. I need to step up. But right now, Kyle's spending all his time with his dad and Jada and the kids. I've never seen him like this, and I was there when his mother died."

"How long ago was that?"

"Mama Jacqui—yet another Jacqui in my life—died when we were 27, I think. Heart attack. She died quickly—that might be part of it. And he's the last parent standing for Kyle. Losing that parent is another thing entirely." He shifted on the bed. "I didn't call to list all the challenges of the day. I just wanted to relax with you for a few minutes. After only ten days, you already make my days better."

"You seem surprised."

"Well, we've only known each other for ten days. And I wish like hell you were right here right now."

"I miss you too. I've been thinking about you." I stopped, embarrassed at how close I was to spilling exactly what I was thinking. It had been only ten days, five of them long-distance. I wasn't sure I was ready to unload the sexual fantasy I was about to indulge in with him as the star.

"What were you thinking? Anything interesting?"

I deflected. "I wanted to talk about my sister, who's trying to move my parents again. She called me for support for some silly reason, knowing I don't agree with her rationale." I quickly explained the situation. "She's going to harp on this during her visit. I don't know if I want to subject you to such pleasant conversation."

Luke laughed. "I think I can handle it. I mean, I'm not saying you have to invite me to meet your family, but if you're so inclined, I'm cool with it."

I smiled at him. "That's sweet. And just for that, you have an open request for me to visit your mother again." I could see the appreciation on his face.

"Would you really? I don't want to impose."

I blew by that comment. "I think I made friends with her so she might enjoy my company. Hopefully she remembers me, because I don't want security dragging me out—"

"Would they put you in handcuffs?"

I pointed at him, laughing. "They might. And don't get any ideas from what I just said!"

"Too late!"

I made a comment about how I could probably get myself out of them since I'd been handcuffed to a headboard before. I stopped as I realized what I was saying… and my cheeks turned bright red.

Then the mood on the call suddenly changed. Gone was the lighthearted joking. Admittedly, my last comment was sexually charged—I didn't even think about that when I let it slip. The way he looked at me set off a firestorm in my core. Like he was already imagining such a scenario and more.

I shifted in bed as I felt wetness between my legs—I didn't have on underwear since my original plan was time with my vibrator. But then I realized my vibrator was in full view. I tried to move it, but eagle eye had already noticed.

"What were you really thinking about before I called?" he said softly, sitting up in his bed.

The blush engulfed my entire body. I didn't know what to say. But he was looking at me so intently, so suggestively, hungrily.

"Okay. I'm so embarrassed. I planned a little me time to try to relax after the hellish call with my sister…"

He arched his eyebrow. "Was I a part of this me time?"

Maybe I would spontaneously combust.

Luke continued. "Why are you so embarrassed? I think it's sexy. Extremely sexy." He dragged out the last two words. "If you're up for it—and that word choice wasn't an accident—I would love to watch you. Maybe provide some verbal encouragement."

"Phone sex? I—"

"Yes, except I just want to watch. I want to watch you come undone while imagining you're coming on my dick." His voice dropped lower, rougher. "You know I've been imagining bending you over and thrusting into your perfect wet pussy over and over until you can't breathe. I've wanted to fuck you every day since we met. While not the same, it'll be a nice appetizer for the real thing."

My breathing became more rapid as his words swirled around my body like a caress. The need for release had moved beyond just taking the edge off to a primal need.

I decided to take the leap.

"Get comfortable," he said. "I can see you've selected a heavy-duty device there..."

"I'm afraid to ask why you know your vibrators so well..." I gasped out.

"There's a lot you don't know about me yet. But you'll learn." His eyes were dark, hungry. "How sensitive are your breasts? I love that they're a perfect handful. I'm not going to ask you to take off your t-shirt... but imagine me sucking and biting your nipples until you feel it in your pussy."

I generally didn't focus on my breasts when pleasuring myself, but tonight I followed his lead. My hands moved under my shirt, cupping myself, thumbs brushing over my nipples. They hardened immediately.

"That's it," he murmured. "Touch yourself like I would. Pinch them. Harder."

I did, gasping at the sensation that shot straight to my core.

"Is your pussy aching for my dick?"

"Y-yes..." I breathed out, reaching for the vibrator.

"Good girl. Put it in position."

I did. I was so wet my vagina made a squishing sound.

Luke moaned. "Fuck, you are so wet for me right now. I wish I was there. Turn it on. I want you to fuck your pussy like you want my dick to fuck you. And I want you to look at me."

My eyes popped open and our eyes met. It was such an intense, intimate moment even though we were thousands of miles apart.

When I turned on the vibrator, my body was immediately flooded with sensations. The dual stimulation—the thick shaft inside me, the suction on my clit—was almost too much.

"That's my girl," Luke said, voice rough. "Let me see you. Show me how you fuck yourself thinking about me."

I started pumping the toy in and out, my hips moving to meet each thrust.

"Faster," he commanded. "I know you can take it harder than that. When I finally get inside you, I'm not going to be gentle. I'm going to fuck you so hard you'll feel me for days."

A moan escaped my lips. The vibrator was hitting that spot inside me, the one that made my toes curl. The suction on my clit was relentless.

"Look at me," he said when my eyes started to close. "I want to watch you come. I want to see your face when you fall apart."

Our eyes locked again. There was something so raw, so vulnerable about this—letting him see me like this, completely undone.

"You're so fucking beautiful," he murmured. "Touch your nipples again. Pinch them while you fuck yourself."

I did, my movements with the vibrator becoming more rapid, more desperate. I could feel the orgasm building, coiling tight in my belly.

"That's it, baby. You're close, aren't you? I can see it. Your breathing's changed. Your hips are moving faster. You need to come."

"Yes," I gasped. "Please—"

"Please, what?" His voice was almost a growl. "Tell me what you need."

"I need to come. Please, Luke—"

"Then come for me, Gimbiya. Come thinking about my dick inside you. Come so hard you can't remember your own name."

The orgasm hit me like a wave, spreading from my core outward. My back arched off the bed, vision dimming as pleasure crashed through me. Wave after wave, sensation after sensation. I lost track of time, lost track of everything except the pulsing pleasure radiating through my entire body.

When I finally came back to myself, I was trembling, the vibrator still buzzing between my legs. I turned it off with shaking hands.

Luke was leaning back on his bed, looking completely satisfied despite the obvious bulge in his sweatpants.

"There you are," he said softly. "That's my girl. I loved watching you unravel. I cannot wait until you get to do that on my dick instead of that toy."

I was still trying to catch my breath. "You didn't—"

"Tonight was about you. Trust me, watching you come that hard was more than enough for me." He grinned. "Besides, I have a list now. Things we need to try. And that handcuff comment you made? Definitely on the list."

I laughed, still feeling the aftershocks. "You're trouble."

"You have no idea, Gimbiya. No idea."

After we hung up, I lay in bed, staring at the ceiling.

That had been... intense. Intimate. Real.

And on Monday, I sat across from Keith at a coffee shop, pretending to be available.

The guilt tried to creep in, but I pushed it away.

Tomorrow I was flying to Miami. This weekend I'd see Gabe. I'd hopefully see Luke when I got back.

And I still hadn't told him.

I turned over, pulled the covers up.

I'd deal with all of it after Miami.

After I figured out how to untangle this mess I'd created.

37

luke

I got up early Thursday morning and went back to the hospital. After last night, I was in a good mood despite being exhausted from traveling around the country all week.

On top of that, I really wanted to see Grace again. But I wasn't going to be in San Francisco until this weekend at the earliest. And she'd be in Miami.

A thought: Could I meet her in Miami this weekend? I wasn't sure how she'd feel about that since she'd be with family, close friends, and exes. I didn't know if she'd be comfortable introducing me to everyone so fast.

If not, I'd fly back to San Francisco. But I had my fingers crossed.

Kyle was alone at the hospital, standing outside his father's room when I arrived.

"Where's the family, Ky?" I asked, giving him a hug.

"Since Dad's doing better, I chartered a flight for them to go home. The kids are going stir-crazy and my father will be transferred to a rehab facility soon. Then I'll move him to San Fran. Which means dealing with his estate, house, everything."

"But he's getting better. That's great."

"I don't want to leave all the work to you. So, we need to do better at managing our meetings—whether we do more Zoom meetings or fly clients to our offices. And we need to search for additional upper-level management." Kyle patted me on the shoulder. "I know you've been juggling your new lady friend and your mom along with work."

"Well, it's kept me from love bombing her too much. But this week has been rather hellish since it felt like I was on a plane almost every day. I might fly to

Miami this weekend to hang out with her. Her son has a swim meet." I ducked my head. "But she may not want me around her friends."

"You can only ask."

We visited with Papa Washington, who'd been moved from intensive care to a regular room. Still on oxygen, he didn't talk much but seemed happy to see us. The doctor came in, and Kyle took her aside to get some specifics so he could start planning in California.

Sitting in a corner of the hospital room, I made phone calls and read emails. Killing time until I called Grace.

A little voice in the back of my mind brought up the Harmony issue.

I couldn't even think about how to broach the topic without sounding like a creepy guy. There was no nice way around this.

So, I ignored it again.

But this phone call—asking to come to Miami—could be a fundamental change for our relationship.

I'd be meeting her son. Her friends. Her ex-husband and his new wife.

I'd be stepping into her real life.

And I was still lying to her about who my sister was.

The irony wasn't lost on me. Every step forward made the lie bigger.

Meeting my mom. Now meeting her son, her people.

Integrating into her life while keeping a big secret.

I pulled out my phone, stared at it.

I should tell her. Before Miami. Before I met everyone.

Grace, I need to tell you something. My sister is Harmony. The matchmaker. I've known since the beginning.

My thumb floated again over her contact.

But I didn't call.

Because once I told her, everything would change. She'd realize I'd been lying for almost two weeks. She'd wonder why I didn't say anything. She'd question everything between us.

And I couldn't lose her.

Not now. Not when I was falling this hard.

I put my phone away.

After Miami. After I'd met her son, solidified our relationship.

Then I'd tell her. When we were strong enough to survive it.

I was a coward. I knew that.

But I called her anyway.

38

grace

It was canon among my friends that I essentially had both a flying and an airport phobia. It wasn't really a phobia according to psychological terms, but it was as close as you could get without my refusing to get on a plane.

If I were flying with family or my son, I'd force myself to stay awake and white-knuckle my way through the airport and flight. An alcoholic beverage on the plane often took the edge off.

If I were flying alone, I'd take an anti-anxiety pill and go to sleep as soon as I got in my seat. I'd stay up the night before, so it'd be easier to fall asleep. I loved those flights. I'd wake up rested, having missed every bit of turbulence, the distressing liftoff, and the jerky landing—all the things that made me uncomfortable.

Making it through security today was better because we didn't have to pull everything out of our carry-ons or take off various items of clothing. I reminded myself I really needed to sign up for pre-check to make this part easier. Finally, airports were upgrading scanning devices, so you didn't have to essentially strip down.

I slept through the entire flight from takeoff to landing. Didn't check any bags, didn't rent a car because I had plenty of friends in Miami.

As I exited the plane, I called Mac, who'd volunteered to pick me up and take me to my hotel to check in. From there, we could go directly to the academy to catch a race or two of the Interclub meet.

She was waiting for me at the curb in a blue Audi SUV. I slid into the passenger seat, gave her a quick hug, and she merged into traffic.

"How was your flight?" Mac asked, looking over. "You look like you had a better ride than your last trip."

"I slept the entire way. This is the way going forward. How are you doing?"

It was still hard to believe that after everything, we'd become friends. We were technically family, but we knew to leave some topics out of discussion to maintain a nice status quo.

"It's been busy. I finally have a regular schedule at the new practice. Not seeing a lot of patients yet but just getting everything organized and licensed is enough. And keeping up with the boys is more work than I expected."

"That makes sense. One kid is a lot. Two athletic kids with schedules to manage is much more." I leaned back. "I can't tell you how much I miss Gabe. How has he been doing? He tells me he's okay, but since I can't see him every day, I worry."

"He's doing so well and constantly talks about missing you. He tells us when he talks to you. Gabe will be so glad to see you!"

"I'm so close to just chucking it all and moving here. But then I wouldn't have anywhere to live or any money to eat with."

Mac laughed. "You can love up on him this weekend. And he's the favorite in a couple of races, which will be fun to watch."

My phone vibrated. "Sorry—let me get this."

It was Luke.

"Hey, sexy. I take it you're in Miami now?"

"Hi, Luke!" I replied.

Mac's head snapped toward me in curiosity. I held up one finger as I continued. "Yes, I'm just leaving the airport."

"Are you heading to see your son?"

"The meet is starting soon. I'm already nervous about the competition." I could feel Mac's eyes burning a hole in my head. I turned toward the passenger door, so she was out of my line of sight. "Are you still in Chicago?"

"For now. But Kyle's father is doing much better. I plan to get out of here soon, since Kyle sent his family back home. He has to make plans for rehab and then assisted living or advanced nursing care depending on how fast Papa Washington recovers."

I smiled. "That's good news, but it sounds like a lot of work."

"It is." He paused. "I have a question I'm afraid to ask..."

"Ask me what?"

"Would you like some company this weekend? I haven't seen you in almost a week. I miss you. I'm probably being too forward. I shouldn't have said anything."

I smiled again, though he couldn't see. *That would be perfect.*

Except.

Luke meeting everyone. Meeting Gabe. Meeting Evan and Mac. Meeting my friends.

All while he still didn't know I'd gone on two speed dates while we were falling for each other. *Hedging my bets...*

"I wouldn't mind a little company. What exactly are you offering?"

Mac almost leaned out of her seat trying to hear.

"I'll fly down tomorrow. If that's okay. I don't know if you want me milling around with all your family and your ex—he's there, right?"

"Yes, he is. But it'll be fine. I think. I don't care. I want to see you, too."

Mac still had her hands on the steering wheel, but her face and ears were on my side of the car.

I shooed her away, laughing. "Back up, ma'am. Pay attention to the road, please."

"What's happening over there?" Luke chuckled.

"Nothing. My friend is being nosy right now. So, you'll probably be interrogated like a criminal when you get here."

"I can dodge questions with the best of them. Oh, thank you again for seeing my mother. She liked you a lot, and she's doing much better. Unfortunately, I finally heard all the details of the activities those 'active' seniors have been getting into."

I burst out laughing. "I warned you!"

"I'm too young to hear such information! I can't believe that. It sounds like these grown-ass older people are acting like teenagers! And multiple partners? I didn't need that in my brain. Anyway, after I make flight plans, I'll call you later to give you details. I'll be there tomorrow morning sometime. I'll let you get back to your friends."

"Thanks. See you tomorrow."

"Bye, Gimbiya."

Before I could disconnect properly, Mac was all in my business. "Who is *that*?"

"My friend Luke. He's going to swing through this weekend, so I expect you'll meet him. And I'm not telling you anything about him right now. Maybe later over some champagne after the races."

We were at my hotel by then. Parking in the lot, Mac said, "I look forward to hearing about him. But you have to give me something to tide me over until I can gossip about your dating life for real."

"I ran into him—literally—in an office building. That's all you get."

She grumbled good-naturedly and followed me in while I checked into my hotel room. I always get a room with a nice tub because after being agitated in the airport and on the plane, I like to either take a long soak or go to the spa. We didn't have time for the spa today. Sitting in the tub was on my list of things to do later.

I dropped off my roller bag and splashed water on my face.

Mac sat on the couch in the room as I freshened up. "Hey, did you pack like your 'friend' was coming to town?"

I frowned. She was stirring shit right now. And no, I hadn't packed beyond watching swimming and casual dinners.

"Oh, yeah. We're having a small party at our place Saturday night. And a Halloween party tomorrow night. No costumes though—unless you want to wear one."

I stuck my head out of the bathroom, annoyed at all the tidbits she forgot to mention before I packed.

Mac laughed sheepishly. "Did I not tell you about that before? Sorry. You have time to shop. I already have to take Ree—"

"Ree is coming? Girl, you have forgotten a lot of things about this trip!"

"I'm terribly sorry! But honestly, you're bringing a whole man down here, and you didn't mention *that*," she replied snarkily. "But I do recognize my errors—I'm not being a good hostess. I'll make it up to you and your 'friend'. I'll arrange a special date night meal before the house party or something. Just give me a chance. I've been struggling lately—a little more forgetful than usual. I'm really sorry."

I looked at her. "Are you alright?"

"Yeah, I'm fine. Just been working extra hard at the clinic. Starting a new business is a full-time job. Not counting the patients I have to see. And I have to hire someone else at least part-time, but I'm dragging my feet. I don't want to pay anyone yet. Evan keeps saying to go ahead and start looking. But I don't know if I agree."

I came out of the bathroom. "Okay, I'm ready," I said, grabbing my daybag. I didn't change since I was wearing jeans and an Elite Academy hoodie. Mac was wearing a similar hoodie. "I don't know. I'm impressed you're creating your own practice. I might have to do that if I move down here next year."

We were both quiet when we left the hotel room.

As we got in the car, Mac snapped her seat belt. "I see what you're doing. Trying to talk about 'safe' topics so I won't ask anything else about Luke."

"Keep hope alive?"

"You should have known better."

I laughed, but inside, anxiety churned.

Luke was coming tomorrow. Meeting everyone.

And I still hadn't told him everything.

This was not going to end well.

39

grace

We pulled up in front of the familiar swimming complex.

The boys had officially started in September, basically at the beginning of their school year. I came down with Gabe the first week and helped him settle into his new ten-plus-month home. After the first three days, he acclimated relatively quickly—faster than Evan and I had thought he would, given his ADHD and issues with change. The first day was a little stressful, all my worries that this might be too much for him coming back. But having Alex there helped. The schedule was pretty rigid at the beginning to help everyone understand expectations and to embed discipline.

I also came down one weekend toward the end of September. Gabe was thriving when I got there. My boy was extremely happy about his opportunity.

I seemed to be the only one still struggling.

As we walked in, we could see Alex talking to a coach. It had only been a month since I'd last seen him. He was taller. We didn't try to get his attention. I noticed a new screen was installed on the wall to allow spectators to see the photo finishes underwater.

Looking around for a seat, we spotted David, who had saved us spots. I hadn't spoken to David since the wedding, which should make this an interesting weekend. I didn't know what he had told Mac, if anything, and he wasn't there when I came down last month. We climbed onto the metal bleachers and inched past the other parents in our row.

Mac leaned down and gave David a buss kiss on the cheek. I gave him an elbow bump and sat on the other side of Mac.

"Hey, you two! Grace, I hope you had a pleasant trip. Good to see you." Like we hadn't almost torched our hard-fought friendship at the wedding. He continued, "Evan won't be here today, right?"

Mac looked at both of us with a slightly perplexed look but didn't push. "Evan has an urgent surgery today, so you might not see him until later. Ree is coming first thing in the morning. And we have a spa appointment for the three of us on Saturday."

I opened my mouth, but Mac held up a finger. "I scheduled the spa services for Saturday late morning during the long-distance races. Neither of the boys will be competing in those." To me, she added, "See if you can find out when your friend is coming. We can pick him up at the airport if he arrives around the same time."

I ducked my head. "I don't think he's going to need us to pick him up. I really didn't tell you about him, did I?"

David was listening to the conversation intently. I continued. "Luke's company has a private jet, which he'll use to get here from Chicago."

Mac cocked her head and raised her eyebrows. "So, his company has, or he has the jet?"

"He and his business partner own the company."

David chimed in. "What's this guy's name? Is he your boyfriend? Do I need to grill him?"

I shook my head. "I don't think that's necessary. But thank you. And we haven't officially given what we have a name yet. It's only been a couple of weeks."

"Wait. A couple of weeks and he missed you so much that he's turning his private jet around to come see you this weekend?" Mac threw her arm over my shoulder. "Girl, that's what I'm talking about! I will need details. But first, I think your baby is heading to the blocks."

Perfect timing.

This meet was for the twelve-to-fourteen-year-olds. The swimmers were preparing for the first races—the shorter distances, Gabe's preferred distances. The first race was the 50 free. Gabe's favorite race of all time. One lap, full out. Exciting because there was no room for error—just fast strokes cutting through water with controlled mayhem.

I was getting nervous, as I did before every race Gabe ever participated in. I grabbed Mac's hand and squeezed—she yelped.

Gabe climbed onto the blocks. David had grabbed programs. Gabe was the youngest in his heat, but similar in weight and height to everyone else.

On your marks, get set, go. The starter gun cracked and everyone hit the water. Gabe's start was a strong point for him—Evan had coached him up on that when he was young. That had been Evan's strength when he was racing too. He just wasn't as fast and twitchy as Gabe.

Gabe was one of the first two swimmers to surface. He was battling with a boy—I checked the program—a fourteen-year-old from a swim club in Orlando.

The three of us were screaming, as were many of the surrounding parents. It was difficult to tell who touched the wall first, and my heart was hammering.

We anxiously looked at the screen.

Gabe for the win.

I stood up yelling, "That's my baby!"

Mac tried to pull me back down into my seat.

Hopefully, I didn't embarrass him.

I checked his time on the scoreboard—it was faster than it had been earlier this summer.

Maybe it had been a good idea for him to come here.

To our surprise, Alex and Gabe both competed in the 100 free—just in different heats. So, if they both made it through, they'd have to compete against each other. That would be a hard race to watch, but we weren't there yet.

They both made it through the first heats.

All in all, the meet was fun. Once the first day concluded, David, Mac, and I climbed down the bleachers and went with the crowd of parents to greet our swimmers.

"Mom! You made it!" Gabe wore his UltraElite warm-up suit, as did Alex. Mac and David stood talking to Alex. Gabe ran over and gave me a huge hug.

"I'm so glad you saw my race."

Tears welled up in my eyes. I was so proud and thrilled.

"I'm so proud of you! Your dad couldn't make it this afternoon."

"Yeah, Dr. Mac told me earlier. It's okay." I hugged him again.

Because there were races tomorrow, the Academy didn't allow the boys off campus tonight. We stood talking to our sons for a few minutes until we had to leave. They had to eat in the cafeteria and then rest.

Mac suggested the three of us grab dinner, but I begged off so I could do my travel self-care. The tub was calling my name. I gave each of them a hug after we all walked out to our cars. Mac was going to drop me off. David had driven himself. During the hug, he whispered in my ear, "We need to talk to clear the air."

I pulled away and nodded. "We're cool. But we can talk tomorrow. Good night." He looked at me peculiarly but backed off.

🔬

Back at my hotel, I immediately ran a full bath with the provided bath bubbles.

I had been in the tub for ten minutes when my phone rang. It was Luke.

"How are you?" I said, settling deeper into the water.

"Fine. Looking forward to tomorrow. What are you doing?" He paused. "I hear water."

"I'm in the tub. I always get in the tub after flying."

"Are you a bad flyer? I was going to ask you to ride back to San Francisco with me on the private jet. But if you're going to throw up—"

I got out "Hey! I'm not—" before I realized he was kidding. "I usually take an anti-anxiety pill on the plane so I can sleep through the entire flight. I haven't been on a private jet before, so I don't know how I'd do."

"Well, I had other plans for the private jet, so sleep would not be the first thing on the menu. It would be an opportunity to join the Mile High Club—in comfort and not wedged into an airplane bathroom."

I brightened as I imagined christening different parts of that plane. "How does that work with Kyle?"

"The plane gets cleaned after each trip. I expect that Kyle and Jada have had many adventures on this plane. I try not to consider what all this plane may have seen." He paused. "So does that mean you'll fly back with me?"

"Maybe. I would be curious to see what you have planned."

"Heh heh. Changing the subject—how did your son do today? I meant to ask sooner before I got sidetracked with thoughts of you under me ten thousand feet in the air."

"Hey. No teasing. Where are you exactly? If we keep this conversation up, are you going to have to take matters into your own hands on your plane? Do you have a flight attendant? Where do they go when the occupants are busy entertaining themselves?"

"I'm at the airport. Waiting to take off in a couple of hours. The flight path between Chicago and Miami is busy right now, so I had to take off later. It should be a three-hour flight or so. I won't call you until after I land. I'll check into my hotel first—unless you want me to come to your room."

"Why are you getting your own room?" Man, I was being very forward. But we hadn't slept together yet, and I wasn't waiting any longer. I still couldn't believe I was brazenly inviting him to stay with me.

"Are you sure? Because if you are, you don't have to ask me twice. What hotel are you in?"

I told him the name and room number. "Now, I'm not in a fancy suite. It's a nice room—probably not what you reserve when you travel."

"I will admit that I do reserve suites with great views and extra amenities. Does that make me a bad almost-billionaire? I don't think about it—I just try to do what I can to make the world better. For foster kids and for people's health. I never intended to have this much money. Billionaires are pretty hated right now. One day when I slow down, I'll really think about what I'm doing."

"You're the first person I've knowingly spoken to who is within breathing range of billionaire status. Except for the plane, I would probably just think you were regular rich. Not Richie Rich rich."

"Richie Rich! Did you read comics as a kid?"

"Not really. Mystery books mostly."

"We'll have to compare reading lists. I like mysteries too. Like you."

"I don't think I'm a mystery though. I wear my heart on my sleeve."

"Maybe so. But it's fun to figure it out." He paused. "I do have to get ready to board. Since I plan to spend time with you in other cities, I'll handle room selection in the future. There will be a nice tub and a king-size bed. Although I don't think we'll need that much space."

I whispered quietly, "Just get here."

He bid me good night.

I was going to have a hard time sleeping while anticipating seeing him tomorrow. I was acting like a schoolgirl.

As I got dressed, I thought about how everything had changed on a dime a couple of weeks ago. I swore I wasn't going to let my heart get away from me. But it was. Luke was kind, sexy, smart, and genuinely interested in my being happy. Most of the time I felt safe on this roller coaster—we were still getting to know each other, no pressure, no real expectations. It was still all fun.

But one day we'd be asking real questions. Making real decisions. He admitted he wasn't a relationship person but wanted to be that for me. Easier said than done.

And I was still lying to him about the matchmaker. About Keith. About Everett. About all of it.

I might be in too deep already to get out.

And I didn't even want to get out. That was the most terrifying part.

40

grace

Friday morning was hectic.

Mac had planned to pick Ree up at the airport around midday. However, Ree took an earlier flight from Houston and arrived around 9 a.m. Ree ended up taking a rideshare to the hotel—we were staying in the same one for convenience. Of course, Mac missed both calls from Ree—the first with the early arrival and the second when Ree and I sat outside by the pool when she got to the hotel. Mac hung out at the airport for about an hour until she finally realized her phone was on silent. Contrite, Mac called and told us she would meet us later.

After Ree checked into her room, she and I were sitting by the pool waiting for people to arrive. I met Ree during June at the trial swim camp that started it all. Ree, or Adrienne, went to medical school with Evan and Mac years ago. The two women had been close during med school but had reconnected a few years ago.

Ree was a neonatologist who had just realized she had spent her life working and needed to figure out what she wanted. Like maybe a baby. She was in her forties too, so time was of the essence. It was a common topic of conversation with Ree right now.

Through Mac, Ree and I had become pretty good friends over the past four months. And while sitting by the pool, we talked about Ree's baby plans and my plans in general.

"We know I want a baby. But what do you want? You helped your ex get to his happily-ever-after. What are you doing to get to yours?"

I wasn't sure where to start, but I was rescued from answering by the look on Ree's face. She was looking over my shoulder.

"What's wrong?" I asked.

"There's a really good-looking, built man heading this way." I turned to see. It was Luke.

I snatched up my phone in a panic to see if I had missed a call or text from him. I hadn't.

"Do you know him? Because if you don't—" Ree started mischievously.

"Sorry. He's here for me." I replied and stood up.

I heard Ree mumble "damn" behind me.

Luke saw me and jogged over. He crushed me to him and gave me a sweet kiss that sent all kinds of improper feelings throughout my body. Improper only because we couldn't do anything about them right this minute.

But *later*.

"Hey, Gimbiya," he said breathlessly. "I'm glad to see you." I realized he called me Gimbiya more than Sunshine these days. I liked it.

"Happy to see you too," I said, wrapping my arms around his neck. "When did you get in?"

"However long it took my driver to get here from the airport. Everything in Chicago and San Francisco is calm right now. I saw no reason to wait for more drama before getting out of town." He looked over at Ree, who was sitting there with an expectant look on her face. "Who is your friend?"

"Oh my God. Sorry, Ree." I led Luke over to the table. "Lucien Sloane—Luke—meet Adrienne Graves, MD. She went to medical school with my ex-husband and his wife."

Ree stood up and shook his hand. "Hi, Luke. Nice to meet you. Everyone calls me Ree." She held out her hand aimed at an extra chair at our table. "Join us for a few minutes before we have to head over to see some swimming."

Luke looked at me and sat down in the chair that Ree indicated.

"So, tell me about yourself," Ree asked.

"Is this an interview?" I frowned at Ree.

Luke laughed. "It's fine. I'll give you a topline history. I'll be here all weekend, so you may learn more about me than you want." At the same time, he reached under the table and placed his hand on my knee. I tried to play it off, especially when he started sliding his hand toward more interesting territory.

He rattled off his basic facts looking as innocent as possible. I could see her approval increasing even with this early information. She had more questions, but I put a stop to the interrogation by redirecting everyone's attention to the swim meet we were supposed to be attending.

"Let's get you settled in your room. Then we can meet back down here and drive over."

"I have a car if you want to ride with me," Luke suggested.

That sounded like a reasonable plan, so we all walked to the lobby and went to our respective rooms. Luke had a roller bag and a shoulder bag. I led the way to the room we were going to share. I was calm on the outside. Inside I was a nervous wreck. This felt like a commitment—one I had no idea I'd be making two weeks ago. I was happy with where things were, but that little voice in the back of my mind was second-guessing my decision.

I hated that voice.

But once I opened the door—giving him the extra key—Luke rolled his luggage inside, kicked the door shut behind him, and gently nudged me against the wall next to the bathroom.

"I know we don't have much time, so I'll maintain my control for now." He looked at me in that way he had—like he was already three steps ahead. "I have been thinking about this moment all morning. I can't go another minute without kissing you. An actual kiss—one that makes us both breathless, you wet, and me hard." He leaned in. "I have plans for you, Gimbiya. Except you won't be acting like a princess."

He kissed me in a way that was becoming familiar and still managed to undo me completely every time. I grabbed his hips and pulled his pelvis against me. The kiss became deeper. I forgot what we were supposed to be doing, where we were supposed to be going. I pulled his shirttail out so I could grab his ass. He ground himself against me—

Knock knock.

Jesus. "Who is it?" I panted out. Luke continued to suck on my neck.

Shit.

"It's Ree. Who else would it be?" she replied exasperatedly.

Luke slipped into the bathroom as I limped my way to the door. I know I looked like someone had just kissed me thoroughly. It couldn't be helped.

Ree came in talking at the same time. "I couldn't find Luke's hotel reser-vati—" She paused as she noticed his luggage inside my door. "Oh, he doesn't need one, does he?" She gave me a crooked smile. "Girl, go freshen up. I got here just in time. You two might have been naked on the floor in a minute or two. And then you would have missed the meet because we ain't waiting."

I looked at her, dazed.

"Snap out of the sex haze." She snapped her fingers at me. "Gabe. Gabriel. Your son. Remember him? Hurry up so we can go!" She then yelled through the bathroom door, "I will be waiting in the lobby. Hurry up. We don't have time for unclothed shenanigans right now." And left.

"Is the coast clear?" Luke asked as he came out of the bathroom, laughing. "Your friend is hilarious. This should be an interesting weekend."

41

grace

I hired a driver to transport us around while I was in Miami. I think I've been getting lazy, because I actually like driving. But driving in other cities wasn't as fun as it used to be when I was younger. Too much traffic. And my patience levels had decreased. Something else I needed to unpack—was I taking money for granted?

When we arrived at the Academy, I had to admit that the facilities impressed me. With the meet going on, there were a lot of spectators and swimmers milling around the state-of-the-art buildings. It reminded me of some college campuses I had visited over the years. More evidence of the vast amount of money in sports.

I helped Grace out of the SUV, but Ree scrambled out of the other side unassisted.

Holding hands, we followed Ree into the building. There was no admission fee. Just inside the door, we were each wanded and asked which swimmer and swim club we were there to support.

Ree spotted the rest of our party immediately, and we wove our way through other parents to find the saved seats. I didn't know any of them, although I recognized Evan from a picture at Grace's home. The pretty woman sitting next to him must be MacKenzie—the couple Grace had played a role in getting back together. I don't care what she said, that had to be hard to do. Feelings don't always follow logic, and even if you aren't in love anymore, the memories still remain. The other man sitting on the other side of MacKenzie must be Grace's partner in crime, David.

Grace quickly introduced me to everyone seated. I got a few measured looks from Evan and David before each of them reached over to shake my hand. Grace had mentioned she hadn't really talked about me, and the men in the group appeared surprised by my presence. However, everyone was polite and we all fell into easy banter about the races, including some friendly ribbing among the men about their personal sports prowess. Of course, attention turned to me as they asked me basic questions about myself. I watched MacKenzie pull out her phone and look me up on Google, her eyebrow raising at whatever she found.

Grace was definitely going to be bombarded with questions later.

I didn't expect these races to be as exciting as they were. I hadn't been to an interclub swimming meet with teenagers, where every swimmer had high aspirations. It was nothing like watching kids at neighborhood swim meets, which I had done in the past for some foster children I knew. These kids were so competitive, you could tell from a distance.

Alex and Gabe had heats for the 50m free almost as soon as we walked in. Fortunately, they were still not in the same heat. But if they both advanced, they would be competing against each other during the next heat.

Both advanced through that round with no real pressure. The next race would be difficult to watch.

Evan and Mac went to the concession stand and brought us all drinks and snacks. We munched on chips and popcorn as we waited for the next race that meant anything to us.

"Oh my! It's almost time for Alex's next race!" MacKenzie said excitedly. I looked toward the pool and spotted a tall, wiry boy who resembled David. Easy to pick out their kid.

And he was really good. I found myself cheering during his 100m heat. There was another swimmer closing in on Alex at the end of the race. Grace had gripped my shoulder as we tried to will him to go faster, hang on, you're almost there.

I had forgotten what it felt like to be included in the small things. I'd been avoiding that kind of connection for so long that I was noticing all the little signs right now. And when Alex touched the wall first, a roar erupted from our little cheering section—including me.

There was a break in the action, and we all went to get something to eat from the concession stand.

Evan and David walked over to me. I expected they would at some point. Hopefully, this wouldn't get too complicated.

"Hey, man. Are you enjoying the meet?"

"Yeah, I haven't been to a meet like this before. These kids are excellent swimmers. Grace mentioned you attended this swim academy when you were younger."

"I did. When I was twelve. I had Olympic dreams too. Did you play any sports? I feel like I should already know this, but Grace didn't give us a real heads-up about you." Evan laughed. "I didn't get to Google you like I would any man dating my ex who might be around my son. Mac just showed me the info about your companies."

I shrugged. "That sounds reasonable to me. What do you want to know?"

"You look like you played sports..." Evan started.

"Yeah. I was an undersized linebacker who left the NFL after three years. Getting hit like that hurt."

Evan nodded and continued. "You're one of the owners of the Sloane-Wash medical device company? I have heard of them and hope that you all come up with something for some conditions I treat." He laughed. "Can I talk to you about that sometime?"

"Sure. If you have device ideas for different medical procedures in other specialties than those we service right now, I'm glad to listen. It's how we grow. We're trying to establish agreements in different areas with different countries. Let me know—we can bounce ideas off each other."

Evan looked a little surprised at how easily that conversation went. I think he expected me to be territorial, but talking business? I'll talk to anyone. He continued with his questions, and I could see Grace talking with MacKenzie and Ree as she kept tabs on our conversation. I shook my head because it looked like she was about to come rescue me, which I didn't need.

"Thanks, man. How long have you known Grace?"

"About two weeks. This is very new, Evan. We're trying to figure it out."

David jumped in then, a little aggressively. "But you flew down here to spend the weekend with her?" Evan elbowed him. I wondered what was behind that bit of aggression. There was clearly some behind-the-scenes information I wasn't privy to yet.

I squinted at David. "My life has been very busy over the last week and a half. I've flown all over the country because my business partner needed me to take up some slack during a family emergency. So, I make time to see her whenever I can. This weekend worked for both of us. I'm going to give her time with Gabe without me around, though. I have plenty of work to catch up on."

Grace had had enough at this point and came over. "Are you two still questioning my friend?" She put her arm through mine. "I think everyone is going back into the natatorium. Let's go."

I kissed her on the cheek as we walked away. She whispered, "Thank you for handling that. I was afraid David would literally challenge you to a race. He did it to Evan."

"I'm not a bad swimmer or basketball player. I can handle myself."

We smiled at each other, each with our own secrets to keep.

42

grace

The plan was to leave after the next set of races. MacKenzie kept saying something about a Halloween party no one seemed prepared for. And given that we were leaving the Academy around 3 p.m., no one was going to have time to get ready for said party either.

We all stood outside in the parking lot to clarify what we were doing tonight.

Evan shook his head. "I told her we shouldn't call it a party. Just a casual get-together at our house. We'll order some food, we already have drinks, and just chill. We haven't seen each other for a few months and don't get together often enough. Some other friends from our practices will be there too. It's just a chat-and-chill Halloween gathering."

But there was a catch. Trick or treaters. The children in the neighborhood were coming by for their share of Halloween candy. There would be a big bin of candy by the door. Mac asked us all to take turns giving out candy at the front door, so nobody missed out on the party all night. That sounded cool.

Everyone jumped into their chosen vehicles. Luke's driver took us to Evan and Mac's new house in Key Biscayne. I had been here last month. Since then, the renovations had finally been completed, and I couldn't wait to see the finished product. Both of them were thrilled with how it turned out. Looking around, the home was gorgeous—nicely sized, really nice neighborhood, beach a couple of miles away, pool in the backyard. I walked over to Mac and complimented them on their work.

With the decorations and music, the party had a cool vibe. However, I didn't really want to hang out too long tonight. I had other things I'd rather be doing.

Evan hadn't lied. About fifteen to twenty other people from their new jobs or the neighborhood were at the house by the time we got there.

For it not to be a 'party', MacKenzie had ordered a lot of food: pizza, wings, sushi, fries, dips, tacos, and more. She had also looked up recipes for Halloween-themed drinks—three that she selected for her guests.

There was some spooky mood music playing in the background and the vibe of the gathering was sexy-moody. Luke and I had volunteered to take one of the earlier shifts for candy distribution. We took note of the candy in the bin to steal some for ourselves. It was nice to meet a partner who had a sweet tooth too.

There was a barstool in the foyer next to the door. He sat down and I stood in between his legs as we waited for the first group of children to ring the bell. Since we were alone most of the time, Luke and I exchanged multiple greedy kisses while we waited.

The first group of kids hit the stoop.

"I love the costumes these kids are wearing," I noted after we dropped candy into the pumpkins of an alien, a cheerleader, and a Grim Reaper.

"I used to be a ghost most of the time."

"A ghost? Why?" I asked.

"Easy, inexpensive costume. But my mom occasionally would make me a gangster suit or a priest costume if my father had an old suit he couldn't wear anymore." He draped his arms around my hips.

"I can imagine you as a little gangster." I leaned in to kiss him. "Like a little godfather."

"What do you know about The Godfather?" He grinned and grabbed my ass.

David walked over to us and said hi. We didn't separate immediately.

"Excuse me," David said. "I didn't mean to interrupt."

Luke looked back and forth between David and me. "I'm going to get a couple of drinks. Watch the door—more kids are probably coming." He kissed me gently on the lips and left.

David stood in front of me as I settled back on the barstool. "Hi there!"

"Hi! What's up?"

"Your friend seems very nice."

"He is." I paused. This could get messy if I didn't head it off. "Is there anything specific you wanted to talk about? Other than the wedding? We don't have to talk about that. We were drunk off our asses and feeling a certain kind of way. We're cool as in-laws. And we can keep it at that." I looked back to see if Luke was heading back yet.

"You've moved on. So, it was just a one-time thing? Nothing to explore further?" He had an odd look on his face.

I cocked my head at him. "You weren't looking for more, were you? You never called or anything afterwards."

The look cleared. "True. But we were there for each other during a really weird time. We will always have this strange bond, you know. From being the 'others' in their relationship."

I put my hand on his arm. "Yeah. But we can't build a romantic relationship on that. Neither of us wants that. We're close friends who understand each other very well. I don't want to lose that—ever."

"So that's it. You moved on." He repeated it, a little less stridently this time.

"Yes, I have. And I bet you have too." Luke reached us and handed me a fluorescent orange concoction. "What is this?" I asked him cautiously as David looked on.

"A fluorescent piña colada." Luke laughed, taking a sip. "Not bad."

David looked at Luke. "I hear you played in the NFL for a couple of years. I played pro basketball overseas."

The ice broke quickly. They chatted about playing pro sports for a few minutes, then another group of children—teenagers who were costumeless—appeared at the door. I tsk-tsked at them, and they dropped their heads in shame as they continued to hold their bags out for candy.

Brazen, weren't they?

I dumped a little less in their bags than in the costumed kids who had visited.

I turned back to the two men, who were now shooting the shit about the life of a professional athlete.

David looked at me and said, "Hey. I need to talk to MacKenzie. Have fun with the trick or treaters." He dapped up Luke and went back into the family room.

"Did you two have something going on?" Luke asked, watching him walk away. He tapped me on the ass to switch seats again. He sat down, and I leaned on the stool between his legs with my back to him. He wrapped his arms around my waist, his face in my hair. I felt comfortable enough to give him a little detail.

"No, not really. We had a moment after the wedding, commiserating about our exes getting married. Nothing really happened. It was just a moment—a weird moment."

"I thought you and Evan had divorced a long time ago."

"We had. But it was weird—and a little painful—to watch him marry someone else and see how that would affect my role in his life and his family. I knew that intellectually before the wedding and even when David and I were helping them get back together. But then, as they said I do, the evidence was right in my face. It threw me."

He kissed my cheek. "I like that you felt comfortable enough to tell me about that situation. That you could trust me." He kissed my neck—a soft moan and escaped from my mouth. "Hopefully, we can get out of here soon."

I leaned against his chest. "Soon."

And tried not to think about how easily he said the word trust.

43

grace

No one else was coming to cover the door. I think my friends planned it that way. Luke grabbed a plate to get us some food since we'd been trapped waiting for late trick-or-treaters. While we ate and fed each other, Luke called his driver back so we could leave. It was getting late, but children and teenagers were still coming by.

These were older kids—sans costumes—this time. Was there no shame?

We were almost finished with our food when MacKenzie finally released us from door duty. She had Ree in a choke hug and pulled me to the side, leaving Luke talking to Evan, David, and another physician colleague who was a sports fan. He was in heaven with two retired professional athletes and a former almost-Olympian all to himself.

"We have spa time scheduled tomorrow. Are you still coming, Grace?" Mac asked, cutting her eyes over to Luke. "I see you have things to do." She smirked.

"I'll be there. Just tell me what time. Are we still having a house party tomorrow night?" I gave her a hug.

"Yes and no. Since I forgot to tell everyone about costumes for tonight, I want a redo. The house party will be adults-only, day-after-Halloween. No food. Just drinks and music. Real talk. Maybe some spades or gin rummy. Dress sexy or costume—whatever makes you feel good. We're keeping it mature." Her double entendres made her giggle.

"What brought this on? Why a redo?" Ree chimed in. She'd been fairly quiet since arriving because she said she was tired. She'd left the Academy early and went back to the hotel for a nap. But Ree looked like she was perking up now that the night was ending.

"It's going to be a much more intimate gathering tomorrow night with a few more people, and I wanted to have a costume party this year." She looked down.

"Something's up with you. Everything okay?"

"Yeah, everything's fine. Really." Mac shot us both a dazzling smile. "So, are you gonna dress up tomorrow night?"

I shrugged. "I didn't bring costume gear, so we'll do what we can. I need to ask Luke. I don't know if he's prepared either."

"It's easy for guys. I don't think he'd have a problem." Ree added. "I will need the story of how you two met."

"I can only imagine." MacKenzie laughed. "No really. I like him. I wish you two the best."

Tears kicked up in my eyes. I gave her and Ree another hug and said goodbye. As I headed over to Luke, Ree ran to catch me.

"I just wanted to say I hate we haven't gotten to talk much. Let's do better tomorrow, okay?"

I hugged her. I felt grateful all weekend. Healthy, happy child, friends, healthy myself, and a new man. What more could I want?

In the car's back seat, Luke and I kissed all the way to the hotel. He whispered sweet words in my ear, making my heart skip a few beats.

Holding my hand, he kissed each finger one by one. "Your hands are so soft. But I can tell they're strong—your hands have purpose. Saving lives, making your patients' lives better. That's sexy."

And: "I want to kiss you all over. Take our time. Everything about you deserves to be cherished."

But with each kiss, I started feeling apprehensive.

When we entered the lobby, Luke stopped me. He nodded to the desk attendant, who came over with a large, filled basket and an additional hotel key. Before I could look at what was in the basket, Luke leaned over and whispered, "I have a few surprises for you. Do you mind if I put a blindfold on you? I promise you're safe—I won't let anything happen to you."

I nodded in wonder as he removed the satiny blindfold from the basket and slipped it on me. We got on the elevator immediately, but I could tell we weren't going to the room I'd originally reserved because we went to a higher floor. The elevator stopped on the top floor. Holding my hand tightly, he guided me off and opened a door.

The balcony door was open—I could hear the ocean and feel the breeze. There was smooth Latin jazz playing in the background. He gently untied my blindfold and put his arm around my shoulders.

"Welcome to the Penthouse Suite."

I looked around the lavishly decorated room with dozens of roses placed in both bedrooms, living area, bathroom, and the balcony—which was huge. There were candles everywhere, rose petals in a path to both beds. Champagne on ice. A half dozen cupcakes, fondue with fresh strawberries and other food I didn't even have a chance to look at. I saw our luggage by the door.

He'd upgraded our room.

I looked back at him with a huge grin. "How did you get this done?"

"I never reveal my secrets," he said, leading me to the bathroom with the most gorgeous tub I'd seen in a hotel, and I was a tub connoisseur. I audibly gasped to his great delight.

"This is amazing!" I threw myself into his arms.

"Hang on. One more thing..." He led me to the balcony. There was a massage table in the middle.

"Who's the masseuse?"

"Me," he said, kissing my neck. "I know you want to freshen up first."

"I just need a minute," I said over my shoulder. As I slid into the bathroom, I began to get nervous. I'd dreamed about this moment, but now that it was here, I was petrified. Looking at myself in the mirror, I turned a critical eye.

I'm forty-two. I had a baby thirteen years ago. I'm near my original weight, but my body isn't what it was. Stretch marks, a little pooch.

He's a former pro athlete and billionaire who's had his pick of beautiful women. Would he be disappointed when he actually sees me naked? We'd been playing around before with no real full view.

I realized I was putting pressure on myself that I never did with anyone else. Maybe because I really wanted this to mean something?

I stripped down to my matching bra and panties. I had an IUD and he had a vasectomy. Pregnancy was off the table.

Then I heard him standing on the other side of the bathroom door. "Are you okay in there?"

I giggled nervously. "I'm fine. Just freshening up."

"Hey, if we're moving too fast, we can wait…"

I opened the door immediately. "No." Then I blushed. "No. I'm fine."

I'd put my robe back on. Tied tightly. Trying to calm my nerves. Standing shyly in the middle of the room, unsure where to go or what to do.

He smiled and handed me a glass of champagne. "Would you like a massage?"

I nodded and he led me to the table. I took a couple of sips of champagne—God, that was good—and took off my robe before laying on my stomach.

"Hey. While your underwear is incredibly sexy, it has to come off." I nodded as Luke draped a towel around my midsection, as I struggled with my bra.

"Let me help you with this," he said, reaching under the towel and sliding my thong down my hips slowly, letting his fingers drag along my ass and inner thighs. I squirmed with anticipation.

He started with my shoulders, down my back to my waist, ass, legs. The most sensual massage. I was like jelly after about fifteen minutes. He rolled me over with little help from me. The towel had gapped open but I didn't care. He massaged my shoulders and legs. Then he bent my knees and slid me toward the end of the table. Both legs went over his shoulders.

"Are you comfortable?"

I nodded.

The first contact of his mouth with my clit jolted me off the massage table.

"You taste even better than last time." After the time in my kitchen, I'd decided that oral sex was something Luke enjoyed and would probably do every day if he got the chance. I was glad to be the recipient because what he was doing to my core had to be illegal. Lips, tongue, teeth, fingers—my senses were on overload. The cool breeze on my skin, warmth enveloping my body, waves crashing both on the beach and throughout my body. Crying out his name at climax, too wrung out to remember I was on the balcony or care who heard me.

After the waves slowed, Luke picked me up and took me to bed.

Kissing my face, he whispered in my ear, "I'm not done yet. I want to feel you come that hard around my dick. Can you do that for me?"

I nodded.

Luke proceeded to drown me in sensations. He kissed and caressed my entire body, learning my curves, setting my skin on fire. I rolled him on his back to return the favor.

He tried to restrain his passion as I explored him, allowing me time. His body was beautiful—tight muscles, smooth brown skin, an African shield tattoo on his back, a few scars from football. And I finally got a good look at his dick, which was glorious. Long, thick, veiny, pulsating. It felt good in my hand as I slid my palm up and down his shaft, watching how he responded. He exhaled loudly and squirmed.

"That feels so good. But I need you on top. Put yourself on my dick."

He didn't have to tell me twice.

I wanted him to fill me, move me, send me rocketing out of my skin, and hold me gently as I returned to earth. I wanted to see him lose control because of me.

I put the tip at my opening and lowered myself so just the tip was inside. Although I was wet, there was a twinge of pain. He saw me wince.

"Hey. You okay?"

"I'm fine. Just have to get used to you."

"You will."

I lowered myself to the hilt. He filled me completely—I had to adjust to his size. His dick felt so perfect I didn't move initially. Just wanted to feel him inside me for a moment. This feeling alone was almost enough to send me over.

Luke flipped me on my back. Then he started moving inside me slowly, gently at first. Then with increased speed and force. With each thrust, he hit the spot that made my toes curl. Driving me closer to oblivion.

"Do you want me to stop? Tell me what you want."

"Harder. Right there... Don't stop. Don't you dare stop," I gasped out.

He laughed low. "I knew you'd be like this. Let go for me. I can feel you contracting around me."

With each thrust, I could feel the waves building, intensifying and spreading. I clutched at his back, digging my nails in as I felt my world careening away. Both our breathing grew rapid. I was almost there—I didn't realize I was whimpering, begging for release.

He took my right leg and pushed my knee against my chest, opening me more. The next thrust hit my clit and I climaxed.

Luke entwined his fingers with mine as my core contracted tightly around him. In my haze, I could feel his movements become more erratic as he chased his own orgasm. As he came, he squeezed my hand and said my name: Grace. Collapsing on me, he kissed me on the lips then dropped his head on my shoulder. I tried to brush my wet curly hair out of my face but my limbs felt heavy and spent.

\#

It took both of us a while to fully collect ourselves from that incredible high. This wasn't my first orgasm from sex. But it was the first time I felt in sync with my partner.

Pulling out of me, he pulled me into the crook of his arm tight against his body, throwing one leg over mine.

He whispered "my Grace" again, pulling me closer.

My heart.

Once he gathered himself, he cupped my face and said, "All day, every day."

I should tell him. Right now. About Harmony. About the matchmaker. About everything.

But I didn't want to break this moment. Didn't want to see his face change when he realized I'd been lying.

So, I kissed him instead.

And buried the guilt a little deeper.

44

luke/grace

luke

We had a quickie in the bathroom around 3 a.m. when she accidentally woke me up. We fucked facing the mirror and then Grace and I made love again as the sun came up.

I kissed her shoulder as she rolled over sleepily and smiled at me. "Hi!"

The way the early morning light hit her face made her look almost aflame. And I made sure every part of her was actually on fire. I took longer this time, trying to know every part of her intimately. Grace was more impatient with my slow build.

"We have plenty of time to learn each other. I want you inside me now." She gently caressed my shaft, sending chills down my spine.

"You're bossy. I like it. Roll over on your back—your wish is my command."

I entered her more slowly this time so I could savor how tight she was around me and how we fit together. I watched her as I entered to see her expression. Lifting one leg to place on my shoulder, which improved my access.

With each thrust, I could feel her coming closer to climax.

"Eyes on me. Eyes on me. I want you to see me when you come," I said, because I was almost there myself. I knew once she came, the contractions would send me over.

And it did. She clutched the sheets and gasped, arching her back. It was so sexy because she kept her eyes on me. It drove me crazy. I couldn't get deep enough, close enough.

Was this what everyone was talking about? I'd had a lot of sex over forty-four years. But I felt like I couldn't get enough of her. I could make love to her all day, every day. Sit and talk to her for the rest of the time. She was like a drug.

Grace curled up against my side. "Are you okay?" I asked, kissing her forehead.

"Honestly, I feel fine. But while I was nervous before, you made sure I was comfortable. I really appreciate that. Thank you."

"Honestly, I've been dreaming about this since I first saw you. If I were still the no-relationship guy, I would have dated you without expectations for the long term. Obviously, the sex would have been incredible. But I would have missed out on *you*. You're beautiful inside and out. I don't know what I'm doing, but I'm in for the ride."

She smiled drowsily at me.

My chest cracked open right then.

I should tell her. About Harmony. About knowing from the beginning.

But she was falling asleep in my arms, trusting me, and I couldn't bring myself to ruin it.

After a few minutes, I could hear her snoring lightly. I slid my arm from under her head so I could reach my phone. I called room service to order breakfast—waffles, eggs, bacon, juice.

I couldn't fall back asleep as my mind raced, trying to understand what was happening to me. After making love to Grace last night and this morning, I really didn't want to be at the house party tonight. I didn't want to go anywhere—just camp out in this suite with her.

Waking up next to her made me feel new feelings—ones I'd heard of but never really experienced. My heart had seemed very insulated before, but somehow this woman had claimed hold of me and wasn't letting go.

And I was still lying to her. Every moment we got deeper, the lie got bigger.

I was going to lose her when the truth came out. I knew that now.

But I still wasn't ready to tell her.

Around nine, Grace's phone started ringing. It took her a few moments to answer. MacKenzie was calling about their spa trip before they went back to the Academy. She was picking Grace up, so she needed to be downstairs within forty-five minutes.

I was going to skip that session, so Grace could spend time with her son and friends without me hovering. We decided to grab dinner afterwards and head to the costume party at MacKenzie and Evan's tonight. I was on my own today. I knew one thing I was going to do—handle the costume portion of the evening.

Grace padded into the bathroom, wrapped in a robe, to take a quick shower. I tried to make a plan for my morning and afternoon, since I had studies and paperwork to review—there was never rest for the wicked. But my mind kept wandering to the woman in the shower.

Even though we'd spent the last twelve hours together, she came out of the shower still wrapped in a robe. I sat in bed watching her gather clothes to carry into the other bedroom.

"You're getting dressed in the other room?"

She blushed. "I didn't want to bother you. I thought you might want to get some rest." She smiled. "You did put in work this morning. And I need to remain focused," she said lightly over her shoulder as she went into the other room.

Probably best if she dressed somewhere else. She might not make that spa date.

grace

I met MacKenzie and Ree in the lobby. I felt ecstatic about last night, but I had to admit I was sore. There were some things I hadn't done physically in a long time.

Maybe spending time in a spa would help with that. Hopefully. Fortunately, I didn't look like I'd been thoroughly fucked as I walked up to my friends.

"There's a wonderful day spa near the Academy. We're doing a short wellness journey today. If we had more time, we could do a full day."

"Well, maybe next time I come back we can," I added.

"I just wanted us to have time to relax and talk. Especially because today is going to be adults-only."

"Can you stop saying that?" Ree lightly punched her shoulder.

We arrived at the spa and checked in for the Route to Reinvigoration. MacKenzie hadn't lied. The place was absolutely gorgeous. All white stone and glass and waterfalls. The young woman at the front desk was as peaceful as her surroundings and quickly led us to the women's dressing room.

Handing each of us a towel, robe, and slippers, the woman bowed and disappeared. We changed quickly and waited until the next attendant led us to the healing pool and sauna room.

The attendant looked at Mac. "Ma'am, we have your special requests ready. No hot stone massage, no deep tissue, avoiding certain essential oils per your instructions."

Ree and I looked at each other. What?

"Perfect. Thank you," Mac said smoothly.

We waited until the attendant left.

Ree and I stood in front of Mac so she couldn't move forward. "Are you pregnant?" Ree hissed.

MacKenzie grinned. "Maybe I am. I'm not taking any chances. I just want to spend time with my friends and relax." She walked around us and sat on the edge of the heated pool.

Ree looked at me and whispered in my ear, "I wouldn't be surprised. From what Mac told me about their sex life, the poor egg never stood a chance."

I scrunched up my face in horror. "Remember who you're talking to. I do not need to think about how they're having sex or not." I shuddered. "It's just too fucking weird. But what you say is probably true, I'll give you that."

To protect my friendship with Mac, I tried to steer clear of those discussions because they were too bizarre, given that he was my ex. I probably knew more than Ree did just from familiarity. But surprisingly, the topic of a potential new baby didn't hurt my feelings. Perhaps I was moving forward a little.

Ree elbowed me. "You're feeling pretty feisty and foul-mouthed today. With a little limp. Seems like you might need to be careful yourself." Ree pointed at my chest, then went to sit by Mac, offering premature congratulations because Mac wouldn't give a firm yes or no on a possible pregnancy.

I opened my robe and looked down at my chest. A fairly large hickey was visible and must have been obvious under the shirt I wore—and planned to wear — to the Academy.

Oh my God, how did I miss that this morning! And I couldn't wear that shirt because Gabe would see it and God knows what he'd think or say.

I sat down on the other side of Mac, beet red.

"I have shirts you can wear," Mac replied, slipping off her robe and sliding into the pool.

Ree and I looked at Mac and then at my chest. The size discrepancy was obvious.

Mac pursed her lips and splashed water in our direction. "I *do* have shirts you can wear. What the hell—you two are messy as fuck this morning. Is it because someone else got fucked this morning?"

I went whatever shade was beyond beet red. As embarrassed as I was, I still gave a smartass answer. "You started it with the 'maybe I'm pregnant' shit. We follow your lead. And we can be messier... don't write checks that your ass can't cash."

We all looked at each other and burst out laughing.

"Who are you? My grandmother? Damn!" Ree barely got the sentence out.

And that was the end of any relaxation at the spa. We kept bursting into peals of laughter—a little punch drunk. As she served us mineral water and fruit, the attendant kept glancing at us with a barely controlled grin and suggested we take it down a notch or two so as not to disturb the other guests.

I'm surprised they didn't kick us out.

45

grace

Watching our children race each other was one of the most nerve-wracking things I'd experienced as a parent.

I felt sorry for Evan. Obviously, he was rooting for our son, but he couldn't appear to completely dismiss his stepson if he wanted a happy life at home.

I asked him about it. "So, how are you handling this?"

MacKenzie had given me a button-up shirt to swap out the revealing one I'd originally walked out of the hotel with. But it was obviously his wife's, so Evan was confused as hell.

"I'm rooting for Gabe, of course. I wish Alex well."

Mac heard him and elbowed him. "It's okay. David's rooting for our son, too. I have matured in my relationship. Clap, please."

Evan laughed and kissed her lightly. "But what's going on here?" He pointed at my shirt. "Why are you wearing my wife's shirt? And where is your boyfriend?"

"I needed a fresh shirt. She was kind enough to let me borrow one. As for Luke, he's working. But he's coming tonight. Oh my God—did I just refer to him as my boyfriend?"

"I think you did. Really, how long has this been going on, and how serious is it?" Mac leaned over Evan to see my face as she quizzed me.

"Only a couple of weeks. And we'll see how serious it is." I was hedging like hell, which they could tell.

"Given that he flew his private jet down here to see you, and didn't you say he flew to San Francisco for a day to see you, I think he's pretty serious."

"Like I said, we'll see." But at this point, I was smiling. I was hoping it was serious, even as I got nervous about it. I wasn't used to a guy being the driver of the relationship.

Probably because I picked guys I felt I needed to fix or manage. Luke didn't appear to need me to convince him he enjoyed being around me. Which was what I wanted but still scared the shit out of me. I was in the great unknown.

And I still hadn't told him about Harmony.

About any of it.

Tomorrow. I'd tell him tomorrow on the plane.

Gabe won the race by a touch. He was a short-distance specialist after all.

46

grace/luke

Back at the hotel, Luke was waiting with the kind of focused attention that made my stomach flutter. When I walked in, he stood and gave me a kiss that reminded me why I'd been thinking about him all afternoon.

"Just so you know, I've been thinking about you," he said against my lips.

"Am I naked in these thoughts?"

He pulled back, studying my face. "Among other things. I thought about having dinner with you, watching the sunset together. Actually talking to you about something other than how badly I want to get you naked."

"Oh." The surprise in my voice was embarrassing.

"You seem shocked that I want more than your body."

"No. Of course not. Sorry. I'm still figuring out how this works." I sat beside him on the couch, dropping my purse. "How was your afternoon?"

"Productive. Kyle's handling the Boston situation well." He gestured to his laptop setup. "How was the spa? And Gabe's race?"

"The spa was the opposite of relaxing—we couldn't stop laughing. Watching the boys compete was nerve-wracking, but Gabe won, which felt like a victory for both of us." I paused, suddenly self-conscious. "The downside is I have a very visible hickey."

Luke looked appropriately sheepish. "I'll be more strategic about placement next time. Though I love marking you."

He pulled me into his lap with an ease that suggested he'd been thinking about this moment. "You've completely destroyed what little restraint I had.

I don't want to overwhelm you, but being close to you, talking to you, just looking at you—it's becoming necessary for my sanity."

I touched his face, feeling the rough texture of his beard against my palm. "I spent today thinking about how different this feels. Usually I'm the one managing relationships, trying to anticipate what the other person needs. I'm not used to someone who seems genuinely content with who I am right now."

"Content?" He leaned me back and kissed me with enough intensity to make me forget we had somewhere to be. "Grace, nothing about you is merely content. You fascinate me."

The words lodged in my throat. It felt too perfect, which terrified me. I understood it was possible to find someone who truly wanted you—I'd just watched Evan and Mac prove it. But accepting that it could happen to me required a leap of faith I wasn't sure I was ready for.

"What am I wearing tonight? Mac keeps emphasizing 'grown and sexy.'"

"I took the liberty of having options sent up." He gestured toward the bedroom. "We can adjust if nothing works."

The rack held elegant dresses and several legitimate costumes that were significantly more provocative than anything I'd worn in years.

I held up the Queen of Hearts outfit. "This is either perfect or completely inappropriate."

"I don't know your friends well enough to judge Mac's expectations. Want to try it on?"

It pushed every comfort zone I had, but something about the way Luke looked at me made me feel capable of carrying it off. I called Ree for a reality check.

"Graves here."

"That greeting makes you sound like you're announcing a death."

"Useful in my line of work. What's up?"

"Costume advice. Are we actually doing this grown and sexy theme, or should I play it safe?"

"We're doing it. This might be our last chance if Mac is pregnant like we suspect. I'm going Catwoman—tight, strategic, but tasteful. You?"

"The Queen of Hearts. More daring than usual."

"If your man approves, own it. We're only in our forties once."

After hanging up, I looked at Luke, who was watching me with an expression I couldn't quite read.

"The Queen of Hearts it is."

luke

Grace and I had dinner on the balcony, lingering over wine as the sun set over the ocean. These quiet moments felt essential before whatever chaos Mac had planned. Her increasingly unhinged texts throughout the afternoon suggested we were in for an interesting evening.

"What's gotten into her?" I asked, after Grace showed me a message about mandatory spades tournaments.

"Pregnancy hormones, I'm betting. She's not usually this outspoken or competitive. Early pregnancy can make you feel slightly insane."

I studied her profile as she looked out at the water. "Any regrets about not having more children?"

"The doctors strongly advised against another pregnancy after Gabe. Emergency C-section, placental abruption—we almost didn't make it." Her voice grew quiet. "So, no more pregnancies for me. But I'd be open to other ways of expanding a family."

"I never wanted biological children. Always thought that made me unusual."

"From what I've seen, you're creating more opportunities for kids than most biological parents do. Your foundation work, the mentoring—that's real impact."

I appreciated that she'd listened when I'd mentioned it in passing. "Most people don't see it that way."

"Most people aren't thinking clearly about what children actually need."

We dozed together on the balcony until it was time to get ready, and I found myself thinking that this—this quiet domesticity with her—felt more natural than anything I'd ever experienced.

After Grace chose the Queen of Hearts costume (my favorite, though I didn't influence her decision), I showed her my matching king outfit.

"Very theatrical," she said, giggling as she examined my crown and scepter.

"I want everyone to know you're my queen tonight."

"I need to shower before we go."

I followed her toward the bathroom, but she pressed her hand to my chest. "Alone, or we'll never leave this room."

Her logic was sound but watching her walk away had me mentally cataloging exactly what I planned to do to that costume later.

The evening stretched ahead of us, full of possibilities, and I realized I was looking forward to showing Grace off to her friends almost as much as I was anticipating getting her out of that outfit afterward.

47

grace

By the time we arrived at Evan and Mac's, I needed to readjust my costume and fix my hair. Luke had found creative ways to access what he wanted during our car ride, leaving me breathless and slightly disheveled. The driver's careful attention to the privacy screen and the small stack of towels near the bar suggested this wasn't his first rodeo with this type of evening entertainment occurring in the back of his limo.

I'd never climaxed in front of another person – someone who was not participating -- before. The thrill was addictive.

When we finally made it out of the car, I had to admit we looked incredible together. The Queen and King of Hearts—theatrical but undeniably striking.

Ree approached in a skin-tight leather bodysuit with strategic cutouts that showcased her runner's physique. "I think we were right about Mac," she whispered. "Her costume is a skeleton with two little skeletons in the belly area."

Mac appeared beside us as if summoned. "Since you're discussing my news—yes, Evan and I are pregnant. Still early, so discretion appreciated. I couldn't resist the announcement costume for you two."

"Congratulations!" I hugged her, surprised by how genuinely happy I felt. No jealousy, no complicated feelings—just joy for friends who'd found their way back to each other.

When Luke joined us, Mac immediately shifted into interrogation mode.

"Do you have children, Luke?"

"No biological children. I was certified as a foster parent years ago, but my travel schedule wouldn't have been fair to a child. I do hire kids who are aging out of the system and run a mentoring foundation."

"That's impressive," Evan said, appearing with drinks. "I'd love to hear more about that. Perhaps there's a chance of expanding that work down here."

"Later," Luke said, sliding his arm around my waist. "Right now, I want to dance with Grace. She looks incredible tonight."

Mac's playlist was everything she'd promised—Parliament Funkadelic, Prince, Earth Wind & Fire, all the music that had soundtracked our childhoods. Luke was a revelation on the dance floor, moving with the kind of natural rhythm that probably should have been illegal.

"Miss Merci made sure her boy could lead a lady properly," he said, pulling me close as we swayed to a slower song. "Salsa, merengue, waltz, line dance—whatever you want. But even if you never want to dance, I'm still your man."

I would have stayed in his arms all night, but Mac conscripted me for a hand of Spades. Normally I took the game seriously, but Luke's hands on my shoulders, his breath on my neck, made concentration impossible.

After I reneged for the first time in my life—much to Evan's loud amusement—I abandoned the card table for more dancing. Luke's hands never left me, and I could feel the promise of the rest of our evening in every touch.

The driver was waiting with fresh towels when we finally called for pickup. Luke's mouth on me during the ride back to the hotel was its own kind of heaven, and by the time we made it upstairs, I was ready to show him exactly what I thought of being his queen.

The night was just beginning.

48

grace

Sunday morning started with crisis management. At 6 a.m., my phone buzzed with a flight cancellation that would have meant missing my time with Gabe entirely. The replacement flight left too early for our planned brunch—unacceptable when I'd only seen my son for barely ten hours this month.

I tried to search for alternatives without waking Luke, but he trapped me in bed with his arm around my waist.

"Flight problems?" he mumbled against my shoulder.

"They want to put me on an earlier flight. I'd miss seeing Gabe."

"Fly back with me."

I turned to face him, confused. "Don't you have meetings in Chicago?"

"Kyle's handling Boston, remember? I'm going back to the coast today. I assumed you were coming with me."

The relief was overwhelming. "What time?"

"Whenever you want. Spend time with your son. Just give me an estimate so I can tell the pilot."

Tears sprang to my eyes. "You're saving my visit with him."

"I'm looking out for what matters to you." He pulled me closer, and I could feel his morning erection against my hip. "Though I should mention—I plan to properly introduce you to flying private. You'll need those anxiety meds, but not for the reasons you think."

The promise in his voice made me breathless. "I have a couple hours before I need to leave."

"Good. You seem stressed about this flight situation. Let me help you relax."

What followed was slow, thorough, and left me wondering how I'd survived forty-two years without this level of physical connection. By the time Luke was finished with me, I was boneless and completely his.

Visiting Gabe was everything I'd hoped for. My son was waiting outside the Academy in the teenage uniform of jean shorts and a hoodie, full of stories about his races, his friends, and the academic challenges that were actually engaging him for the first time in years.

But watching him across our restaurant table—noting the deepening of his voice, the way he'd grown into his features—hit me with devastating clarity.

I was missing everything. Voice changes, growth spurts, the daily conversations that shape a person. Ten hours this month with the child I'd fought so hard to bring into the world.

"Are you planning to stay at the Academy another year?" I asked, trying to keep my voice steady.

"Probably. The coaches think I have real potential, and I like the structure here." He looked so much like Evan, but taller, broader. "Why?"

"Just planning ahead." But inside, my heart was breaking. Another year of missing his life, of being a weekend visitor in my own son's childhood.

When he asked about my dating life—casual, the way teenagers probe for information they're not sure they want—I deflected. How could I explain that I was falling in love with someone when I wasn't even sure I could stay in the same state as my child?

The ride back to the hotel after dropping Gabe off was a blur of tears and tissue boxes courtesy of a sympathetic driver. I wasn't just crying because I missed my son—I was mourning the impossible choices that seemed to define every aspect of my life.

How do you choose between love and motherhood when both feel essential to who you are?

49

grace/luke

grace

I cried during takeoff, a combination of flight anxiety and emotional overload from the weekend. Luke noticed immediately, setting aside his work to sit beside me.

"Talk to me. What's going on?"

"I can't miss another year of Gabe's life." The words came out broken. "But that affects everything we're building. I don't know how to choose between being his mother and being with you."

"You shouldn't have to choose." He pulled me closer. "We're two weeks into this, Grace. We don't have to solve everything right now."

"But I do have to solve it. I can't keep splitting myself between San Francisco and Miami, and I won't ask you to rearrange your entire life for someone you barely know."

"What if I want to rearrange my life?" His voice was quiet, serious. "What if you're not someone I barely know, but someone I've been waiting for without realizing it?"

I studied his face, looking for signs that he was just saying what he thought I wanted to hear. Instead, I saw the same certainty I felt when I looked at him—terrifying and absolute.

"You're remarkably calm for someone whose girlfriend is having a breakdown at thirty thousand feet."

He laughed, the sound rumbling through his chest. "I spent my teens and part of my twenties angry at the world and my father. Didn't solve anything, just made me miserable. Now I know what I want—I'm doing work that matters, I have enough money for several lifetimes, and I found the woman of my dreams. Why would I be anything but calm?"

"Even when that woman comes with a teenage son and geographical complications?"

"Especially then." He swung my legs across his lap. "Now, I believe I promised to distract you from your flight anxiety."

What followed was my official induction into the Mile-High Club—and several other memberships I hadn't known existed. By the time we landed, I was thoroughly relaxed and slightly scandalized by my own behavior.

luke

Grace slept against me for most of the flight, and I spent the time studying her face in the changing light. She was classically beautiful, but it was her expressiveness that captivated me—the way emotions played across her features, how her entire being seemed to engage with the world around her.

And something she didn't know about me yet. The conversation where I explained about Harmony, about knowing she was working with a matchmaker, about the information I'd had before our first date—that conversation was coming, and I had no idea how it would go.

I'd been waiting for the right moment. Now I wondered if I'd waited too long, if the foundation of lies would make it impossible for her to trust that my feelings were real.

I'd finally found the woman I wanted to spend my life with, and I might lose her because I'd been too afraid to tell her the complete truth from the beginning.

Looking down at her sleeping face, I made a promise to myself and to her: no more secrets. Whatever it cost me, she deserved honesty. Even if it meant losing the best thing that had ever happened to me.

The plane began its descent toward San Francisco, carrying us back to reality and all the complications waiting there.

50

grace

After Miami, Luke and I settled into what felt like a real relationship. Tuesday nights at his place, Thursday nights at mine, weekends together—the rhythm of two people consciously making space for each other in lives that were already full.

His house in the Marina District was everything I'd expected from a successful entrepreneur—gorgeous views, designer everything, a chef who left perfectly prepared meals in the freezer. But it was meeting Fitz that sealed the deal. Luke's chocolate lab greeted me with paws to the shoulders and immediate devotion, the kind of unconditional affection that made me understand why Luke had rearranged his life around this dog's needs.

"He likes you," Luke said, watching me get thoroughly sniffed and approved.

"How can you tell?"

"He hasn't tried to steal your shoes yet. That's his usual move with women he's not sure about."

We took Fitz for runs around Luke's neighborhood, showered together afterward, ate dinner prepared by his chef while discussing everything from neurosurgical innovations with Evan to the best wine pairings for Tuesday nights. It felt domestic in a way I hadn't experienced since the early days of my marriage—but without the underlying tension of trying to be someone I wasn't.

Thursday nights at my house were different but equally comfortable. Luke would arrive exhausted from meetings or calls with Kyle, collapse on my couch, and let me take care of him. I'd prep dinner before my afternoon patients, pour wine, and watch him decompress in my space. Sometimes he'd fall asleep during football games, and I'd cover him with a blanket, oddly satisfied by this evidence that he felt safe enough to be vulnerable in my home.

Friday morning brought coffee in bed, lazy lovemaking, and the kind of pillow talk that made me understand why people wrote romance novels. I was reading one, actually—something I'd grabbed at the airport during one trip with Gabe—and kept thinking that this kind of connection didn't happen to real people.

Except it was happening to me.

The only disruption in our perfect routine was my family. Celeste called repeatedly Friday morning while Luke was on a call with Kyle, and I ignored her with the dedication of someone who'd learned that boundaries required enforcement.

When my mother called—using the universal code for 'your sister is making me crazy'—I knew I was trapped.

"Family dinner tomorrow," she announced. "Everyone's expected."

"Can I bring someone?" The question slipped out before I could stop it.

"Bring whoever you want. Maybe having outsiders will keep the temperature down."

After I hung up, Luke appeared with coffee and a knowing smile. "Let me guess—I just got voluntold for family dinner?"

"You could say no. Celeste is in town, which means there will be drama."

"And miss the chance to see you navigate family politics? I wouldn't dream of it."

That afternoon, while Luke worked and I caught up on patient notes, I found myself thinking about how seamlessly he'd integrated into my life. He got along with my friends, my ex-husband, my brother. He somehow managed to make even my most mundane routines feel special.

It was terrifying how quickly I'd gotten used to having him around. How much I looked forward to his calls, his texts, the way he looked at me like I was the most fascinating woman in the world.

Because the truth was, I was falling in love with him. Hard, fast, and completely against every rational instinct I'd developed since my divorce. And for the first time in years, I was allowing myself to believe that maybe, just maybe, I deserved this kind of happiness.

The family dinner would be a test—not of Luke, who I already knew could handle anything, but of whether I was ready to fully commit to this thing between us. Ready to stop protecting myself and start building something real.

Saturday couldn't come fast enough.

51

luke

Saturday morning arrived with the kind of anticipation that meant everything was about to change, though I didn't know it yet.

Grace and I had planned a full day—the Ferry Street Market, followed by my regular chess humiliation courtesy of Kyle, then dinner with her family. It was the kind of domestic routine that would have terrified me six months ago. Now it felt like the foundation of something I wanted to build my life around.

"You realize Kyle is going to destroy you in front of me," Grace said, selecting a gray dress and boots since we wouldn't be returning before Berkeley. "Doesn't that bother you?"

"I must really trust that you're not going anywhere if I'm willing to let you watch me get systematically dismantled by my best friend."

She'd checked with me multiple times about the family dinner, making sure I was comfortable meeting her parents under potentially volatile circumstances. I wasn't worried—I was good with parents, and besides, she'd already met my mother under considerably more stressful conditions.

The Ferry Street Market was Grace's Saturday ritual, and I found myself charmed by her interactions with vendors who clearly knew her well. We were discussing bringing my chef here for inspiration when someone behind us called her name.

"Grace?"

We both turned. Grace's face immediately shifted into polite wariness, which put me on alert. A man about our age stood there with the kind of smile that suggested he thought he was owed something.

"Curtis. Hello." Her tone could have frozen wine.

I slid my arm around her shoulders, a protective gesture that felt entirely natural.

"Haven't seen you around for a few weeks," Curtis said, his eyes tracking my movement. "I see you've been busy."

Grace's posture changed completely. "Curtis, this is Luke. We met here last month—he lives in Oakland. How have you been?"

"I thought you were going to call me." He looked directly at me. "But I see you're staying on the bougie side of things."

Grace's exhale was controlled but sharp. "Thanks for confirming my initial impression. We have somewhere to be." She turned to leave, clearly wanting distance from this man.

"Of course you do," he called after us. "These women won't give a regular brother a fair shake."

Once we were out of earshot, Grace was quick to clarify. "I had coffee with him once. Fifteen minutes I'll never get back."

"He won't bother you again," I said, meaning it completely. Something about her trust in me, the way she'd immediately sought the protection of my presence, made me want to promise her safety from all the Curtis's of the world.

"Tu es mienne. Je protégerai ton cœur."

The words came from somewhere deeper than conscious thought. A promise I'd never made to anyone except my mother.

Kyle demolished me at chess, as expected, but seemed frustrated that the match lasted longer than usual.

"Grace must be your good-luck charm," he said afterward. "Jada wants to meet her soon. She doesn't believe you actually found someone who tolerates you."

"Why would that be so hard to believe? Luke seems perfectly reasonable to me," Grace asked with a smile.

Kyle laughed but quicky got serious and said, "You have a point. I have to confess—he is the closest thing I have to a brother. He means a lot to me. Be good to him, please." He looked away as he gathered his belongings to leave.

Grace suddenly looked as overwhelmed as I felt by the emotion in his words and voice.

I could feel it – we were both deep in this now. But I also knew we were both keeping secrets – mine more devastating than hers. Bu now, I realized that there was no good time to tell her. And if there had been, I missed it. I remained hopeful that this would work out...

Somehow.

Driving to Berkeley, I found myself thinking about the domesticity of the day—how natural it felt to include Grace in my routines, how easily she'd integrated into the rhythms of my life. When she apologized for volunteering me for potential family drama, I realized I was looking forward to it.

"Your mother will love me," I assured her. "She wants to see you happy."

"Are you nervous?" she asked as we pulled up to her parents' house.

"Should I be?"

Her sister's rental car was already in the driveway, and I watched Grace steel herself for whatever confrontation awaited. But as we walked to the door, I found myself thinking that this—supporting her through family complexity—was exactly what I wanted to be doing for the rest of my life.

Her mother answered the door and gave me the kind of appreciative once-over that would have embarrassed Grace under other circumstances. But when her father appeared and immediately started discussing Sloane-Wash with the enthusiasm of someone who'd been following our work for years, I knew the evening would go well.

Even Celeste, after some initial provocation about Grace's dating patterns, settled into something approaching civility once she realized I wasn't there to judge anyone.

Watching Grace navigate her family dynamics—the way she deflected her sister's comments, the obvious affection between her and her parents and her and Vic Jr—I saw her in complete context. This was a woman with deep roots, complex relationships, people who loved her fiercely and imperfectly.

Driving home afterward, her hand on my thigh tracing patterns that were making concentration difficult, I realized the day had been a kind of test I hadn't known I was taking.

"We had dinner with my parents," she said. "I think tradition demands we make out in the car afterward."

By the time we reached my garage, she'd already shed her underwear. What followed was urgent, desperate, and felt like a claiming on both sides. When she sank down onto me in the driver's seat of my car, her hand on my cheek, I saw forever in her eyes.

It was the last perfect day before everything changed.

52

grace

The week following dinner at my parents' house settled into a rhythm that felt almost too good to be real. Luke traveled briefly—Boston for follow-up meetings, preparations for a ski trip that would combine work with client entertainment. But even when he was gone, his presence lingered in my house, in my routines, in the way I found myself planning my days around his schedule.

I should have been happy. I was happy. But there was a part of me waiting for the inevitable complication, the revelation that would prove this was all too perfect to last.

When Autumn called Wednesday afternoon while I was luxuriating in a rare bath on my day off, I knew my period of blissful avoidance was over.

"So, she lives," Autumn said without preamble. "This is completely predictable behavior from you."

"What are you talking about?" Though I knew exactly what she meant.

"You're obviously getting thoroughly satisfied by someone right now. When you're between relationships, you call constantly—checking in, making plans, needing reassurance. But the moment you start getting regular dick, you disappear completely." She paused for effect. "We set you up with a matchmaker, you go on some initial dates, then vanish. I need details. How did this work out?"

"It's complicated."

"Everything's complicated with you. Details about the matchmaking process. Come on—you know all my intimate business. Share yours."

"We don't need to share every detail of our lives, Autumn."

"Do I need to call Harmony directly and ask how you're progressing?"

The suggestion made my stomach clench. "Don't do that. She doesn't know about my current situation."

Silence on the other end, followed by a sharp intake of breath.

"So, this man isn't through the matchmaker? Grace, what the hell? Please tell me you haven't gone back to someone we already ruled out. Or is this the phone-destroying incident from that building?"

I could hear her moving around, probably looking for her shoes. "I'm coming over. We're not handling this conversation over the phone."

"I suppose I can't avoid this forever. Come over. But promise me you won't contact Harmony until I explain."

An hour later, I found myself trying to explain to Autumn how I'd fallen in love with someone I'd met by accident on the same day I'd committed to professional matchmaking services.

"Let me understand this," Autumn said, sitting across from me in my living room. "You literally collided with this man in the lobby of the matchmaker's building?"

"Knocked his phone right out of his hand."

"And you've been seeing him for a month without telling your matchmaker?"

"Yes."

"While paying for services you're not using?"

"Yes."

She stared at me with the expression of someone trying to solve a particularly frustrating puzzle. "Grace, do you understand how this looks? You paid for professional help finding love, then got distracted by the first attractive man you bumped into?"

"It wasn't a distraction. This is real."

"Real enough that you're hiding it from the woman you hired to help you find exactly this?"

The question hit harder than I'd expected. "I kept meaning to call Harmony, but the longer I waited, the more awkward it became."

"So, you avoided it entirely. Like you're avoiding it now."

She wasn't wrong. "I don't know how to explain this without sounding like I played her."

"Then you call her and tell the truth. You're a grown woman, not a teenager. You don't ghost your service provider because you're embarrassed."

"What if she thinks I wasted her time?"

"Did you?"

"No. Maybe. I don't know." I looked at my friend, this woman who'd supported me through my divorce and subsequent dating disasters. "Autumn, I think I'm in love with him. Really, genuinely in love."

"Then you owe it to yourself—and to Harmony—to handle this properly." She stood up, gathering her purse. "And you owe it to us to introduce him. I'm planning a dinner party for this weekend. Time for Luke to meet the committee."

"The committee?"

"The women who've watched you survive your marriage, rebuild your confidence, and learn to believe you deserved better. If this man is as wonderful as you think, he won't mind being properly vetted."

After she left, I sat in my quiet house and forced myself to confront the truth. I hadn't just been avoiding Harmony because of embarrassment. I'd been avoiding her because some part of me was afraid that acknowledging Luke to her would somehow break the spell, would make this perfect thing I'd found subject to analysis and judgment.

But Autumn was right. I was too old to be handling my relationships like a teenager. It was time to face the music with Harmony, and it was time to let my friends meet the man who'd turned my careful, controlled life completely upside down.

The question was whether he'd survive their inspection—and whether what we had was strong enough to withstand being exposed to the light.

53

grace

I spent more time getting ready for Autumn's impromptu dinner party than I had for any date in recent memory. This wasn't just social entertainment—this was Luke being formally presented to the women who'd supported me through the worst years of my life and celebrated every small victory since.

Their opinion mattered more than I wanted to admit.

Luke found me in my closet, holding up two dresses with the indecision of someone who understood the stakes.

"The burgundy," he said without hesitation. "You look incredible in that color."

"Are you nervous?" I asked, noting that he was already dressed in what appeared to be his most expensive suit.

"Should I be?"

"They're going to analyze everything about you. Autumn may have run a background check. There could be questions about your financial stability, your relationship history, your intentions regarding me."

"Grace." He stepped closer, adjusting my necklace with steady hands. "I went through the NFL combine. They measured *every* inch of my body and made me run drills for twelve hours straight while scouts took notes on my every movement. Plus they tested my brain and asked about every rumor they may have heard. I think I can handle your friends."

"This is different. These women know me in ways those scouts never knew you. They've seen me at my absolute worst—sobbing in Autumn's kitchen at 2 a.m. because Evan forgot my birthday, crying over men who didn't deserve five minutes of my attention, questioning whether I was capable of being loved properly." I met his eyes. "They're not just evaluating you. They're protecting me."

Something in his expression shifted. "What are you afraid of?"

"That you'll decide I come with too much complexity. That meeting the people who know all my damage will make you realize this is more complicated than you bargained for."

"You think the people who love you are complications?"

"I think I come with a lot of history, opinions about how I want my life to look, and friends who won't hesitate to tell you if they think you're not good enough for me." I smoothed down his lapels. "Not everyone wants to sign up for that level of scrutiny."

Luke took my hands, stilling my nervous fidgeting. "Grace, I'm forty-four years old. If I wanted uncomplicated, I'd date twenty-five-year-olds who don't know what they want yet. Your history is what made you who you are. Your friends' protectiveness tells me you're worth protecting. And their scrutiny?" He smiled. "It tells me you're surrounded by people who understand your value."

When we arrived at Autumn's house, conversation literally stopped. I was grateful we'd both dressed up—everyone else had clearly gotten the memo that this was a formal inspection.

Theo approached first with the gravity of a man welcoming someone into his family. "I suggest you get a drink," he told Luke with twinkling eyes. "My wife intends to thoroughly investigate your character and intentions. Consider yourself warned." He was chuckling as he walked away.

Autumn, Claudia, and Zoe approached with coordinated precision.

"Lucien Benoit Sloane," Autumn said, extending her hand. "We meet at last."

Luke kissed her hand lightly. "The pleasure is mine. I assume you have questions about my intentions toward your friend?"

"Among other things. You've appeared very suddenly in Grace's life, and she's clearly quite taken with you. I researched your professional background—impressive. But I noticed no history of serious relationships. How does a man reach his forties with your resources and remain unattached?"

"I was waiting for the right woman. Someone who wanted me for who I am, not what I could provide or how I might enhance her social position."

"Reasonable answer," Claudia murmured approvingly.

"It's a nice answer," Autumn said, "but I found an old interview where you explicitly stated you didn't believe in marriage and weren't built for long-term relationships. Have your fundamental beliefs about commitment evolved?"

Luke's smile was easy, unperturbed. "That interview was from my twenties, before I understood the difference between being unready for commitment and being unwilling to settle for the wrong person. I'd never met anyone who made me want to reconsider my position on relationships." He looked directly at me. "How could I not want something deeper with Grace? She's extraordinary."

When they finally dispersed, Luke pulled me close. "Are we done with the formal interrogation?"

"That was just the opening round," I warned, but I was smiling.

Later, when the men were discussing football and biomedical innovations, Autumn cornered me in her kitchen.

"How do you feel with him?" she asked.

The question brought unexpected tears to my eyes. "Like I'm someone's first choice for the first time in my adult life. Not convenient, not just suitable, not just good enough—but actually chosen." I wiped my eyes quickly. "He seems genuinely excited to see me, to figure out how to make me happy. I don't feel like I have to perform or become someone else to earn his attention."

"That's exactly what we wanted to hear," Autumn said, hugging me. "As long as that continues, you have our blessing."

"He must be taking *excellent* care of you," Claudia added, appearing with Zoe. "You look completely at peace."

I felt myself blushing. "The physical connection is..." I searched for appropriate words. "Extraordinary. I never understood what all the fuss was about until now."

"Welcome to the club of properly satisfied women or how they say it in my old neighborhood: The Good Dick Club," Autumn said with a grin.

That night, back at my place, Luke and I celebrated passing the first round of friend approval in ways that definitely secured my membership in Autumn's exclusive club.

But as I fell asleep in his arms, I couldn't shake the feeling that the easy part was over. Soon I'd have to face the conversation I'd been avoiding with Harmony, and something told me that revelation would test everything Luke and I had built together.

54

grace

Monday morning arrived with a voicemail box so full it could barely accept new messages. All from Harmony, and all carrying the increasingly sharp edge of a professional whose patience was wearing thin. I'd been avoiding her calls for two weeks, unable to find adequate words to explain why I needed to discontinue services I'd barely started using.

I'd hired a matchmaker to help me find love, then stumbled into it accidentally in her building's lobby. How do you explain that level of cosmic coincidence to someone who'd invested time, energy, and professional reputation in creating a strategic plan for your romantic future?

I forced myself to listen to all seven messages while hiding in my office between patients. Harmony's tone evolved from professional concern to barely contained frustration, and by message four, she was explaining that Keith the dentist had contacted her multiple times about scheduling a "proper" second date—one where we could actually talk without the speed-dating time constraints.

The thought made my stomach revolt. What could I have possibly done during our brief encounter to suggest genuine interest? I'd been late, distracted by thoughts of Luke, and admittedly operating at about thirty percent of my usual social capacity. Yet somehow, this man had interpreted our interaction as promising enough to pursue.

The guilt was becoming unbearable. While I'd been falling deeper in love with Luke—sharing intimate dinners, meeting his friends, introducing him to my family—Harmony had been working diligently on my behalf. She'd been screening online profiles, coordinating potential matches, probably staying up late crafting strategies to help me find exactly what I'd already found.

By lunch, I couldn't postpone the conversation any longer. I called her back, armed with excuses that sounded hollow even to me.

"Harmony, I'm so sorry I've been impossible to reach. My sister's visiting from Korea, and the family dynamics have been completely overwhelming."

"Dr. Grace!" Her relief was immediate and genuine. "I was beginning to think something terrible had happened to you. I know you mentioned family obligations, which I completely understand, but we really need our weekly check-in. Things have been moving forward on this end, and I don't want you to miss important opportunities."

The word "opportunities" sent another spike of guilt through my chest. "What kind of opportunities?"

"Well, Keith is very interested in setting up a real date—somewhere quiet where you can actually have a conversation. He's contacted me three times since your speed-dating session, which suggests you made quite an impression." I could hear papers rustling on her end. "Plus, I've established your profiles on the dating sites we discussed, and the response has been excellent. After screening out the obvious problems—the men who clearly didn't read your preferences, the ones whose photos are obviously twenty years old—there are several genuinely promising prospects I'd like you to review."

My throat was closing. "Harmony—"

"And I'm eager to discuss your journal entries about the dating process. How you've been feeling, what you're learning about yourself, what patterns you're noticing." She paused, and I could hear the enthusiasm in her voice. "This is exactly the kind of momentum we want to maintain. Strike while the iron is hot, as they say."

The phrase hit me like a slap. Momentum. She thought we had momentum, when in reality, I'd been completely checked out of her program for weeks.

"I think we need to meet in person," I said carefully. "There have been some changes in my situation that we need to discuss."

"Changes? What kind of changes?" Her tone sharpened with professional concern. "Grace, if you're feeling overwhelmed by the process, that's completely normal. A lot of people get nervous when things start moving forward. But that's exactly when you need support the most."

"It's not nerves. It's more fundamental than that." I closed my eyes, steeling myself for what was coming. "Can you meet this afternoon?"

We arranged to meet at her office at five—the earliest she could escape from her full-time job. Walking through the lobby of her building that afternoon felt surreal. This was where my life had changed direction so dramatically, though I was only beginning to understand the full implications of that collision with Luke.

Surprisingly, the security guard actually nodded at me with the familiarity of someone who'd seen me here before, and I found myself wondering what he'd observed that first day. Had he noticed Luke watching me? Had there been some sign, some indication that our "accidental" meeting was more complicated than it appeared?

Harmony met me at the office door with a professional smile that didn't quite mask her anxiety. She led me into her office and gestured to the chair across from her desk.

"Before we start," she said, settling into her chair and pulling out a thick folder I recognized as my file, "I want you to know that what you're experiencing is completely normal. The closer we get to finding real connection, the scarier it becomes. It's human nature to sabotage ourselves when we're on the verge of getting what we actually want."

The assumption that I was self-sabotaging made the guilt even worse. "Harmony, this isn't about fear of success."

"Then help me understand what's going on. Are you unhappy with Keith? Because we can absolutely explore other options. The beauty of having multiple approaches—the speed dating, the online profiles, the curated matches—is that we're not putting all our eggs in one basket."

I watched her flip through my file, probably reviewing notes about my preferences, my history, my hopes for the future. The care and attention she'd invested in understanding what I needed felt like a weight on my chest.

"I need to discontinue your services," I said quietly.

The words hung in the air between us. Harmony's hand stopped moving across the page, and when she looked up, her expression had shifted from professional concern to something much more personal.

"I see." She closed my file with deliberate care. "May I ask why? If it's a financial concern, we can absolutely adjust the payment structure. Or if you're feeling rushed by the timeline, we can slow things down."

"It's not about money or timing." I twisted my hands in my lap, searching for the right words. "I met someone."

Her face went through a series of micro-expressions—surprise, confusion, then something that looked like professional hurt.

"You met someone? Through one of the dating apps? That would be unusual, since we haven't officially launched your profiles yet."

"No, not through your services." The words felt heavier as I prepared to explain. "I met him here, actually. In this building."

"Here?" Her voice was carefully controlled, but I caught the flicker of something in her eyes.

"The same day I came for our first consultation. I was running late—you remember—and I literally collided with him in the lobby. Knocked his phone right out of his hand." The memory of that moment felt different now, tinged with questions I hadn't thought to ask at the time. "We started talking, and it just... developed from there."

I watched Harmony's face as I continued, looking for any sign of happiness or acceptance. I knew this was a disappointment, but I hoped she could be a little happy that I was happy...

"He's tall, probably six-two or six-three. Went to Stanford, which I know you'll appreciate since you're Cal people." I attempted a light tone. "Works in biomedical engineering. Very successful, actually—he co-owns a company called Sloane-Wash."

The change in Harmony's expression was instantaneous and devastating. Color drained from her face, and her carefully maintained professional composure cracked completely.

"Sloane-Wash," she repeated slowly.

"Yes. His name is Lucien Sloane, though everyone calls him Luke." I leaned forward, suddenly alert to the shift in energy. "Do you know him?"

The silence that followed contained the seeds of everything that was about to change between Luke and me. I watched Harmony's internal struggle play out across her features—surprise giving way to something that looked like anger, then settling into what I could only describe as disappointed resignation.

"Yes," she said finally. "I know him."

"Is he a client of yours? That would be an incredible coincidence—"

"No, Grace. He's not a client." She sat back in her chair, and I saw the exact moment she made the decision to tell me the truth. "Luke is my brother."

The words didn't make sense at first. I stared at her, waiting for clarification, for this to somehow become less impossible than it sounded.

"Your brother?"

"My half-brother, technically, but we've been close since we were children." Her voice had taken on a flat, professional tone that somehow made the revelation more devastating. "Luke came to my office that day to pick up some preserves our mother had made. He saw you were a client."

The room started to tilt. "He saw that I was a client?"

"Your intake photo was on my whiteboard. Along with your basic information—doctor, divorced, teenage son. I was excited about working with someone who seemed so clear about what she wanted." She was watching my face now, probably seeing my world reconstruct itself in real time. "We talked about you."

The words "we talked about you" hit like physical blows. Every conversation Luke and I had shared, every moment of vulnerability, every time I'd opened up about my fears and dreams—all of it had been informed by information I hadn't provided him.

"What did you tell him about me?" My voice sounded strange, distant.

"That you seemed genuine. That you were serious about finding a real relationship, not just dating for entertainment." She paused, and I could see her beginning to understand the full implications of what she was revealing. "I mentioned that you deserved someone who would appreciate what you brought to the table."

I pressed my hands to my temples, trying to process what this meant. "So, when Luke asked me out, he already knew I was looking for love. He knew I was working with a matchmaker."

"Grace, I don't think he intended to deceive you—"

"But he did deceive me." The anger was building now, hot and clean and clarifying. "He let me believe our meeting was coincidental. He listened to me talk about my fears of not being enough, my worries about finding someone who could love me properly, and he never once mentioned that he'd had advance information about my emotional state."

"I'm sure he didn't see it as deception—"

"What else did you tell him?" I was standing now, though I didn't remember getting up. "Did you share details from my intake interview? My relationship history? My concerns about dating?"

"No!" Harmony's response was immediate and emphatic. "I would never share confidential information like that. Our conversation was general—the kind of thing you might say about any new client."

"But it was enough." I began pacing the small office, pieces clicking into place with horrible clarity. "It was enough for him to know exactly how to approach me. A woman actively seeking a committed relationship, divorced, probably vulnerable and grateful for attention from someone genuinely interested."

"Grace, you're making this sound more calculated than it was—"

"Was it calculated?" I stopped pacing and faced her directly. "Tell me honestly, Harmony. Is this something Luke has done before? Pursued your clients?"

The pause before her answer told me everything I needed to know.

"Luke has never been serious about anyone," she said quietly. "He dates, but casually. He's never shown interest in settling down or building something lasting."

Each word landed like another piece of evidence in a case I didn't want to be building against the man I'd fallen in love with.

"So, I'm what—a novelty? An interesting challenge? Someone different enough from his usual type to hold his attention for a few weeks?"

"I don't know his motivations," Harmony admitted, and the honesty in her voice was somehow worse than deflection would have been. "But Grace, you have to understand—you've been participating in my program at maybe twenty percent capacity because of him. You've missed follow-up calls, avoided scheduling dates, dismissed promising matches. That's not fair to either of us."

The professional hurt in her voice cut through my own emotional turmoil. She was right—I had been treating her services as an expensive safety net while investing all my emotional energy in Luke.

"I'm sorry," I said, meaning it completely. "You deserved better from me as a client. This isn't about your methods or your program. Under different circumstances, I think you would have found exactly what I was looking for."

"Under different circumstances, you mean if my brother hadn't interfered with the process?"

The bluntness of the question stunned me. "Is that what you think happened?"

"I think Luke saw an opportunity and took it, probably without considering how it would affect my business relationship with you." Her professional mask slipped entirely, revealing frustration that had clearly been building. "And I think you got swept up in something that felt exciting and spontaneous, without realizing it was built on information asymmetry."

Information asymmetry. The clinical phrase somehow made everything worse, reducing my relationship with Luke to an economic principle about unequal access to knowledge.

"What should I do?" The question escaped before I could stop it.

"That depends. Do you think what you have with Luke is real, or do you think you're responding to someone who knows exactly which buttons to push?"

The question hung in the air between us, and I realized I didn't have an answer. How do you separate genuine connection from skilled performance when you don't know where one ends and the other begins?

"He could have told me," I said quietly. "At any point over the past month, he could have explained how we really met. But he didn't."

"No, he didn't," Harmony agreed. "And that's something you'll have to decide if you can forgive."

I sat back down, suddenly exhausted by the weight of what I'd learned. "What would you do? If you were in my position?"

"I'd probably be exactly as confused and hurt as you are right now." She leaned forward, her expression softening from professional to personal. "But Grace, I need you to know something. When Luke does care about someone—which is rare—he's completely devoted. I've never seen him rearrange his life for anyone the way he seems to have for you."

"How do I know the difference between devotion and performance?"

"I wish I could answer that for you. But I think that's a conversation you need to have with Luke."

I stood up again, needing to escape this office, this building, this epicenter of revelations that had turned my understanding of everything upside down.

"I need time to think about all of this."

"Of course you do." Harmony stood as well, and for a moment, we just looked at each other—two women whose professional relationship had become collateral damage in whatever game Luke had been playing.

"For what it's worth," she said as I reached the door, "I don't think Luke set out to hurt you. But I also don't think he considered how his choices would affect anyone else."

In my car in the parking garage, I sat motionless for thirty minutes, staring at my phone. Luke had called twice since I'd been in the meeting, probably wondering how my day had gone, maybe planning our evening together.

How many evenings had we shared where I'd opened my heart to him, believing I was sharing myself with someone who was discovering me organically? How many times had I been vulnerable with a man who already knew the landscape of my hopes and fears?

The worst part wasn't that Luke had lied to me—it was that he'd made me complicit in my own deception. Every time I'd marveled at how perfectly we fit together, how naturally he seemed to understand what I needed, I'd been celebrating his ability to respond to information I hadn't known he possessed.

I started my car and drove home through the familiar streets of a city that suddenly felt foreign. Tomorrow, I would have to decide whether to confront Luke with what I'd learned, or whether to simply disappear from his life before he had the chance to explain away what felt increasingly impossible to justify.

For tonight, I just needed to sit with the devastating possibility that the best relationship of my adult life had been built on a foundation I'd never consented to create.

55

luke

The pounding on my door at five-thirty Tuesday morning pulled me from the kind of sleep that comes only after hours of staring at the ceiling, replaying every conversation I'd ever had with Grace and wondering how badly I'd miscalculated. Trying to determine the right conversation that would have allowed me to plead my case and apologize for not telling her everything when we met.

I stumbled downstairs in pajama pants, expecting some kind of emergency. Instead, I found Harmony on my doorstep, her face a mask of professional fury that I hadn't seen since she was a teenager, and she'd discovered I'd borrowed her car without asking when mine was in the shop.

"We need to talk," she said, pushing past me into my living room. "And before you ask, yes, I'm alone, and yes, this is about Grace."

I disabled the alarm and closed the door, my stomach dropping as the implications of her early morning visit settled in. "What happened?"

"What happened is that your girlfriend came to my office yesterday to cancel my services." She turned to face me, and I could see the exhaustion beneath her anger. "She told me about this wonderful man she'd met in my building's lobby. It took me exactly thirty seconds to realize she was talking about you."

The floor shifted beneath my feet. "Jesus. What did you tell her?"

"The truth. That you're my brother, that you knew she was my client, that we'd discussed her situation." Harmony's voice was steady, but I could hear the hurt underneath. "She looked at me like I'd just explained how magic tricks work—like something beautiful had just been revealed as manipulation."

I sank onto my couch, the weight of what I'd set in motion finally hitting me completely. "How did she react?"

"How do you think she reacted? She realized that every conversation you've had, every moment of intimacy, every time she opened her heart to you—it was all happening with information she hadn't given you." Harmony sat across from me, her professional composure cracking. "Luke, she thinks you used insider knowledge to manipulate her emotions."

"That's not what I did." But even as I said it, I realized how hollow it sounded. "I mean, yes, I knew she was your client. Yes, I knew she was looking for someone. But I didn't use that information to—"

"Didn't you?" Harmony interrupted. "Think about it, Luke. Really think about it. How many times did you say exactly the right thing, move at exactly the right pace, provide exactly the kind of relationship experience she was hoping to find? How much of that was genuine intuition, and how much was you responding to information you knew she needed?"

The question hit like a physical blow because I couldn't immediately answer it. Did I shape my approach based on what Harmony had told me about Grace being serious, ready for commitment, deserving of real love? Honestly, how would I know either way?

"I fell in love with her," I said quietly. "Whatever else happened, whatever mistakes I made in not telling her about you, my feelings were – are -- real."

"I know that. That's what makes this so devastating." Harmony's anger was giving way to something that looked like grief. "Luke, I've watched you date casually for twenty years. I've never seen you rearrange your life for anyone, never seen you introduce someone to our family. I bet you have never looked at a woman the way you look at Grace."

"Then why did you tell her I was just playing games?"

"Because I was angry and hurt, and I spoke before I thought." She dropped her head into her hands. "I told her you were a serial dater who never settles down. I may have suggested that you were just entertaining yourself until you got bored."

The devastation was complete. "She thinks I saw her vulnerability as an opportunity."

"Yes. And the worst part is, I can see why she'd think that. Put yourself in her position—she hired me to help her find love, then accidentally found it in my lobby. Except it wasn't accidental at all, was it? You knew exactly what she was looking for."

I stood up and began pacing, needing movement to process the magnitude of what I'd lost. "I should have told her about you from the beginning."

"Yes, you should have. But more than that, you should have trusted her to handle the circumstances." Harmony's voice was gentle now, sad. "You made the decision for both of you that the truth was too dangerous to share."

"I was afraid she'd think I was calculating. That she'd assume I was playing some kind of game."

"And now she thinks exactly that anyway, except worse—because now it looks like you were calculating enough to hide the calculation."

In trying to protect what we had from appearing manipulative, I'd created the exact situation I'd been afraid of.

"What did she say when you told her? Exactly?"

"She asked how much information you had, whether you'd seen her file, if everything between you was built on lies." Harmony met my eyes. "Luke, this woman came to me because she wanted to find real love. She trusted my process, trusted that I would introduce her to people who genuinely wanted what she wanted. Instead, she found out that the best relationship she's ever had was compromised from the beginning by information asymmetry."

"Information asymmetry?" I repeated the phrase, hearing how clinical it sounded.

"That's how she'll think about it. She's a doctor—she understands power dynamics, informed consent, the importance of equal access to information in any relationship." Harmony stood up, preparing to leave. "You didn't just lie to her, Luke. You made her unknowingly complicit in her own manipulation."

After she left, I sat in my kitchen as the sun rose over the city, trying to process the complete destruction of everything I'd been building with Grace. The Heavenly trip stretched ahead of me—client meetings I couldn't cancel, board presentations that suddenly seemed meaningless.

I'd spent weeks imagining a future with Grace, thinking about rings and timelines and how to blend our lives together. Now I had to face the possibility that the woman I'd fallen in love with might never speak to me again—and that

I'd lost her not because I didn't love her, but because I'd been too afraid to trust her with the complete truth.

The worst part was understanding that she was right to feel betrayed. It looked like I had used information she hadn't given me, even if unconsciously. Like I had shaped our relationship based on previous knowledge of what she was looking for, even if my feelings were genuine.

How do you apologize for a betrayal you didn't intend but can't deny? How do you prove that love built on imperfect foundations can still be real?

I didn't have answers, and I wasn't sure I was going to be given time to find them.

56

grace

Tuesday morning dawned gray and cold, matching the emptiness I felt after a sleepless night of trying to process the revelation that had turned my understanding of everything upside down. Luke had called twice the previous evening, and I'd let both calls go to voicemail, unable to trust my voice or my judgment.

The questions circled endlessly through my mind: How much had Luke known when he'd first asked me out? Had he crafted his approach based on information I hadn't given him? Was our connection genuine, or had I fallen in love with someone who understood exactly which buttons to push because he'd been given the manual?

I forced myself through my morning routine—coffee, shower, the careful construction of professional composure that would get me through a half-day of patients. But underneath the familiar rituals, my mind was working through the implications of what Harmony had told me with the same methodical analysis I'd apply to a complex medical case.

The facts were stark: Luke had known I was working with a matchmaker before he'd asked me out. He'd had information about my relationship status, my readiness for commitment, my desire for something serious. He'd pursued me armed with information about me while letting me believe our connection was entirely organic.

The parallel to my marriage was unavoidable and devastating. Evan had withheld crucial information about his feelings for MacKenzie, letting me make decisions about our relationship without knowing where I stood. Now Luke had done something similar, though in reverse—instead of hiding information that would have changed my choices, he'd used information I hadn't known he possessed to shape those choices.

But there was a crucial difference, and my analytical mind couldn't ignore it. Evan had actively concealed something that directly threatened the foundation of our relationship. Luke had failed to disclose something that had given him insight into what I was looking for. The deception felt similar, but the mechanics were different.

Was I conflating two very different types of betrayal because they both involved information asymmetry?

And I had to consider the fact that I didn't tell him that I was working with a matchmaker. I had been hedging my bets. But if I had told him the truth, his relationship with Harmony would have come out sooner, and I wouldn't be trying to understand what the hell just happened. I reserved some of my ire for myself for playing a small role in feeding my own deception.

By lunch, I'd made a decision that surprised me with its clarity. I needed to see Luke face-to-face, to look into his eyes when I asked him to explain himself. Not to end things dramatically, but to understand what had actually happened between us and whether it was salvageable.

I cleared my afternoon schedule and threw together an overnight bag, then called Autumn while driving through the city toward the highway.

"This better be an emergency," she answered on the second ring.

"It might be. I'm driving to Heavenly to confront Luke."

"About what? Grace, you sound terrible."

"I found out yesterday that Luke is Harmony's brother. He knew I was working with a matchmaker before he asked me out."

The silence stretched long enough that I wondered if the call had dropped.

"When did he find out?" Autumn asked finally, and I was grateful for her directness.

"According to Harmony, the day we met. They discussed me briefly—nothing detailed, but enough for him to know I was serious about finding someone." I navigated through traffic while trying to organize my thoughts. "He knew this entire time, Autumn. Every conversation we've had about my fears, my hopes, my relationship history—he already knew the context."

"That's complicated," Autumn said carefully. "But Grace, complicated isn't the same as malicious. What do you think his motivation was?"

"I don't know. That's what I need to find out." I merged onto the highway, the familiar rhythm of driving helping to calm my racing thoughts. "Harmony suggested he might have seen me as an interesting challenge, someone different from his usual casual dating pattern."

"Well, that was shitty of her. And what do you think?"

"I think I fell in love with someone who may have been performing a version of himself designed to appeal to what he knew I wanted." The words tasted bitter. "How do I separate what was authentic from what was calculated?"

"By talking to him. By looking at his actual behavior over the past month, not just the circumstances of how you met." Autumn's voice was gentle but firm. "Grace, I watched Luke with you at the dinner party. That man wasn't performing—he was completely, genuinely smitten. Whatever information he had at the beginning, his feelings now are real."

"But how can I trust my judgment? I've been wrong before about what was real and what was wishful thinking."

"Because this situation is fundamentally different from your marriage. Evan actively deceived you about something that directly affected the viability of your relationship. Luke failed to disclose something that gave him insight into your readiness for exactly the kind of relationship you ended up building together."

The distinction was subtle but important, and I found myself turning it over as I drove through the changing landscape toward the mountains.

"Are you telling me I should just forgive him?"

"I'm telling you that you should find out what actually happened before you decide whether forgiveness is relevant." Autumn paused. "Grace, you've been happier in the past month than I've seen you in years. Don't destroy something that might be fixable because you're afraid of making the same mistake twice."

"What if I am making the same mistake? What if I'm so desperate to be chosen that I'm ignoring obvious red flags again?"

"Then talk to him and find out. But go in with an open mind, not predetermined conclusions."

After hanging up, I drove in relative silence, letting my mind work through the questions I needed answered. Not accusations or ultimatums, but genuine inquiries into what Luke had known, when he'd known it, and why he'd chosen not to tell me.

The three-hour drive gave me time to separate my emotional reaction from the facts of the situation. Yes, Luke had information I hadn't given him. But what had he actually done with that information? Had he manipulated my responses, or had he simply been more confident in pursuing someone he knew was available and interested in commitment?

By the time I reached Heavenly, I'd achieved something approaching clarity. This conversation would determine whether Luke was the man I'd fallen in love with, or whether I'd been in love with a guy prepped to win over a woman whose vulnerabilities had been mapped out in advance.

The stakes couldn't have been higher, but for the first time since leaving Harmony's office, I felt prepared to handle whatever truth was waiting for me.

57

grace

I pulled up to Luke's rental as darkness settled over the mountains, my hands shaking with a combination of adrenaline and fury that had been building for the entire three-hour drive. I had sent him a text asking for the address, not trusting my ability to speak to him. When Luke appeared on the porch—shirtless, worried—I fought the urge to fall into his arms. I needed to maintain the cold clarity that comes before you destroy something beyond repair.

"Grace, what's—"

"Inside. Now." I had to maintain my edge or I would never get through this. "We need to talk about your sister and what the fuck you've been doing to me."

Luke's face turned ashen. He led me into the main room, and I didn't bother admiring the view. I spun around to face him before he'd even closed the door.

"Harmony Zee. Your sister. Ring any bells?"

"Grace, let me explain—"

"Explain what? How you've been playing me from day one? How you knew I was desperately looking for love before you ever asked me out?" The words were coming out in a rush, fueled by weeks of feeling perfectly understood by a man who'd apparently been working from my emotional profile. "Or maybe you want to explain how you sat there listening to me pour my heart out about being afraid I'd never find anyone while knowing your sister had already given you the fucking cheat codes?"

"It wasn't like that—"

"BULLSHIT!" The word exploded out of me. "It was exactly like that! You knew I was working with a matchmaker, Luke. You knew where I was vulnerable and that I was probably desperate enough to fall for the first decent man who showed genuine interest. And you used that!"

Luke's jaw tightened. "I didn't use anything. I met you, I was attracted to you—"

"Before or after you saw my photo on Harmony's whiteboard? Before or after she told you I was divorced and finally ready for something serious? Before or after you learned I'd been hurt in my marriage and wanted someone who wouldn't take me for granted?"

His silence was answer enough.

"Oh my God." I stared at him as the full scope of his deception crystallized. "She told you I'd been hurt. She told you I deserved better. You didn't just know I was available, Luke—you knew exactly what wounds to heal, exactly what kind of man I was hoping to find."

"Grace, you're twisting this—"

"I'm twisting it? I'm TWISTING it?" My voice was rising beyond any professional composure I'd ever maintained. "You crafted yourself into exactly what you knew I needed! The patient man who didn't rush me. The successful man who didn't need anything from me. The emotionally available man who introduced me to his friends and family because you knew that's what I'd see as proof of genuine interest!"

"That's not—those feelings were real!"

"Which feelings, Luke? The ones you had, or the ones you performed?" I was pacing now, too angry to stand still. "Because from where I'm standing, it looks like you saw a lonely, divorced woman working with a matchmaker and thought, 'Easy target. I know exactly what she wants to hear.'"

"That's not who I am!" Luke's composure finally cracked. "I don't prey on vulnerable women! You should know me better than that."

"No? Then what do you call this? What do you call pursuing someone when you have insider information that they don't know you have?"

"I call it falling in love!"

"With what? With me, or with the challenge of making the matchmaker's client fall for you instead of her setups?" The accusation hung in the air, and I watched Luke flinch like I'd slapped him.

"Jesus Christ, Grace. Is that really what you think of me?"

"I don't know what to think of you! I don't know who you actually are!" The words were coming out raw, unfiltered. "I thought I knew you, Luke. I thought you understood me in this incredible, organic way. But it turns out you understood me because your sister gave you my fucking psychological profile!"

"She didn't give me your profile—"

"She told you I'd been hurt! She told you I deserved better! She told you I was ready for something serious!" I stopped pacing and faced him directly. "How is that not a profile? How is that not you having information about my emotional landscape before I even met you?"

"Because I was already attracted to you before I knew any of that!"

"Were you? Or do you just tell yourself that to feel better about what you did?" The question came out crueler than I'd intended, but I was past caring about his feelings. "Because the timeline seems pretty convenient, Luke. You meet me, you're attracted, you go upstairs and learn I'm exactly the kind of woman who's vulnerable to your particular brand of charm, and suddenly you're motivated to pursue me?"

"It wasn't like that!"

"Then what was it like? Explain to me how this isn't you seeing an opportunity and taking it!"

Luke was quiet for a long moment, and when he spoke, his voice was deadly calm.

"You want to know what it was like? Fine. I saw your picture on Harmony's board, and yes, she told me you were a client. And yes, that information gave me confidence to pursue you because I knew you weren't playing games." He met my eyes. "But Grace, you need to ask yourself something. Are you this angry because I had information, or are you this angry because the information was accurate?"

The question hit like a physical blow. "What the hell is that supposed to mean?"

"It means maybe you're not upset that I knew you were looking for love. Maybe you're upset that you were so easy to read. That your needs were so obvious that a casual conversation with my sister was enough to give me a roadmap."

The words hung in the air like poison, and I felt something break inside my chest.

"Are you seriously blaming me for being transparent about what I wanted?"

"I'm saying that if you were as strong and self-possessed as you like to think, my sister's amateur analysis wouldn't have been enough to help me 'manipulate' you."

The cruelty of it stole my breath. This was Luke—the man I'd fallen in love with—suggesting that I'd been complicit in my own deception because I'd been too emotionally obvious.

"Fuck you." The words were quiet, deadly. "Fuck you for making this my fault."

"I'm not making it your fault—"

"Yes, you are! You're standing there telling me that the problem isn't that you used information I didn't give you—the problem is that I was pathetic enough for that information to be useful!"

"That's not what I said—"

"It's exactly what you said!" I was screaming now, past caring who might hear. "You're telling me that if I'd been less desperate, less obvious, less fucking needy, your little advantage wouldn't have worked!"

"Grace—"

"Did you laugh about it? When you realized how easy I was going to be?" The question came from some dark place I'd been trying not to explore. "Did you and Harmony have a good laugh about the lonely doctor who was so desperate for love she'd pay someone to find it for her?"

"Stop it."

"Did you make bets about how fast you could get me into bed? About how long it would take me to fall for the caring, stable man routine?"

"STOP!" Luke's voice filled the room. "You're being cruel now."

"I'm being cruel? I'M being cruel?" I laughed, and it sounded bitter even to me. "You want to know what's cruel, Luke? Cruel is letting someone think they've finally found their person. Cruel is listening to me tell you about my fears and insecurities when you already knew exactly what they were. Cruel is making me fall in love with a version of yourself that now I am not sure is the real you!"

"I never designed anything—"

"Bullshit! You just admitted that knowing I was serious gave you confidence to pursue me! You just said that understanding I'd been hurt made you approach me differently! That's design, Luke! That's calculation!"

"It's also falling in love!"

"With what? With me, or with your ability to be exactly what you knew I was looking for?" I grabbed my purse, suddenly desperate to escape before I said something even worse. "Because I can't tell the difference anymore, and apparently neither can you."

"Grace, don't leave like this."

"Like what? Angry that I've been played? Hurt that the best relationship of my life was built on lies?"

"It wasn't built on lies!"

I turned back to look at him, and for a moment, I saw the man I'd fallen in love with—vulnerable, afraid, genuinely devastated by what was happening between us.

Then I remembered that I'd never actually known him at all.

"Yes, Luke. It was. It was built on information asymmetry and your willingness to use. It was built on you knowing things about me that I hadn't told you." I opened the door, cold mountain air and snowflakes rushing in. "And the worst part? I'm not even angry about the advantage anymore. I'm angry that you were right. I was that easy to read. I was that desperate. I was exactly the kind of pathetic woman who would fall for the first man who seemed to genuinely want her."

"Grace—"

"Don't. Just... don't." I stepped outside, then turned back one final time. "I hope it was worth it, Luke. I hope having the inside track on landing the lonely doctor was everything you thought it would be."

"Grace..." He reached out, grabbing my arm. He looked like he was looking for the right words to say but all he could muster was. "It's too late for you to drive all the way back home. Please just stay here tonight."

58

grace

After that brutal fight, we sat in Luke's living room like survivors of a car crash, both of us staring at the wreckage of what we'd just done to each other.

"You can't leave in this," Luke said quietly, the first words either of us had spoken in twenty minutes. The snow was falling harder now, making the decision for me—I wasn't driving back to San Francisco in this weather, no matter how much I wanted to escape.

I looked out at the white emptiness beyond the windows and felt something inside me crumble completely. Trapped. With the man who'd just told me I was pathetic enough to manipulate. With the man I'd just accused of playing elaborate games with my heart.

"I'll sleep on the couch," I said, my voice hoarse from screaming.

"Grace—"

"Don't." I held up a hand. "Just don't. I can't do any more talking tonight. I can't process any more truth or lies or whatever the hell that was. I just need to not think."

Luke ordered Chinese food while I sat on his couch, staring at nothing, feeling the full weight of what we'd revealed to each other. He'd been right about one thing—I had been easy to read, desperate enough for love that his sister's crude analysis had been sufficient to give him a roadmap to my heart.

And I'd been right too—he'd used that information, consciously or not, to become exactly what he knew I was looking for.

We ate in silence, the wine loosening nothing except my grip on the control I'd spent forty-two years building. By the time we'd finished the bottle, the snow had stopped, but something else had started—a dangerous loosening in my chest, a reckless need to stop thinking about information asymmetry and trust foundations and whether love could survive deception.

"I should go to bed," I said, standing unsteadily.

"Grace." Luke's voice was raw. "I know you hate me right now, and you have every right to. But I need you to know that I love you. Whatever I did wrong, whatever information I had—I love you."

The words might have well been a slap to the face. "Don't. Don't make this about love when we just spent an hour explaining to each other why it was all bullshit."

"It wasn't all bullshit—"

"Luke, stop." I turned to face him, and something in his expression made my chest ache. "I can't do this. I can't keep having this conversation. I can't keep thinking about whether you manipulated me or whether I was just desperate enough to be manipulated. I can't—"

My voice broke, and suddenly Luke was standing in front of me, close enough that I could smell his cologne, could see the pain in his eyes that matched what was tearing me apart inside.

"I know," he said quietly. "I know you can't. I can't either."

We looked at each other for a long moment, both of us standing on the edge of something that would make everything worse. I should have walked away. Should have gone to the guest room and locked the door and spent the night staring at the ceiling, processing what had just happened to us.

Instead, I reached for him.

"Don't talk," I said against his mouth. "Don't say anything. Don't make this mean something it doesn't mean."

The kiss was nothing like the desperate claiming from our earlier encounters. This was angry and sad and tasted like grief, like two people trying to fuck away the pain of what they'd just lost.

Luke's hands were in my hair, and I was pulling at his shirt, and neither of us was pretending this was about love or connection or building something together. This was about escaping, about not thinking, about using our bodies to avoid the devastation of what our minds and words had just done to each other.

"Grace—"

"I said don't talk." I pushed him toward the bedroom, my movements full of desperation.

What followed was raw and urgent and completely divorced from the careful intimacy we'd built over the past month. This was sex as anesthesia, as temporary amnesia, as the kind of destructive choice you make when the alternative is falling completely apart.

Luke seemed to understand that this wasn't about us—it was about me using him to escape from the pain of us. And maybe he was using me the same way, because when I pulled him down onto the bed, when I wrapped myself around him like I was trying to disappear into his skin, he didn't try to make it beautiful or meaningful.

He just helped me forget.

Afterward, we lay in the dark without speaking, both of us knowing we'd just made everything infinitely more complicated. The physical release was temporary, but the emotional damage was more lasting. We'd just used intimacy to avoid dealing with betrayal, and now we had to live with both.

"I should go to the guest room," I said eventually.

"Stay." Luke's voice was barely audible. "Please. I know this doesn't fix anything but stay."

I should have said no. Should have maintained whatever small boundary I had left. Instead, I let him pull me against his chest, let myself have one more night of pretending that the man I'd fallen in love with still existed.

In the morning, I woke up first and lay there for several minutes, looking at Luke's sleeping face and understanding that I'd made everything worse. The pain I'd tried to escape was still there, but now it was accompanied by shame and the knowledge that I'd reverted to destructive choices to avoid dealing with emotional reality.

I was getting dressed when Luke woke up.

"You're leaving."

"Yes." I didn't look at him. "I have to get back."

"Grace." He sat up, and I could hear the hope in his voice that last night had changed something between us. "Can we talk about—"

"No." I turned to face him. "Luke, last night was me making a mistake I knew better than to make. It wasn't forgiveness. It wasn't us working through anything. It was me being unable to handle the pain and using you to make it stop temporarily."

The hope died in his eyes. "So, it meant nothing?"

"It meant I'm still in love with you although I hate what you did, and I'm not strong enough to walk away cleanly." I picked up my purse. "But it doesn't change anything about who knew what when or trust or whether we can build something real from here."

"Then what happens now?"

"Now I go home and figure out whether the woman who slept with you last night is someone I can respect, or whether I'm still the kind of person who makes horrible decisions when I'm upset."

I left him sitting in that bed, both of us understanding that some forms of escape only make the things you're running from more powerful. The drive home stretched ahead of me—hours to live with what I'd just done, and the growing certainty that loving someone and being good for them weren't always the same thing.

59

grace

The drive back to San Francisco Wednesday morning passed in a haze of self-recrimination and the kind of emotional hangover that comes from making choices you know are destructive while you're making them. Every mile between Heavenly and home gave me more time to process what I'd done—not just the fight with Luke, but my decision to have sex with him when I should have walked away.

By the time I reached my driveway, I understood that I'd managed to make an already complicated situation infinitely worse. The woman who'd driven to Heavenly seeking truth and clarity had returned as someone who she thought she had evolved past. At forty-two, I was apparently still capable of reverting to the worst possible coping mechanisms when relationships became difficult.

I'd barely gotten into my robe and opened a bottle of wine when my phone rang. MacKenzie's name on the display reminded me that the world had continued functioning while I'd been destroying my relationship in a mountain cabin.

"Grace! I have updates about Gabe's holiday schedule from the academy—" Mac's cheerful voice stopped abruptly. "Are you okay? You sound terrible."

"I'm fine. What about Gabe?"

"Thanksgiving break starts Wednesday, he'll be home Thursday morning." Her voice shifted from informational to concerned. "Grace, what happened? You sound like you've been crying."

I gave her the abbreviated version—Luke's connection to Harmony, the information asymmetry, the brutal fight that had revealed exactly how cruel we could be to each other when pushed.

"Wait," Mac interrupted. "Back up. You drove three hours to confront him about this?"

"Yes."

"And you had a fight so bad that you're now questioning the entire relationship?"

"Among other things, yes."

Mac was quiet for a long moment. "Grace, I'm going to say something that might be unwelcome, but I think you're making this about your marriage when it's actually about your fear of your own judgment."

The observation hit uncomfortably close to home. "What do you mean?"

"I mean that Luke having information about your emotional availability isn't the same as Evan hiding his feelings for me. One gave someone confidence to pursue something real, the other was active deception about fundamental compatibility." Mac's voice was gentle but firm. "You're treating them as equivalent because they both involved information asymmetry, but the intentions and outcomes were completely different."

"He still used information I didn't consent to share—"

"Did he? Or did he use information that gave him confidence that you were someone worth pursuing seriously?" Mac paused. "Grace, you hired a matchmaker because you wanted someone who understood you were ready for commitment. In a weird way, that's exactly what you got."

The logic was uncomfortable because it highlighted something I'd been avoiding—my anger might be less about Luke's actions and more about my embarrassment at being so transparent in my needs.

"There's something else," I said quietly. "After our fight, I... made some poor choices about how to handle my emotions."

"What kind of poor choices?"

"The kind where you involve having sex."

Mac's silence was telling. "Oh, Grace."

"I know. I know it was destructive and stupid and probably made everything worse between us." The shame was fresh and sharp. "I just couldn't bear the pain of what we'd said to each other, and I wanted it to stop."

"And did it work?"

"For about thirty minutes. Then I woke up realizing I was back to making shitty decisions to cope, which is exactly the kind of pattern I thought I'd outgrown."

"Have you talked to Autumn about any of this?"

"Not yet. I came home planning to hide under the covers with wine until I felt capable of rational thought."

"That's also not healthy coping, Grace."

Before I could respond, my doorbell rang with the insistence of someone who wasn't going away. Through the security window, I could see Autumn on my porch, keys in hand with the determination of someone prepared to use them.

"Speaking of Autumn," I told Mac. "She's here. I should go."

"Grace? For what it's worth, I think you're making this more complicated than it needs to be. But I also think you need to figure out whether you're running from Luke or from your own fear of trusting your judgment about him."

After hanging up, I let Autumn inside, and she took one look at me—robe, wine glass at two in the afternoon, obvious signs of emotional devastation—and followed me straight to my bedroom.

"Start from the beginning," she said, settling onto my bed with the patience of someone prepared for a long conversation.

I told her everything. The fight, the brutal things we'd said to each other, Luke's accusation that I'd been easy to manipulate because I was so obviously desperate, my own cruel suggestions that our entire relationship had been a calculated performance.

"Grace. That sounds like you two had a street fight."

"And then I made it worse by sleeping with him afterward."

Autumn's eyebrows rose. "Explain that decision-making process."

I gave her a 'you already know' look.

Autumn exhaled. "How do you feel about that choice now?"

"Ashamed. Stupid. Like I reverted to the worst possible coping mechanism when I should have been strong enough to just leave." I took a large sip of wine. "I'm forty-two years old, Autumn. I should—I do—know better than that."

"But you're also human, and you were in pain." Autumn's voice was gentle. "The question is what you learned from making that choice."

"That I'm still capable of self-destructive behavior. That maybe Luke was right when he suggested I was pathetic enough for his sister's amateur psychology to be effective."

"Stop." Autumn's tone was sharp. "Stop using Luke's cruel words as a weapon against yourself. He said that to hurt you, not because it was true."

"But what if it was true? What if I was so obviously desperate for love that basic information about my situation was enough to help him win me over?"

"Grace, listen to yourself. You're taking responsibility for Luke's decision. That's not about you being desperate—that's about him having an advanced scouting report and not telling you about it."

I sat with that for a moment. "But I was desperate, wasn't I? I consented to the hiring of a matchmaker. I was actively seeking love in a way that was apparently obvious to anyone who met me."

"You were ready for love. There's a difference between desperation and readiness, between being open to connection and being pathetic." Autumn shifted to face me fully. "Grace, do you think there's something inherently shameful about wanting to find someone to share your life with?"

The question caught me off guard. "No, of course not."

"Then why are you treating your readiness for a relationship as evidence of weakness?"

"Because..." I paused, trying to articulate something I'd been feeling but not thinking clearly about. "Because Luke was right that I was easy to read. Because apparently my situation was so obvious that a casual conversation with his sister was enough to give him directions to win me over."

"Or because you were emotionally mature enough to know what you wanted and honest enough not to hide it." Autumn reached for my wine glass and took a sip. "Grace, what if instead of seeing your transparency as weakness, you saw it as strength? What if being easy to read isn't the same as being easy to manipulate?"

The reframe was subtle but significant. I'd been treating my emotional availability as evidence of desperation, but what if it was actually evidence of growth?

"I'm still angry that he had information I didn't give him directly."

"You should be. That was unfair, and he should have told you about it much sooner." Autumn handed back my wine. "But Grace, you need to decide whether that lie – because that's what it was—is unforgivable, or whether it's something you can work through with someone whose feelings for you are genuine."

"How do I know his feelings are genuine? How do I separate what was real from what was performance?"

"By looking at his actual behavior over the past month. By thinking about whether someone who was just playing games would have introduced you to his family, rearranged his travel schedule several times to see you, made sure you had time with your son, subjected himself to interrogations by all your friends and exes." Autumn was quiet for a moment. "By asking yourself whether the man who held you while you cried about missing Gabe's childhood was performing, or whether he was just someone who loves you."

I pulled my knees to my chest, feeling the weight of everything I needed to process. "I said terrible things to him, Autumn. I accused him of making bets about how fast he could get me into bed. I suggested he and Harmony had laughed about my desperation."

"And what did he say?"

"That I was being cruel. And he was right—I was." The memory of Luke's face when I'd made those accusations made my chest ache. "I wanted to hurt him the way he'd hurt me, so I said the most vicious things I could think of."

"Do you think any of those accusations were true?"

"No. I think they were the words of someone in pain lashing out at the person who'd caused that pain." I took another sip of wine. "I think Luke genuinely loves me, and I think I wanted to punish him for not telling me what he knew."

"So, what happens now?"

"I don't know. I don't know if we can come back from the things we said to each other. I don't know if I can trust someone who knew what he knew and kept it a secret, even if his feelings were real." I looked at my oldest friend. "And I don't know if I can respect myself for using sex to hide from how I was feeling."

"The sex thing is easy," Autumn said pragmatically. "You made a mistake, you recognized it as a mistake, you won't make the same mistake again. Growth."

"And the rest of it?"

"The rest of it depends on whether you think love requires perfect beginnings, or whether it requires genuine feelings and the willingness to work through difficulties." Autumn stood up, apparently having said what she'd come to say. "Grace, I've watched you in relationships for fifteen years. This is the healthiest dynamic I've ever seen you in, even accounting for the information asymmetry and the brutal fight."

"How can you say that after everything I just told you?"

"Because you're processing it like a mature adult instead of making excuses or pretending it didn't happen. Because Luke told you the truth when you demanded it, even when that truth made him look bad. Because even your fight was about real issues instead of petty grievances." She paused at my bedroom door. "You two actually confronted your problems – not in a nice way. But baby steps. Now you need to see if you can deal with them to move forward. That's the healthy part, even when it's painful."

After she left, I sat in my quiet house with the weight of everything I needed to decide. Mac had suggested I was conflating Luke's situation with my marriage when they were fundamentally different. Autumn had suggested that my emotional transparency was strength, not weakness. Both had implied that the question wasn't whether Luke was perfect, but whether he was worth the effort of working through imperfect circumstances.

The wine was warm in my hands as I considered the possibility that I'd been so afraid of repeating my pattern of ignoring red flags that I'd started seeing deal-breakers where complications existed instead. The question was whether how we started was an insurmountable obstacle to trust, or whether it was something two people could acknowledge and work through if their feelings were genuine enough to justify the effort.

For the first time since walking out of Harmony's office, I had to consider whether I'd been running from Luke, or whether I'd been running from my own fear of trusting someone who'd seen my emotional availability and chosen to pursue me because of it, not despite it.

The distinction, I was beginning to understand, might make all the difference in whether we had a future together.

60

luke

After Grace left, I sat in that empty rental for an hour, staring at the place where she'd stood when she'd called me pathetic and suggested I'd made bets about how fast I could get her into bed. The cruelty of her words was matched only by my own—telling her she'd been easy to manipulate, that her desperation had made Harmony's amateur psychology effective.

We'd eviscerated each other with surgical precision, finding exactly the words that would cause maximum damage. And then, in a moment of mutual desperation, we'd used sex to avoid dealing with the wreckage we'd created.

The memory of that choice sat in my chest like a weight. Grace had been clear about what it meant—escapism, not forgiveness. She'd used my body to temporarily numb the pain I'd caused her, and I'd let her because I was equally desperate to pretend we hadn't just destroyed something irreplaceable.

By the time I forced myself to get ready for the day, I understood that I might have lost the love of my life not through any single lie, but through a series of choices that had culminated in us saying things to each other that couldn't be taken back. And I couldn't act surprised about how it turned out – I knew this would likely be the outcome and yet I still let fear dictate my choices.

Kyle was waiting at the ski rental shop with several board members when I arrived, and I could see him clock my distress immediately. We'd been friends long enough that he could read the signs—the careful professional mask hiding complete internal devastation. Typically, it wasn't about a woman though.

"What's going on with you?" he asked quietly while we fitted boots.

"I think I destroyed my relationship last night," I said, focusing on equipment I didn't need to rent but was renting anyway to have something to do with my hands.

"What happened?"

I gave him the abbreviated version. I had gone over the events in my head so many times that I didn't want to repeat the entire brutal sequence again.

Kyle was quiet for a long moment. "Jesus, Luke. You two really went nuclear."

"I told her she was easy to manipulate because she was so obviously desperate for love." The words tasted bitter even in repetition. "I made her pain about her emotional openness instead of acknowledging that I had information she didn't give me."

"And what did she say?"

"That I'd made bets about how fast I could get her into bed. That I'd probably laughed with Harmony about the lonely doctor who was pathetic enough to pay someone to find her love." I adjusted bindings I'd already adjusted twice. "She wasn't wrong to be angry, Kyle. I did have an unfair advantage. I did know some information about her before I met her. I don't think I used it maliciously or anything. But I can see how it looks."

"And you fell in love with her."

"Yes. I think I was falling before I even found out about her connection to Harmony. But I'm starting to understand that doesn't matter." I straightened up, finally meeting his eyes. "Grace is a doctor. She understands informed consent, power dynamics, the importance of equal access to information in any relationship. I violated all of that without realizing it."

"So, what's your plan?"

The question I'd been dreading. "I don't know if there is a plan. I don't know if you can rebuild trust when it was really established on equal terms in the first place."

Kyle was quiet as we joined the group heading toward the slopes. "Lightning doesn't strike twice, Luke. You know that, right?"

I did know that. I knew that what I'd found with Grace was unprecedented in my life, that the connection we'd shared was the kind most people spend their entire lives hoping to experience. I also knew that I'd potentially destroyed it through a combination of cowardice, poor judgment, and my own inability to understand how my actions could feel like manipulation to someone who valued transparency above almost everything else. She had told me about the dynamics of her marriage. It's my fault that I didn't realize I was exhibiting the same types of behavior.

The skiing helped, in the way that physical activity sometimes provides temporary relief from emotional pain. But every run down the mountain was accompanied by the understanding that Grace was driving back to San Francisco, probably processing the worst fight of her adult life and trying to figure out whether the man she'd fallen in love with had ever actually existed.

The board meetings that afternoon required a level of professional performance I wasn't sure I was capable of maintaining. But somehow, I managed to discuss expansion plans and hiring strategies while my personal life imploded in the background. Work had always been my refuge during difficult times, but this felt different—like using business to avoid dealing with the reality that I might spend the rest of my life wondering what would have happened if I'd trusted Grace with the complete truth from the beginning.

"You seem distracted," Chuck Evans, one of our board members, mentioned during a break between sessions.

"Sorry. Personal issues. Won't affect our plans moving forward."

But even as I said it, I wondered if that was true. How do you focus on building a business empire when you've just lost the only person who'd ever made you want to share that empire with someone?

Kyle found me on the balcony of the conference room during another break, looking out at mountains that reminded me of Grace's profile when she'd turned away from me in anger.

"You're going to have to deal with this eventually," he said.

"Deal with what?"

"The fact that you're in love with someone who may never speak to you again." His voice was gentle but direct. "The fact that you're going to have to figure out how to live with knowing you had something extraordinary and lost it through your own choices."

The words hit harder than I'd expected. "She might call."

"She might. But Luke, you need to prepare for the possibility that she won't. That the things you said to each other crossed lines that can't be uncrossed."

Friday morning brought one final ski run before we all headed back to the city. I found myself thinking about Grace's accusation that I'd made our entire relationship feel like performance art specifically designed to meet her needs.

The accusation stung because there was some truth in it. By not telling her everything, I knew that's how she would feel – even if that's not what was happening.

But I'd also fallen genuinely in love with her—with her sharp wit, her fierce protectiveness of her son, her ability to see through pretense to what actually mattered. The question was whether she could trust me and my feeling or not moving forward.

The drive back to San Francisco felt like traveling toward an uncertain future. I had business to attend to, meetings to schedule, a life to continue living. But underneath all of that was the growing understanding that I'd changed in fundamental ways during my month with Grace, and I didn't know how to be the person I'd become without her.

I didn't call her during the drive home. Kyle was right that she needed space to process what had happened between us. But I did stop to send flowers with a simple note—not because I thought flowers could fix what happened, but because I needed her to know I was thinking about her.

Sitting in my empty house that evening, surrounded by reminders of the life I'd been building toward sharing with her, I finally allowed myself to feel the full weight of what I might have lost.

For the first time in my adult life, I'd found someone who made me want to be better than I'd ever been. Someone who'd seen my professional success and been more interested in my work with foster kids. Someone who'd challenged me to think about relationships as partnerships rather than temporary entertainment.

And I'd lost her because I'd been too afraid to trust her with the truth, too cowardly to risk her reaction to information that had sounded worse the longer I held on to it.

Some mistakes, I was learning, couldn't be fixed with explanations or flowers or time. Some violations of trust might be too fundamental to overcome.

61

grace

Saturday morning, I was supposed to be running errands. Instead, I was sitting in my car outside a coffee shop, staring at my phone like it might explode, trying to work up the nerve to make a call that would either help me understand what the hell had happened with Luke or confirm that I'd fallen in love with a mirage.

Three days of replaying our brutal fight had left me with more questions than answers. Yes, Luke had information I hadn't given him. Yes, that was fucked up. But the more I thought about it, the more I wondered if I was angrier about that or about the fact that I'd been so goddamn transparent.

Because let's be honest—I had been desperate. Not pathetic, like Luke had cruelly suggested, but definitely ready in a way that was apparently obvious to anyone with functioning eyes. It's why I kept latching onto the wrong men, hoping something would click, then wallowing in my latest mistake. My friends could see it. It's why they suggested the matchmaker in the first place.

I dialed Harmony's number before I could chicken out.

She answered on the first ring. "Oh, thank God. Grace, I've been afraid to breathe wrong since Tuesday. I think I may have given you a wrong impression about what Luke and I talked about. I am so sorry—"

"Stop." I cut her off. "I don't need apologies right now. I need information. And I need you to tell me the truth, not what you think I want to hear."

"Okay." Her voice was careful, professional.

"That day Luke came to your office. Walk me through exactly what happened. What did you tell him about me, what did he say, how did he react. Every detail."

Harmony was quiet for a moment, and I could practically hear her organizing her thoughts.

"Luke came to pick up preserves my mother had made for his mom. When he walked in, he told me that a woman had just knocked his phone out of his hand in the lobby, and that she had given him her card and that he was planning to call her. Then he saw your photo on my whiteboard—I had it up there because I was excited about working with you." She paused. "He asked who you were."

"And?"

"I told him you were a new client. That you were a doctor and divorced, I think. That he needed to stay away because he would mess with your mind." Another pause. "I said that I couldn't believe that you needed my services."

I frowned. While that was still more conversation about me than I was comfortable with, this version didn't seem as bad as originally advertised. If that was all that was said...

"What was his reaction?"

"He got this look on his face—I had to turn the board to get him to stop looking at your picture. He had already said he was going to call."

"Before or after you gave him my emotional profile?"

"That was *all* I said. I mean I guess it is likely too much, and I will do better in the future. But he walked into the office talking about you. That's what I'm trying to tell you, Grace. He was already interested. Any information I gave him didn't create his attraction—it gave him confidence to pursue it."

I sat with that distinction for a moment. It felt important, though I wasn't sure why.

"Harmony, I need you to answer something honestly. Do you think your brother was performing for me? Do you think he crafted a version of himself based on what you told him?"

"No." Her answer was immediate and firm. "Grace, I've watched Luke date for twenty years. He's charming, he's successful, women love him. But he's also been completely emotionally unavailable that entire time. What I saw when we talked about you was different."

"Different how?"

"Like he couldn't believe his luck. And I saw the fear when he realized that he might lose you." Her voice grew softer. "Grace, my brother introduced you to my stepmother. He's never done that with anyone. Ever."

"But if he knew I was looking for commitment—"

"And maybe that's exactly what he needed to know to let himself want more too." Harmony's voice was gentle but direct. "Luke has spent his adult life avoiding serious relationships. He's been trying not to become our father. Maybe meeting you and knowing you were ready gave him permission to try to be that for you."

I leaned back in my car seat, processing what she was telling me. "You really think he loves me?"

"I think Luke is more in love with you than he's ever been with anyone. I think he's spent the last three days freaking out because he's terrified he ruined the best thing that ever happened to him." She paused. "Grace, what are you going to do?"

That was the million-dollar question, wasn't it? Was I going to let these circumstances destroy something that might be real, or was I going to fight for a man who'd seen my emotional status and chosen to pursue me because of it, not despite it?

"I don't know yet," I said honestly. "But I'm tired of analyzing this to death. I'm tired of trying to figure out what was real and what wasn't. Maybe it's time to just decide whether Luke Sloane is worth fighting for."

"And?"

I thought about the flowers on my kitchen counter. About the way Luke had looked at me when I'd walked away from him in Heavenly. About the fact that in a month of being with him, I'd felt more chosen, more valued, more genuinely loved than I had in years of marriage.

"Yeah," I said quietly. "He's worth fighting for."

"What do you need from me?"

For the first time in days, I felt something like hope unfurling in my chest. Not because I thought Luke and I could pretend all of this – the pain, the fight, everything—hadn't happened, but because I was finally ready to stop punishing both of us for it.

"I need help planning something that will either bring us back together or give us both the closure we need to move on." I started my car, suddenly energized by having a plan. "And Harmony? It's going to involve a scavenger hunt and a train trip."

After hanging up, I sat for a moment longer, feeling the weight of the decision I'd just made. I wasn't choosing Luke because I'd decided to overlook what had happened between us. I was choosing him because I was strong enough to fight for this love even though it was complicated.

The question now was whether he was brave enough to fight for me too.

62

luke

The days after Grace left me standing in that rental felt like walking around with a hole in my chest. I kept expecting her to call, kept checking my phone like an idiot, but nothing.

I sent flowers twice. Simple arrangements because anything bigger felt like I was trying too hard after the shit we'd said to each other. No response to those either.

Work helped during the day but coming home to my empty house was brutal. Grace's perfume still lingered on the bathrobe she'd borrowed, and I found myself holding onto it like some kind of pathetic asshole, trying to remember what it felt like when she was here.

"Get it together, Sloane," I told myself, but getting it together proved harder than I'd expected.

By the Monday of the week of Thanksgiving, I was desperate enough to visit my mother, thinking she might provide some distraction. Big mistake.

"You look like hell," she said when I showed up that evening with takeout. "What's wrong with you?"

I gave her the basic story—Grace finding out about Harmony, our fight, the possibility that I'd fucked up the best thing that had ever happened to me.

"Did you lie to this woman?"

"I didn't tell her about Harmony being my sister."

"Why not?"

"Because I thought it would sound weird. Like I was some kind of stalker or something."

Mom set down her fork and looked at me like I was twelve years old again. "Luke, what exactly did you say to her when she confronted you?"

So, I told her. Everything. I should have known my mother would not be impressed with my behavior.

"You told her she was easy to manipulate?" Mom's voice was flat.

"I was pissed off. She was acting like I'd planned some elaborate scheme."

"So, when she was hurt and confused, you made it her fault for being hurt and confused."

"It wasn't like that—"

"It was exactly like that." She shook her head. "I raised you better than that, Luke. When someone you care about is in pain, you don't kick them while they're down."

The words hit harder than I wanted to admit. "I know. I've been replaying that conversation for days, wishing I could take it back."

"Have you told her that?"

"She said she needed space to think."

"Space to think about whether you're worth forgiving, probably." Mom's assessment was brutal and probably accurate. "You really screwed this up, didn't you?"

"Yeah. I think I did."

"Do you love her?"

"More than I knew I could love anyone."

"Then figure out how to prove it. And Luke? Flowers aren't going to cut it after what you just told me you said to her."

On Tuesday evening, I was going stir-crazy in my house when Harmony called.

"I've been afraid to call you," she said.

"Why? You think I blame you for this?"

"Don't you?"

"We both fucked up, Harm. But Grace asked for space, and I'm trying to respect that."

"Luke, I need to tell you something. I have to apologize to you. I made the situation sound worse than it was when I originally talked to Grace. I was angry, and I probably made it seem like you knew more about her than you actually did."

"What do you mean?"

"I mean I told her we 'discussed' her, which made it sound like we strategized about how you should approach her. But that's not what happened. You asked about the woman on the whiteboard, I said she was a client that you needed to stay away from, and that was basically it."

"Think that matters to her?"

"I think Grace is processing a lot more than just what happened with you. I think she's trying to figure out if she can trust herself not to make the same mistakes she made in her marriage. But I think you know that."

That was true. Grace had been burned before by someone who hadn't been completely honest with her. Now I'd done something similar, even if it wasn't as deliberate.

"So, what do I do?"

"I don't know. Wait, I guess. Hope she decides you're worth another shot."

"And if she doesn't?"

"Then you learn from this and try not to screw up the next good thing that happens to you."

After hanging up, I sat on my couch and stared at my phone, wanting to call Grace but knowing that pushing her right now would only make things worse.

I'd never been in this position before. Usually when things got complicated with women, I just walked away. But I didn't want to walk away from Grace. I wanted to fix this, wanted to prove that what we had was real despite how it started.

Problem was, I had no idea how to do that. I was good at solving engineering problems, business challenges, things with clear solutions. But emotions? Relationships? This was uncharted territory for me.

All I knew was that I'd found something extraordinary with Grace, and I'd potentially destroyed it by being too much of a coward to tell her the complete truth from the beginning. Then I'd made it worse by attacking her when she'd called me on it.

The woman I loved thought I'd manipulated her, and I'd basically confirmed her worst fears about herself instead of reassuring her that being open and honest wasn't the same as being desperate.

I missed her. I missed everything about her—the way she argued with me about football, the way she made me want to be better than I'd ever been, the way she looked at me like I was exactly what she'd been hoping to find.

Now she probably looked at me like I was exactly the kind of man she'd been trying to avoid.

My phone buzzed with a text, and for a split second, I thought it might be Grace. Instead, it was Kyle, checking in from New York.

"How are you holding up?"

"I'm not," I typed back. "I think I lost her."

"Give it time. If it's real, she'll come around."

But sitting in my empty house, surrounded by reminders of the future I'd been planning with Grace, I wasn't sure time was going to be enough to fix what I'd broken.

63

grace

The week of Thanksgiving became a study in chaos, both externally and internally. While my family prepared for the invasion of grandchildren and I coordinated desserts and logistics, I was simultaneously planning what might be either the most romantic gesture of my adult life or the most sophisticated form of closure I'd ever attempted.

The decision to fight for Luke hadn't been dramatic or sudden—it had been the slow accumulation of realizations that what we'd shared was worth the effort to try to get us back on track. But deciding to fight and knowing how to fight were entirely different challenges.

"You're distracted," my mother observed Tuesday evening as I stood in her kitchen, supposedly helping with Thanksgiving prep but actually staring at my phone, wondering if Luke was thinking about me too.

"Just work stuff," I lied, continuing to chop vegetables with the mechanical precision of someone whose mind was elsewhere.

"Grace." Mom's voice carried the authority of someone who'd raised two daughters and could smell deception from three rooms away. "What's really going on? You've been strange since you got back from that trip last week."

I set down my knife and looked at her—this woman who'd been married to my father for forty-five years, who'd weathered their own relationship storms and come out stronger. If anyone could understand the complexity of what I was contemplating, it might be her.

"I'm in love with someone," I said quietly. "And it's complicated."

"How complicated?"

"The kind of complicated where you have to decide whether trust can be rebuilt when it was never established on equal terms to begin with."

Mom set down her own prep work and gave me her full attention. "Tell me." So, I did. I told her about the fight Luke and I had, and the way we'd eviscerated each other with surgical precision. I told her about my fear that I was repeating patterns from my marriage, and my growing understanding that some patterns were worth breaking.

"You love him," she said when I'd finished.

"Yes."

"And he loves you?"

"I think so. I hope so." I resumed chopping, needing something to do with my hands. "But Mom, he knew things about me before he should have known them."

"Grace, when your sister decided to move to Korea with Liam, I was completely against it."

"I remember. You and Dad fought about it for months."

"The culture, the language barriers, trying to keep working there as an American woman—I knew it was going to be hard on her."

"But she went anyway."

"She did. And I had to decide whether to keep fighting her because I could see what she was walking into, or whether to trust that she was grown enough to handle it."

"What did you decide?"

"I decided that wasn't my battle to fight. She was in love, she was determined, and just because I knew how difficult it could be didn't mean I got to make her choices for her." She met my eyes. "Grace, your sister was so happy she didn't want to hear about any of the hard parts. But you know what? She's been figuring it out as she goes."

"This is different, though. Luke knew things..."

"And I knew things about Korea that Celeste didn't want to consider. The point is, baby, sometimes things don't start perfectly and still work out. This is something that you didn't encounter in your marriage – the problems there were fundamental and you couldn't fix them. Here, there is something tangible that you can work on if you choose to." Mom's voice was gentle. "You have to decide if you love him enough to work through it. Or at least try to."

Wednesday morning brought Celeste's children—my nephews and nieces, ages eight through fifteen, speaking a mixture of English and Korean and bringing the kind of chaos that only multiple children in a new environment can create. Watching my parents transform into doting grandparents was both heartwarming and exhausting and provided perfect cover for the phone calls I needed to make.

"How are you holding up?" Autumn asked when I called her from my childhood bedroom, hiding from the family mayhem downstairs.

"I've decided to fight for him, for us."

"Good. What's your plan?"

I told her about the scavenger hunt idea, about the train tickets, about my hope that I could show Luke I'd processed our fight and chosen him despite the complications.

"Grace," Autumn's voice was careful, "are you sure you're not just trying to skip past the hard part? The part where you both acknowledge what happened and figure out how to rebuild the trust?"

"I'm not trying to skip past anything. I'm trying to show him that I'm done analyzing this to death. That I've decided he's worth the effort of rebuilding trust for we can see if we can move forward."

"And what if he's not ready for that? What if he needs more time to process the things you said to each other?"

In my focus on my own decision-making process, I hadn't fully considered that Luke might still be reeling from the cruelty we'd both displayed.

"Then I guess I'll have my answer about whether we can come back from what we did to each other."

Thursday brought Gabe home from the academy, and seeing my son—taller, more confident, full of stories about training and friends and the life he was building in Florida—reminded me why I'd been so afraid of missing his childhood in the first place.

"You look different, Mom," he said as we set the table for Thanksgiving dinner. "Happier, maybe? Or sadder. I can't tell."

"Both, probably."

"Is it about that guy? Luke?" Gabe's directness had always been one of his most endearing and challenging qualities.

"Among other things, yes."

"Do you love him?"

The question, coming from my thirteen-year-old son, stopped me cold. "Why do you ask?"

"Because you've been different since Miami. Like, more relaxed but also more worried. Like when something really important is happening."

I looked at my son—this young man who'd inherited his father's perceptiveness and my tendency to cut straight to emotional truth—and realized he deserved honesty.

"Yes, I love him. But it's complicated, and I'm trying to figure out if love is enough when other things are difficult."

"What kind of difficult?"

"The kind where you have to decide whether to trust someone who made mistakes, but whose feelings are real."

Gabe considered this with the seriousness of someone who'd watched his parents navigate divorce and co-parenting with varying degrees of success.

"Dad says the hardest part about loving someone is knowing when to fight for them and when to let them go."

What type of conversations were these two having? "What do you think?"

"I think if you love him and he loves you, the other stuff is just stuff you figure out together."

The simplicity of thirteen-year-old wisdom hit me harder than all of Autumn's careful questions and my mother's diplomatic advice. Sometimes the most profound truths came from the people who hadn't yet learned to overcomplicate everything.

Friday morning, while my family recovered from Thanksgiving excess and prepared for a day of shopping and football, I drove to Harmony's office to finalize the plans I'd been making all week.

"Are you sure about this?" she asked as we reviewed the scavenger hunt route. "Grace, what you and Luke said to each other was pretty vicious. Are you prepared for the possibility that he might not be ready to move past it?"

"I'm prepared for the possibility that this might be closure instead of reconciliation," I said, though saying it out loud made my chest ache. "But I'm more prepared for the possibility that if I don't try, I'll spend the rest of my life wondering what might have happened if I'd been brave enough to try to rebuild us."

The scavenger hunt would take Luke through various shops around the Wharf. Besides the picnic items I had selected, he'd receive clues and small gifts that had meaning for us and that referenced conversations we'd had, private jokes we'd shared, places that we visited like the pier where we'd had our first date, the Saturday morning chess spot, and the bookstore where we'd spent a Sunday afternoon that had felt like the beginning of forever. These were moments that we had which felt too genuine to be a performance.

The final location would be the park near Fisherman's Wharf, in celebration of our first date when Luke and I had first talked about his work with foster children and I'd begun to understand the depth of his character beneath the handsome and successful exterior.

That's where I'd be waiting—with Fitz, with a picnic, and with train tickets for the Great American Southern Trail trip we'd once talked about taking together. Six stops along the Southern United States, seventeen days of learning each other outside the context of our usual lives. Not as a way to pretend our fight hadn't happened, but as a way to show him I was ready to build something new from the complicated foundation we'd been left with.

"What if he doesn't show up?" Harmony asked.

"Then I'll know he's not ready to try again, and I'll have to respect that choice."

"And if he does show up?"

"Then we'll find out if love really can survive the kind of truth that almost destroyed us."

The logistics were surprisingly complex. The scavenger hunt company needed detailed instructions for each location, the gifts had to be prepared and positioned, the final location had to be reserved. But by Friday evening, everything was arranged. All that remained was the phone call that would set everything in motion—or confirm that some relationships couldn't survive complete honesty, no matter how much love existed between the people involved.

I sat in my car outside Harmony's office, phone in hand, ready to make the call that would either bring Luke back into my life or give us both the closure we needed to move forward separately.

The number rang twice before he answered.

"Grace?"

Just hearing my name in his voice made my chest ache with possibility and regret in equal measure.

"Hi. I have something I want to show you. Tomorrow, if you're willing."

"What kind of something?"

"The kind that will either fix us or help us figure out how to say goodbye."

The silence stretched long enough that I wondered if he'd hung up.

"Grace, after what we said to each other—"

"I know what we said. I know how cruel we were. But Luke, I also know that I love you, and I think you love me, and maybe that's worth one more try at getting this right."

Another pause, and when he spoke, his voice was rough with something that sounded like hope.

"What do you need me to do?"

"Be at Fisherman's Wharf tomorrow at ten AM. Look for a woman with a clipboard who'll have an envelope with your name on it."

"Grace—"

"Luke. Trust me. One more time."

"Okay," he said quietly. "I'll be there."

After hanging up, I sat for several more minutes, feeling the weight of what I'd just set in motion. Tomorrow would either be the beginning of rebuilding something with the man I loved, or it would be the end of the most complicated relationship of my adult life.

But for the first time since our fight in Heavenly, I felt ready for either outcome. I'd chosen to fight for Luke not because I'd decided to overlook what had happened, but because I was strong enough to work to build a solid relationship with someone whose feelings had turned out to be genuine, even if those feelings had developed under complicated circumstances.

The question now was whether Luke was ready to do the work with someone who'd seen his worst moment and chosen him anyway.

Tomorrow, I'd find out.

64

luke

Saturday morning, I woke up feeling something I hadn't felt in over a week—hope. Grace had called. She wanted to see me. Whatever she had planned for today would either fix us or give us both the closure we needed, but at least I'd get to see her again.

Fitz seemed to sense my improved mood, bouncing around the kitchen while I made coffee and tried to figure out what to wear to meet the woman who might be about to break my heart or put it back together.

I'd replayed our phone conversation a dozen times since last night. "The kind that will either fix us or help us figure out how to say goodbye." The words could have been terrifying, but there'd been something in Grace's voice—determination, maybe even affection—that made me think she wasn't planning to destroy me today.

By the time I'd showered and changed into black jeans, boots, and a cashmere turtleneck under my leather jacket, I was actually nervous. Not just hopeful, but genuinely anxious about what Grace had planned and whether I'd measure up to whatever test she'd devised.

When I arrived at the Wharf a few minutes before 10 AM, there were people enjoying the holiday weekend with some searching for sales heading into the holiday season. It took me a few minutes to find the woman with the clipboard that Grace had told me about. The young woman wore a uniform with the logo of the scavenger hunt company that Grace and I had used on our first date. Once we made eye contact, she waved at me and hurried over.

"Hello. You're Mr. Sloane, correct?"

I nodded as she made a couple of notes on her clipboard. "Good morning. Can you tell me what is going on?" I asked.

She smiled. "I need you to take this envelope and put it in your pocket. You can open it after you finish everything. Now I would like to see your phone for a moment. Could you pull up your scavenger hunt app, please?"

I took the envelope which had my name on it in Grace's distinctive handwriting and tucked it into the inner pocket of my jacket. Seeing her script felt like a kick in the chest but I purposefully put it out of my mind as I pulled up the requested app on my phone.

The young woman entered some information into the app and handed the device back to me.

"Just follow the clues. Thank you for your business – we appreciate it. Have a lovely day." She turned and merged into the crowd.

Curious about what Grace had planned for me, I checked the phone.

Within the scavenger hunt app, there were questions and riddles designed to lead me to different locations. The first clue read: "Where seafood meets sourdough, find the baker who's been expecting you."

Despite my confusion, I found myself smiling. This was elaborate, even for Grace.

The pier was getting busier with the usual mix of tourists and locals, but I started following the clues, each one leading me to specific shops where clerks seemed to be waiting for me. At the bakery, I received fresh sourdough and a bottle of wine. At the cheese shop, an assortment of cheeses and crackers. At the seafood market, smoked salmon and crab cakes.

Each stop included a small gift or note that referenced something from our relationship—a book of poetry from the bookstore where we'd spent a Sunday afternoon, a Stanford keychain with a note that said "Go Bears anyway" in Grace's handwriting, a small bottle of the cologne she'd mentioned liking.

After an hour of following clues through the wharf, I was loaded down with what had become a complete picnic feast, plus a basket, blanket, and even a wireless speaker. The attention to detail was incredible, and with each stop, I felt more certain that Grace wasn't planning to say goodbye today.

The final clue was simple: "Where we first worked together to solve a problem, your patient companion waits with one more surprise."

The park near the Wharf, where we first combined forces to solve the clues and puzzles we were given, where we first learned that if we worked together, we could make things happen, where she'd first heard about my work with foster kids and I'd started to understand that she saw something in me beyond just success and charm.

I made my way there, heart pounding harder with each step, carrying enough food for a small party and hoping desperately that this elaborate gesture meant what I thought it meant.

And there she was.

Grace stood in the clearing where we'd once talked about dreams and futures, looking as beautiful as ever in jeans and a sweater that made her light brown eyes look impossibly green. She wasn't alone—Fitz sat next to her, tail wagging.

I stopped walking, just taking in the sight of her. If this wasn't her way of telling me she wanted to try again, the disappointment might actually kill me.

My heart was in my throat as I walked toward her, loaded down with picnic supplies and carrying more hope than I'd felt since our fight in Heavenly. Whatever happened next, at least I'd get to look at her again, to hear her voice, to remember why I'd fallen in love with her in the first place.

"Hi," she said when I was close enough to hear, taking a tentative step toward me.

"Hi, Gimbiya," I replied, still hardly believing she was really there. "You look great, as usual."

I was afraid to move, afraid to assume anything about why she'd arranged this elaborate reunion. But she was here, and she was looking at me like maybe, just maybe, we were going to be okay.

65

grace

When Luke didn't immediately move toward me, panic shot through my chest. Maybe this had been a terrible idea. Maybe he'd only come because he wanted to have full closure, not because he actually wanted to see me.

"You got here," I said, trying to keep my voice light. "I hoped the clues were clear and a little nostalgic. I thought it was a good way to reach out."

"You could have called me yourself," he replied, still standing several feet away with that picnic basket. "You know I would have answered."

The distance between us felt enormous, and I could see something guarded in his expression that hadn't been there before our fight. I'd done that—I'd made the man I loved wary of me.

"I wasn't sure you would want to come," I admitted, walking toward him with Fitz following behind me. "And I wanted to do something that would show you this was really me reaching out."

Luke set the basket down but didn't move to close the gap between us. "Grace, we had a problem, and you needed to think. Which meant you walked away and shut me out completely. I sent you flowers, I sent notes, and you didn't reply or even acknowledge them." His voice was careful, controlled. "I may be new to serious relationships, but I'm pretty sure that's not how people work through problems together."

The criticism hit hard because it was completely deserved. I dropped my head, feeling the full weight of how poorly I'd handled everything after Heavenly.

"You're not wrong. I'm sorry I left you hanging like that. I panicked—all I could see was my marriage, all the ways Evan had hidden things from me.

It wasn't fair to you." I gestured toward the blanket I'd already spread out. "But you hit my weak spot by not being completely honest with me from the beginning. Can we set up the picnic? I know you must be hungry after your hunt."

We walked to the clearing and began unpacking all the food from his scavenger hunt. Every time our hands brushed while arranging containers and bottles, I felt electricity, but Luke seemed determined not to react. The lack of his usual immediate response to my presence made my heart sink.

Had I really ruined this? Had the cruel things we'd said to each other killed something that might have been extraordinary?

We sat on the blanket and tried to pretend we were interested in the elaborate spread, though I could barely taste anything. Even Fitz seemed to sense the tension—I handed him a chew toy I'd brought, but he just lay down next to us and watched with worried eyes.

"How did you get my dog?" Luke asked, tugging at Fitz's toy with what looked like nervous energy.

"Harmony helped," I said with a weak smile. "She seems to want to clean up whatever part she played in our problems. Though maybe this whole thing was a bad idea."

"I don't know yet," Luke said, and his honesty was both brutal and reassuring. "Grace, I've missed you like I've never missed anyone in my life. I'm so glad to see you. But we truly fucked up how we handled our first real disagreement, and we need to figure out how to do better."

I nodded, relief flooding through me that he was being direct instead of pretending everything was fine.

"The only reason I haven't taken you in my arms right now," he continued, "is because I know if I touch you, I won't want to have the conversation we need to have. So, me keeping my distance has nothing to do with how I feel about you."

That admission actually made me feel better, not worse. It meant he was taking this seriously instead of just trying to smooth things over with physical closeness.

"I was trying to be more proactive than I've been in past relationships," I said. "But I think I went too far in the other direction. When push came to shove, I reverted to bad patterns and habits. Instead of talking to you calmly about what happened, I accused you of horrible things, said even worse things. Then I just shut down and ran away."

"I need you to talk to me when something's wrong," Luke said firmly. "We have to be able to discuss problems without you disappearing or me getting defensive. Grace, I'm not Evan. You can't let your marriage dictate how we handle disagreements. Or who I am or why I do things."

"I know that. In my head, I know that." I picked at the edge of the blanket. "But when I found out about Harmony, it felt so similar to the way Evan would hide things that I couldn't think straight."

"I get why it felt that way." Luke's voice grew gentler. "I should have told you about Harmony much earlier, but I was scared it would sound calculating or weird."

"That's what bothered me most," I said. "Not that you were calculating, but that you didn't trust me to handle the information. You made the decision for both of us about what I could manage knowing."

Luke was quiet for a moment, and I could see him processing that observation.

"You're right," he said finally. "I did make that choice for both of us, and that wasn't fair. Grace, I need you to know that everything I felt for you was real. My feelings developed completely naturally, even if my approach may have been informed by what Harmony told me."

"I think I know that now," I said softly. "I think that's why I wanted to see you today—because I realized I was letting fear of repeating past mistakes prevent me from fighting for something worthwhile despite the complications."

Luke's expression shifted at that, something hopeful flickering in his eyes for the first time since I'd seen him standing there with the picnic basket.

"What does fighting for us look like?" he asked.

"It means I spent the last week and a half analyzing every conversation we ever had, trying to figure out what was real and what was performance. And you know what I realized?"

He shook his head, waiting.

"I wasn't completely honest with you either. I didn't tell you about using a matchmaker, about knowing Harmony. So, I can't completely claim the high moral ground here. I also realized that even if you had advance information about what I was looking for, you couldn't have faked the way you looked at me. You couldn't have performed how you were with my friends, or how you handled my impossible family, or the way you held me when I cried about missing Gabe's childhood."

I reached over and touched his hand for the first time since Heavenly, and I felt him relax slightly under my fingers.

"Luke, I said terrible things to you in that cabin. I accused you of making bets about me, of laughing about me with Harmony. I suggested our entire relationship was some kind of game, and I meant to hurt you when I said it."

"You did hurt me," he admitted. "But Grace, what I said was worse. I made you feel pathetic for being emotionally honest. I turned your openness into something shameful instead of recognizing it as one of the things I love most about you."

We sat in silence for a moment, both of us acknowledging the damage we'd done to each other when we'd felt cornered and afraid.

"We really went for the throat, didn't we?" I said quietly.

"Yeah. We did." Luke's thumb traced across my knuckles. "The question is whether we can get past it. Whether we can build something better from here."

I looked at this man who'd somehow become essential to my happiness in just a few weeks, who'd seen me at my worst and was still sitting here trying to figure out if we could make this work.

"Luke, I need to tell you something. This elaborate gesture today? It's not me trying to skip past what happened or pretend our fight didn't matter. It's me choosing you despite everything that happened."

His eyes widened slightly.

"I'm here because I decided that information asymmetry and hurt feelings and even cruel words don't matter as much as the fact that I love you. That what we have is worth fighting for, even when it's messy."

"Grace..."

"I'm not done." I took a breath, needing to get this all out. "I spent days being angry that you had an advantage in pursuing me. But maybe the real question isn't whether you had information I didn't give you. Maybe it's whether you used that information to love me better."

Luke was staring at me now like I was saying something he'd desperately hoped to hear.

"And I think you did. I think knowing I was ready for something real gave you permission to be real with me too. To introduce me to your family and friends, to rearrange your life to include me, to love me like you'd never loved anyone before."

I could see tears in his eyes, which made my own chest tight with emotion.

"So that's what fighting for us looks like," I finished. "It looks like me choosing to trust that your feelings are genuine, even if the foundation was more complicated than I originally understood."

Luke lifted our joined hands and kissed my knuckles, and I felt something fundamental settle between us—not the complete erasure of what had happened, but the decision to build something new from where we were now.

"I love you," he said simply. "More than I knew was possible."

"I love you too," I replied. "Which is why I have one more surprise for you."

I pointed out the envelope that I could see inside his jacket. "You can take out the envelope now."

"What is it?"

"Open it."

epilogue

grace

With some help from Kyle, we were able to schedule the train trip during December. The train trip had been everything I'd hoped it would be and more. Seventeen days of uninterrupted time to really learn each other, to practice the kind of complete honesty we'd promised in that park, to prove that what we'd built was strong enough to survive both scrutiny and intimacy. By the time we'd reached Atlanta, Luke and I weren't just back together—we were better together than we'd ever been.

The months that followed were a study in intentional relationship-building. We'd kept our regular schedule of Tuesdays at Luke's, Thursdays at my place, weekends together, but we'd added something new: couples therapy that had gradually morphed into premarital counseling by April. Learning how to communicate about difficult things before they became crises, how to handle disagreements without attacking each other's vulnerabilities, how to build the kind of partnership that could weather whatever complications life threw at us.

Luke had also spent considerable time with Gabe, who'd decided his mother's boyfriend was "cool enough" since he'd played college and professional football and, more importantly, made his mother genuinely happy. Watching them develop their own relationship—Luke asking Gabe about training, Gabe teaching Luke about the latest video games—had been one of the most beautiful aspects of blending our lives.

By late spring, we both knew we didn't want to live without each other. More than that, we wanted to make it official.

"Eloping to Hawaii sounds perfect," I'd told Luke when he'd brought up the idea of a small, private ceremony. "Just us, the beach, and no one else's opinions about our timeline or choices."

It had sounded like a beautiful plan—quiet vows on a Maui beach, a honeymoon spent enjoying each other's company without having to navigate anyone else's expectations about our admittedly rapid progression from crisis to commitment.

But it didn't go that way.

Now I stood on that white sandy beach as the sun set over the Pacific, looking at a crowd of family and friends who'd somehow managed to board planes and arrive in time for our "private" ceremony.

"One nosy soul," I muttered to my father as he prepared to walk me down the makeshift aisle Kyle had arranged after discovering our elopement plans. "Kyle couldn't keep his mouth shut for five minutes."

"Are you disappointed?" Dad asked, adjusting his hastily purchased linen shirt.

I adjusted my Boho lace wedding dress and looked at the assembled crowd—my mother dabbing her eyes, my brother Vic offering her a shoulder, Gabe looking proud in his crisp white linen outfit, Harmony beaming with satisfaction at her role in our love story, Autumn, Claudia, and Ree practically bouncing with excitement. Even Evan and MacKenzie had made it, despite her being eight months pregnant with twins and requiring a private jet and an on-call obstetrician to get here safely.

"No," I said honestly. "I thought I wanted it to be just us, but having everyone here feels right. They've all been part of this story somehow."

Luke waited for me at the wooden arch Kyle had somehow arranged overnight, decorated with gauzy white fabric and tropical flowers, string lights beginning to twinkle as dusk settled over the water. He wore a white linen outfit that captured the wedding vibe perfectly, no shoes on the sand, and the kind of smile that made my heart race even after everything we'd been through.

When Dad and I reached the end of the aisle, Luke's expression made me feel like the most cherished woman on earth.

"You look incredible," he whispered as Dad placed my hand in his.

"You clean up pretty well yourself," I replied, though what I was really thinking was that I'd never felt more certain about anything in my life.

During our vows, I could hear sniffling from the crowd, but I only had eyes for Luke.

"It's hard to believe we've only known each other for eight months," he began, his voice carrying easily over the sound of the waves. "But I can honestly say that when you ran into me in the lobby of my sister's office building, I knew you were going to have a profound impact on my life. Besides the literal impact you had on my phone."

Laughter rippled through our guests.

"As my friend Kyle says, I was struck by lightning that day. I was completely captivated at first sight—by a brilliant, accomplished, sharp-tongued doctor who challenged everything I thought I knew about love. I hit the jackpot, and I knew it immediately." His voice grew more serious. "Grace, I promise to spend the rest of my days earning the happiness you've brought into my life, proving every day that you chose the right man to love you the way you deserve to be loved."

When it was my turn, I looked into the eyes of the man who'd seen me at my worst and chosen to fight for me anyway.

"I didn't want to fall in love with you—I thought I was too smart for that kind of immediate, overwhelming connection. But I couldn't fight what was clearly written in the stars, even if those stars had a twisted sense of humor about timing. It happened so fast it terrified me." I grinned. "And yes, in spite of the fact that you went to Stanford, which should have been an immediate disqualifier."

"Hey!" Luke protested, earning more chuckles from our friends.

"Luke, I love how completely you love me, how you see the world as something to be improved, how passionately you work to make that difference, especially in the lives of children who need advocates. But most of all, I love how you helped me learn to trust my own judgment again, how you gave me the courage to move beyond my past." I reached up to touch his face. "I can't wait to spend our lives together—working hard, loving deeply, and leaving this world better than we found it."

When the officiant pronounced us husband and wife, Luke's kiss tasted like salt air and new beginnings and the promise of a future we'd both been brave enough to choose.

"I love you, Mrs. Sloane," he whispered against my mouth.

"I love you too, husband," I replied, and meant it with every cell in my body.

The reception Kyle had somehow arranged at a beachfront restaurant was everything I hadn't known I wanted—casual enough to match our beach setting, elegant enough to honor the significance of what we were celebrating. Instead of wedding gifts, we'd asked for donations to Luke's foundation that matched foster children with business mentors, and Evan had surprised us by announcing his plans to start a Miami branch with similar goals.

"I guess we really are going to be family after all," I told MacKenzie during dinner, both of us laughing at the complicated ways our lives had woven together.

"The best kind of family," she replied. "The kind you choose."

Our first dance was to D'Angelo's "Lady," and as Luke spun me around the makeshift dance floor, I marveled at how perfectly this imperfect day had turned out.

Later, as I made my way through conversations with everyone who'd made the sacrifice to be here, I felt overwhelmed by gratitude for the people who'd supported me through the hardest and best year of my adult life.

"My eldest daughter is finally whole," my mother said through tears when Luke and I stopped to thank her and Dad for making the trip. "I watched you struggle for so long, wondering how to help. But you figured it out yourself, baby. You learned to trust your heart again."

"Take care of our girl," Dad told Luke, though it was clear he already trusted Luke completely.

When we reached Evan and MacKenzie, Luke squeezed my hand and stepped away to give us privacy for what we both knew would be an important conversation. MacKenzie followed him.

"I'm really happy for you," Evan said, and I could see he meant it completely. "You found the right person, Grace. Someone who gets how extraordinary you are."

"Thank you. And I'm happy for you and Mac too—seeing you two together, it finally makes sense why we couldn't make it work. I didn't get to tell you that at y'all's wedding." I looked over at Luke, who was diplomatically distracting a very pregnant MacKenzie. "We both ended up exactly where we were supposed to be."

"You and I weren't all bad. We had Gabe. You're still family," Evan said quietly. "Whatever happens, you're Gabe's mom and you'll always be important to me. I hope you know that."

"I do know that. And I hope you know that I want you to be happy—really, genuinely happy—in a way we never could have made each other."

When Luke returned to my side, wrapping his arms around my waist, I leaned back against him and felt the completeness I'd been searching for my entire adult life.

"Ready to start our honeymoon, Mrs. Sloane?" he asked, kissing the top of my head.

"More than ready, Mr. Sloane," I replied, turning in his arms to kiss him thoroughly.

As we said goodbye to our guests and headed back to our hotel, I reflected on the journey that had brought us here. A chance collision in a lobby, information asymmetry that had nearly destroyed us, the courage to fight for something real despite its complicated beginnings.

Luke took my hand as we walked along the beach, our wedding clothes getting sandy, both of us grinning like teenagers who'd gotten away with something wonderful.

"Any regrets about having an audience for our private ceremony?" he asked.

"None at all," I said honestly. "It turns out having everyone we love witness us choosing each other made it even more meaningful."

"Good," Luke replied, stopping to kiss me under the Hawaiian stars. "Because I plan to keep choosing you every day for the rest of our lives, and I want everyone to know it."

For the first time in my adult life, I believed that the happily-ever-after I'd been hoping for was not only possible but already beginning. Not because we'd found each other perfectly, but because we'd learned how to choose each other imperfectly, with complete honesty and the kind of love that grows stronger through challenges rather than despite them.

I'd finally found my match.

Also by D.W. Brooks

The CHAOS Universe

I Do CHAOS (#1)
Homecoming CHAOS (#2)
Dating CHAOS (#3)
Model CHAOS (#4 – coming late 2026)

Meet Your Match Series

Late Match (#1)
The Match Game (#2)
The Mis-Match (#3 – coming late 2026)
Game, Set, Match (#4 – coming 2027)

About D.W. Brooks

Author, Physician, Kidney Transplant Survivor

I have always been an enthusiastic reader. Breakfast in my childhood home was a slow process as I would read any object on the table—newspapers, cereal boxes, milk cartons, anything. Taking away my books was an effective punishment.

As part of this interest, my cousins and I created a neighborhood of preteen and teenage characters who had adventures and solved mysteries. We drew out this neighborhood, identified where everyone lived, and created character profiles for each one. We were well ahead of our time and wrote a lot of unfinished stories which disappeared into the attic as we got older. After this failed experiment, I still had thoughts of writing my own stories one day.

Becoming an author was an early dream pushed aside by practical thoughts and fears. I decided to take a more surefire route of going to medical school and residency. While I didn't write my own stories, I spent time writing in a medical and education capacity.

A health crisis awakened the desire to write again. And the ability to self-publish, I could see a path to getting my words and stories out of my head and into a bound book others can read and hopefully enjoy.

The author lives in Texas with her husband and children. She enjoys trying to stay in shape, sporadically cooking, reading (still), writing, and working on her blog. She is eternally grateful to the woman who donated a kidney to her over 8 years ago and continues to advocate for organ donation as much as she can.

To learn more about D. W. Brooks and future publications and events, visit https://authordwbrooks.com.

www.ingramcontent.com/pod-product-compliance
Lightning Source LLC
Chambersburg PA
CBHW051138130726
47988CB00005B/1888